Snowboots & Sunglasses

Caroline Johnston

To Joy
My amazing
author friend
enjoy the snow
Love Caroline
x

IC⁴

IC⁴ Publishing

ISBN: 978-0-9570039-5-8

For more information about Caroline Johnston, please access the author's website at: www.carolinejohnston.co.uk

Cover design: Tanya Rochat

Published by IC[4] Publishing

Dedication

To Innes, Calum, Cameron and Cara

KIRSTY

Fear flashed through me. My stomach clenched. My breathing shallowed and my vision blurred. Flight mode demanded immediate escape. But I was trapped in the confines of a department meeting.

For the last six weeks, panic attacks had plagued me. They would strike without warning or regard for my surroundings. If I could get to a quiet place, I could ride them out. But there was no escape this morning. I was trapped. The meeting room only had one door and I would need to squeeze past several colleagues to reach it.

'God! Help me!' I prayed.

I looked down at my notepad, doodling with my pen in a bid to distract myself and stop the panic attack. But the doodles weren't working. The panic was rising. My skin prickled with heat. Perspiration sticking to my body. I needed to get out. I needed to breathe.

"Kirsty!" I looked up from my notepad, trying to work out who was talking to me. "Kirsty, would you mind going and getting some water for us all? It's quite stuffy in here."

I gazed over at Irene. My mind darting between my need to escape and figuring out the current situation. My legs wobbled as I began my journey to freedom. My eyes fixed firmly on the door.

As I reached the door, I glanced over at Irene. Had she picked up on my fear and given me an out? How different our interactions over the last few weeks. Previously, Irene was the reason I disliked my job. As my section manager, she was always finding fault with my work. Nothing I did was ever good enough. But after my traumatic October, she had become my closest ally at work. Only Irene knew what had happened and the ghosts that haunted me. She sat beside me in HR when I registered my complaint and protected me in the department until Gary left. And now she was looking out for me again.

When I left the meeting room, I went straight to the toilets. Resting my hands against the cool of the sink, I looked in the mirror. The reflection staring back at me was pale, with dark shadows around the eyes.

I ran cold water over my wrists in an attempt to cool myself down. As I kept my wrists in the water, I worked through some breathing exercises. Finally, I felt my body calm down. When would this end?

With the peak of the panic over, I returned to the meeting room before anyone noticed my absence, grabbing some bottles of water and glasses on my way. Irene cast me a concerned glance as I sat back down. I'm not sure how reassuring my smile was.

Finally, the meeting ended. As soon as I was back at my desk, I fired off an SOS text to my friends - Jo, Lynn and Carol. 'Help! Another panic attack at work. Are you free to come to mine tonight?' Almost as soon as the text left my phone, my phone pinged with three text messages to say they would be at mine later.

"Are you okay, Kirsty?" whispered Irene, as she came over to my desk.

"I'm fine now, thanks."

"Do you want to go home?"

All I wanted to do was go home, but then he would still be winning. I attempted a smile. "No, I'll be okay."

"If you need anything, let me know."

The rest of the day passed in a blur. Work and conversations surrounded me like shadows, but I was empty and exhausted. When would I beat these panic attacks? I switched off my computer, feeling only hopelessness.

***

Friendship and pizza were the perfect combination to ease my nerves. The conversation flowed and laughter lightened my mood. I am so grateful for these friends, especially Jo. We both moved to Glasgow about the same time for college and university. We quickly bonded over childhood stories of rural village life, Jo from The Borders and me from Argyll. "So what happened?" asked Jo.

"I don't know. Out of nowhere, I got slammed with a panic attack at work. I was sitting in a department meeting and it just came over me."

"What did you do?" asked Carol.

"Can you believe Irene once again came to my aid? She must have noticed and sent me out to get water for everyone. That gave me the chance to get to the toilets and calm myself."

"That sounds awful, Kirsty," said Carol.

"It was. Plus, it makes me feel like he is still winning and I'm the one paying the price for his actions."

Jo put her arm round me. "I'm sorry it feels like that. But you were the strong one. You did the right thing. But I guess it takes time to get over it. Why don't you talk to Irene and see what she suggests. Maybe go down to a shorter working week and put some fun into your days off."

"Thanks. I feel better already just talking to you. I'll chat with Irene next week and see what she suggests."

"And I've just thought of a brilliant idea that will give you something else to look forward to," said Lynn, who had been uncharacteristically quiet until now.

"Should I be worried?"

"Not at all. You'll love this. Why don't we go on a ski holiday?"

"What?" we all chorused.

"I'm not seeing the connection," said Jo.

"Isn't it obvious?" continued Lynn. We all shook our heads. "You need something to look forward to so that the next time you start to feel the panic rise you can think of the fun thing instead."

"But I can't ski," I replied. "I've never had a lesson or even tried on skis before."

"All the better. You can focus your attention on learning something new."

"I don't know…"

"I'm telling you, Kirsty," said Lynn. "This is just what you need. Let's start planning it now."

I looked at Jo and Carol. They were both smiling at the prospect of a ski holiday. Lynn picked up her phone. "Jo, you're the one with the set schedule. When is the long weekend in February and what days are you off?"

Jo picked up her phone. "It starts the second weekend in February. I get the Monday and Tuesday off."

"So we could go Saturday to Saturday and Jo comes home early? Or do we all go Saturday to Tuesday?"

"I would hate to be the reason you cut the holiday short," said Jo. "Also, it's fun to go in a bigger group. Why don't we ask Paul and Matt if they want to come with us? Although, Matt has the same time restrictions as I do."

"That would be fun," said Lynn. "And it'll give Paul and Kirsty time together."

As the others giggled, I did my best to look annoyed. They were always teasing me about Paul. It got annoying at times, especially as I didn't know where I stood with him. In amongst all the trauma of October, Paul had proved himself a genuine friend, as had Matt. But with Paul, I hoped it was more than mere friendship.

"Will we go to one of the Scottish centres or to the Alps?" asked Jo.

"The Alps, of course," responded Lynn.

"Won't that be too expensive?" asked Carol.

"If we're going to do it, let's do it right and go to France."

"I like Val Thorens," suggested Carol.

"Oh, me too!" said Jo.

"I've not been there before," said Lynn. "Let's look at resorts in that region and decide which one looks best. We can talk to the guys and see if they're up for it too."

"Sounds like a good plan," said Jo. "Kirsty, maybe you should do lessons at the indoor ski slope. Means you won't be starting from scratch on holiday."

"Okay. But are you sure skiing is a good idea for me? You all know my safety record. I'm likely to fall and break a leg or an arm."

"As long as it's just your own limb you break and not anyone else's," joked Lynn. She held her phone up to my face. "Look, you can do private lessons or group lessons. I'm going to phone and book you in."

Before I could reply, she was on the phone to the ski centre. "And you're booked in for lessons," announced Lynn, as soon as she ended the call. "They had a cancellation, so you start on Tuesday night. Two lessons before Christmas and a third lesson after Christmas."

As the others got excited about a winter holiday in snowboots and sunglasses, I wondered if I was the only one who remembered we already had plans for Tuesday night.

PAUL

My lungs and muscles all screamed at me to slow down. But I needed to run out the frustration.

In two days I would be launching my dream. The Smith Salon. I couldn't wait to open the salon and be my own boss. For the last few weeks, I'd been working flat out with Brian, Trish and Jennifer as we worked on the salon and set up our new businesses. And Tuesday was supposed to be the celebration of all our hard work and the dreams ahead of us. But how could I fully celebrate without Kirsty by my side?

With all the hours I'd been pouring into the salon, I'd barely seen Kirsty for weeks. Our time limited to our Sunday routine of church and lunch. And it was at our lunch today that Lynn had confessed her oversight and told me Kirsty wouldn't be at the salon launch.

I pushed my burning muscles harder, trying to wipe out the irritation.

To be fair, Lynn looked more flustered than I've ever seen her before. So I knew it wasn't intentional. But it still stung. Kirsty's face had been red with embarrassment. I wasn't sure if their invitation for me and Matt to join them was their way of saying sorry or if they had planned to ask us all along. But by then I was so frustrated I can't even remember how I answered.

As my thoughts turned to a potential ski holiday, my frustration lessened and I slowed down to a sustainable jog. The thought of going away was appealing. It's far too long since I was last snowboarding. Although the timing isn't great, as the salon will only have been open for a few months and money is tight. But time in the Alps with Kirsty is an alluring thought.

In the early darkness of a November afternoon, I turned round and headed for home. The Christmas street lights fought against the gloom to brighten up the centre of Glasgow. And shop windows sparkled with Christmas trees and decorations reminding me of Ben's sermon from this morning. He'd preached on Advent. I thought Advent was just a reference to chocolate calendars. But it turns out it starts four Sundays before Christmas. Ben explained it all as he lit the first candle of Advent. He told us each candle represented a different aspect of the season, one for hope, one for joy, one for peace and one for love. Today's candle represented hope.

As I continued my run, I thought about the hope that filled every part of my life. This Christmas I had hope and faith. I only became a Christian nine months ago, and since then I've been on a journey of discovery. Faith wasn't something I had been searching for. It was more of a chain of events. My flatmate, Matt, invited me along to an Alpha group he was running. At first I'd declined, but the more he talked about it, the more intrigued I became. The clincher was when he told me the weekly meetings started with food.

There was also hope in my new salon. Until a few months ago, I'd been relatively happy working as a senior designer in one of the top hair salons in Glasgow, but a number of factors and conversations had pointed towards this new path. A venture that included my ByDesign colleagues, Brian and Trish. Life was exhilarating. Every morning I leapt out of bed, eager to get on with the day's tasks.

I had also been feeling hopeful about my love life. Six months ago I went from being a serial dater to being single. It's the longest I've been single since I was twelve, but a lifestyle of one-night stands had to be broken. And now there is only one woman I want to be with - Kirsty. The first time I saw her, she captivated me. I was used to seeing tall, slim, gorgeous women at ByDesign, but Kirsty was a natural beauty. I nearly asked her out a few weeks ago, but the timing wasn't right. I still needed time to get over my serial-dating habit and she needed time to get over the trauma of her manager, Gary, and his clumsy attempts to get her into bed.

I had been hopeful, but now I'm wondering if something is wrong.

PAUL

Launch night! This is where my past, present and future converge. The past brings experience. The present brings excitement. And the future brings hope.

It had been a fraught couple of months. Transforming the salon from the shabby place we had leased to its current designer appearance. Jennifer had worked her magic on the space and it looked amazing. And, she had paid for everything and we would pay her back interest-free. I didn't deserve her kindness, but I'll be forever grateful for all she's done.

Over the last few weeks, we'd learned so much about dealing with suppliers, utility connections, managing cash flow and projections, a real challenge when you don't have a clue about business. And this was where Scott, my friend, and Jennifer's husband, stepped in. As an accountant, he's already come to my rescue several times. He's giving me mate's rates to put our books through his company. But he's also giving us lots of free advice and input.

If this salon is a success, it will be down to the practical, emotional and spiritual support that Jennifer and Scott have poured into it. A big reason for tonight is to thank them for all they've done for us.

And now here we are; on the eve of December and launching The Smith Salon.

Last week we delivered flyers around the neighbourhood inviting people to our launch and offering a discount code on their first appointment. But would it be enough to entice people in? Would anyone even come along tonight? I was grateful it was a dry, mild night. Hopefully, that would help with the numbers.

After a few anxious minutes of wondering if anyone would arrive, the door opened, announcing the arrival of Jo, Lynn, and Carol. It was hugs all round, but I was still disappointed that Kirsty wasn't with them. However, there was no time for negativity as the door opened and a crowd of folks from church came in, quickly followed by my mum.

The next time the door opened, a couple of strangers walked in. This was starting to get more exciting. It was brilliant to have the support of friends, but having strangers walk in gave me hope of new clients and business. Next to enter were a couple of my old clients from ByDesign. As a city centre salon, ByDesign took in clients from all over Glasgow, but if these people lived in the South Side there was a good chance they would become regulars at The Smith Salon.

For the next twenty minutes, the door kept opening to welcome in more people. Trish, Brian and I mingled, making sure everyone had drinks and nibbles and people to talk to. Our nervousness melted into smiles.

"Hi everyone," I shouted over the bubbling chatter. "My name is Paul, and I'd like to welcome you to The Smith Salon. We're excited to launch our new salon and get to know you over the coming weeks and months. We want The Smith Salon to be a place for you to relax and enjoy your hairdressing experience. I think you'll agree that the style and décor of the place are inviting. And for that, I'd like to thank my friend Jennifer." I looked over to Jennifer and raised my glass to her. She responded in kind.

"If any of you are looking for an interior designer, I would highly recommend Jennifer. I also want to thank Jennifer's other half, Scott. Scott, thanks for all your accounting help and support. I know I'll have lots more questions for you." I looked over to Scott and raised my glass.

"Now, The Smith Salon isn't just about me and I wouldn't be doing this without my teammates Trish and Brian." I turned to face my colleagues. "Why don't you guys introduce yourselves?"

A very nervous sounding Trish stood beside me and introduced herself. Next up was Brian, who had everyone laughing as peppered his speech with jokes about hairdressers.

"So now you've met us. Why not come and chat with us and book an appointment. And remember, there is ten percent off for December and January. Please help yourselves to more drinks and nibbles."

As everyone clapped, I made my way over to my appointment book. I had a few appointments already, thanks to church friends. My hope for tonight was for more bookings and I wasn't disappointed. My old ByDesign clients who had come along booked appointments for their Christmas cuts and styles. And I also got some brand new bookings too. Nothing is guaranteed, but based on my appointment book and the people still mingling in the salon, I'm convinced it will all work out.

Scott and Jennifer came over to say their goodbyes. "Sorry, we need to leave," said Jennifer. "We're already past the time we told the babysitter we needed her for."

"Thanks so much for everything. For tonight, for the advice, for the design. I'll never be able to thank you enough."

"Our pleasure, Paul. We're excited to see this new venture work for you. And don't hesitate to give me a shout any time you need accounting input."

Jo and the girls made their way over to me to add their congratulations to the evening and reiterate their wishes for salon success. I wished Kirsty was with them. She was the only thing missing from this perfect evening.

JENNIFER

How do you put into words the feeling of being surrounded by your dream? A few months ago, I had been stumbling around. Lost and unsure of myself. But now, here I stood in Paul's salon, knowing where my future lay.

I had arrived at the salon early with Scott and Matt. We wanted to pray with Paul before the launch got underway. As he chatted now with Brian and Trish, I took the time to walk around, savouring the coming together of my ideas. This salon would be a success because of Paul's hairstyling skills. But I liked to think that my creativity gave the salon the look to complement his style.

The workstation wall was navy blue. Three large, old mirrors reflected the cream colour of the other walls. Spotlights in the ceiling provided the main lighting with small chandeliers providing a quirky lighting style. The reception desk was an old chest of drawers that I had upcycled. An old bookcase by the window displayed styling products and nick-knacks. The warm wood effect of the vinyl floor planks added to the ambiance of the salon. The flooring, spotlights, chairs and work trolleys were the only new items in the salon. I had acquired most of the purchases at car boot sales and auction houses. Even the sinks were all individual pieces bought via online searches. If you knew where to look, you could find bargains that transformed a space from the commonplace to exceptional. But it took time.

The main action point for future projects is to work on my timings. For a few days, I'd lost track of time and had to call in favours with other mums to collect my daughters from school. However, tonight was about celebrating what we had achieved, not focussing on the things I'd got wrong. I was looking forward to a night of socialising and witnessing the start of Paul's amazing new venture.

With instrumental music playing and drinks and snacks being enjoyed, the atmosphere swelled with hope and possibilities. I watched Paul work the room. He was a natural. The Smith Salon would be a success.

I spent some time mingling with strangers, then walked over to Jo. "It's so good you're all here to support Paul. But where is Kirsty?"

Jo filled me in on the group's decision to go on holiday and Lynn booking Kirsty in for ski lessons. "To be honest, I think Kirsty was quite happy for the out," said Jo. "You know Kirsty, she's all insecure about Paul again and avoidance is her way of dealing with it. It's only been a few weeks since they had their chat about the future, but she's already got it all twisted in her head."

"That's exciting you're all going on holiday. Hopefully the thought of the ski holiday will help. And the lessons will be an excellent distraction. We'll just pray she doesn't break any bones!" We laughed, both a bit nervous as to whether Kirsty would survive ski lessons.

Carol and Lynn walked over to join us. "We were just talking about your ski holiday," I said.

"I'm so excited," replied Lynn. "I can't wait."

"It's a lovely thing to look forward to."

"You and Scott should come with us," suggested Lynn.

"No. This is for you younger folks."

"I've seen you on church activity days, Jennifer. When it comes to activities you don't hold back," joined in Carol.

"Say you'll come," added Jo.

"It would be lovely to go skiing. Let me talk to Scott about it." My thoughts drifted to previous ski holidays. Days spent on the slopes and evenings relaxing by a cosy fire; the holidays of the pre-parenting phase of life.

"The salon looks amazing," commented Lynn, bringing me back to the present.

"Thanks. I had so much fun working on it."

"First Kirsty's living room and now Paul's salon," said Carol. "What's next?"

"Well, I have been thinking of interior design as a potential career. And today I signed up for an Introduction to Interior Design course. It's ten weeks of evening classes at the college in the city centre."

"That's fantastic," enthused Jo. "You've obviously got a genuine talent for it."

"I hope so. It's been fun working on projects for friends, but now I need to figure out if I can make a career out of it."

"So, do you launch your business once you've finished your course?" asked Lynn.

"I don't know yet. I'm not sure if the evening course will be enough or if I should follow up with a college course. So I'm not making any business plans yet."

"Well, it's exciting you're taking this first step," said Jo.

I was grateful for the words of encouragement from the girls. Working on Kirsty's flat and Paul's salon had energised me and helped me work out that interior design was a passion worth pursuing into a career. But did I have what it takes to succeed?

By the time we got home, I was shattered. It had been an exciting, but long day. As we waved off the babysitter, Scott put his arm around me and kissed me on the cheek. "The salon looks wonderful. You're amazing."

"Well, thank you, Mr Thomson. It has been lovely to see it all come together."

Scott tilted my face towards him, this time kissing me on the lips. "And now it's time to concentrate on your birthday. I'm not going to tell you what I have planned, but I'm taking you out Friday night."

"Now I am intrigued," I said. We made our way upstairs with a spark of promise that the evening wasn't over yet.

"I'll be working late the next couple of nights," said Scott, as he got ready for bed. "I need to get a client's year-end accounts finished."

An all too familiar spark of annoyance flared up within. Scott's matter-of-fact statement was one I heard too often. He was the boss, and he worked hard. I didn't want to make an issue about the time he spent at the office, but it was constant. Tonight he'd almost been late for the salon opening, because he stayed at work later than we had arranged. And now he'd be missing from home for the next two nights. Another week of the girls barely getting to see their dad.

But before I could push back on him about his working hours, our door flew open. "Mum, my tummy really hurts," cried Chloe.

I put my hand on her forehead. She felt hot. "Let's get you a drink of water."

No sooner were we in the kitchen than she threw up.

Tonight had been a time to celebrate. A chance to dream of my future career as an interior designer. But standing in the kitchen, all those hopes and dreams seemed futile. My husband worked too many hours and my children were still at the stage of childhood illnesses and bugs. This is my reality. Was interior design only a dream?

KIRSTY

What was I thinking? Why had I agreed to this?

I held on to the ski pull for dear life. My knees feeling wobblier with each jerky inch.

Why, oh why, had I agreed to go on a ski holiday? Why had I agreed to ski lessons? I thought taking lessons would equip me for the holiday, but right now, it felt like the worst idea ever. And I was only on the tiny little practice slope! If this felt too high, how would I cope in the Alps!

The ski instructor was trying to be helpful and encouraging, but I was struggling. We were only halfway through the lesson and I had fallen more than anyone else. I wasn't feeling much enthusiasm for skiing or the holiday.

The instructor told the rest of the group to keep practising, then he came over to me. "Okay, Kirsty. Get rid of all those feelings of doubt. I'm going to have you going up and down this slope in no time at all. Trust me, I've taught people more terrified than you."

I laughed. I'm not sure if it was because he was funny or because I was nervous. Or maybe a bit of both.

"We're going to ski down this slope together. We'll take it nice and slowly and if you follow directly in the tracks my skis make, you'll do just fine."

His comments didn't convince me, but I trusted him enough to give it a go. I put all my concentration into following him and kept my eyes fixed on him the whole way down. I was so focussed I didn't even realise we'd reached the base of the slope. I did it! I made it down without falling.

"See, I told you you could do it," he said. "Now back up and let's do that one more time. Then we'll see how you do without having me to follow."

I completed the second run fall-free. But as soon as I started the third run, on my own, I fell over at my first turn. "Kirsty," he shouted over, "you can do this. Keep your eyes up and look ahead. You can do it."

I got myself back up, none too glamorously, and set off. But I did it. I got to the bottom without another fall.

"Good. Now back up and do it again." Wow, this guy was quite the task master.

My fourth time down went without a fall. Was I actually getting it? But the next time, I took another tumble. I wasn't sure if it was because of a wrong move or exhaustion.

"Okay, everyone," shouted our instructor. "You've all done really well tonight. We'll see you back here same time next week."

I shuffled out to the changing area, glad to be leaving the chill of the snowy air. Muscles that had been dormant for years complained at suddenly being forced into action.

My whole body was crying out against skiing. Who was I to argue?

The next morning, my body was still aching. I had tried to appease my complaining muscles by languishing in a warm, scented bubble bath as soon as I got home last night. But as the bus hit another pot hole, the vibration let me know my muscles were still in pain. The cold, grey December morning was conspiring against me too, reminding my body of the chill of the snow.

I limped into the office. As usual, I was the first person to arrive in the department. The lights flickered, trying to decide whether or not to work for me. Hobbling over to my desk, something about my surroundings triggered memories that I longed to forget. Memories of Gary. Memories of unwanted attention and forced kisses. What if I hadn't been able to get away from him? My breathing shallowed, my heartbeat started rising and I felt light-headed. I leaned on the desk beside me and took some deep breaths. The breathing exercises doing enough to calm the panic. 'How much longer, God? When will I be free of this?'

The ping of the lift doors opening brought me back to the present. I was relieved to see it was Irene. She took one look at me and whisked me over to my desk, taking my coffee cup out of my hand before I dropped it.

"Take some deep breaths," instructed Irene.

I went through some more breathing exercises and felt a bit calmer. But as the lift heralded the arrival of more people to the department, the panic returned.

Irene ushered me away from my desk. "Let's go to the meeting room." As soon as we reached the empty room, my tears started.

"Will I never get over this?" I asked through my tears.

"It's only been a few weeks. It will take time."

"Sometimes I think I'm getting there and getting over it and then some random thing brings it all back. I don't even know what set me off this morning."

"You're recovering from a bad experience. These things take time."

"But it's not fair!" I hadn't meant to shout, but frustration and fear had me on edge. Irene glanced out to the department to see if my outburst had attracted any attention. But I wouldn't apologise for my behaviour. I was fed up apologising. "It's not fair. He's the one in the wrong and he gets to move on with his life while I'm the one in tears."

"It is unfair. But at least you don't need to see him at work anymore."

"That is true. And I am grateful he is no longer here. But it feels as if the ghost of Gary is in every shadow."

Gary was only our head of department for a few months. But in that time he caused quite a stir. There was no denying he was a good-looking guy and decked out in designer brands he had the attention of most of the women in the department. I kept my head down and avoided him until he picked me to take over the final admin arrangements for the department's rebranding. Over the weeks we worked together, a strange working relationship developed between us, but in the end, it took a more sinister role. At the rebranding event, he kissed me and expected me to go back to his hotel room with him. My friends had insisted I report him to HR, and with Irene's support, I put in my complaint. However, the smooth-talking Gary negotiated his resignation with no repercussions and was now doing very well for himself working for his new fiancée's mother's company.

"It's not fair. But you stood up for yourself. You confronted Gary. It might not feel like you won, but you blocked his career aspirations here. At times, it will feel like he got away with it all, but he didn't. You made sure of that. Now you need to find your way through this. Reclaim the strength that enabled you to confront him."

Irene's words provided the reassurance I needed. "Thanks, Irene. You've helped me so much through all this. You protected me his last week here, and I'll always be grateful for that. But maybe it's time for me to transfer to another department. Somewhere I don't feel everyone is pointing at me and whispering about me. Somewhere I'm not known as 'that girl'."

"I can understand that. But why not wait a bit longer. I really don't think anyone else in the office knows. Enjoy Christmas. Wait and see who our new manager is and how that changes things around here."

Back at my desk, a thousand questions swirled around my head. The ski lesson should have been my happy distraction. But it hadn't worked. My body was aching and the panic attacks were still happening. Plus, going to the lesson meant I had let Paul down. Would he forgive me?

Kirsty

There were two things I didn't want to talk about at house group - work or Paul.

Lynn was the answer to my prayers. "How did your ski lesson go last night?"

"Well, let me tell you what I've learned so far about skiing." Jennifer, Jo and Carol joined Lynn with expectant expressions, waiting to hear how much fun I'd had at my lesson.

"First of all don't do lessons at the same time as a kids' lesson is happening. As soon as they are on the slope, they are experts with no fear. I won't even comment on how expert they were on the tow rope compared to me." As my friends all laughed, I continued. "Next up we have the equipment. Unwieldy skis that will not comply and constantly cross over each other. And don't even get me started on the sticks, or as I call them, trip hazards." By this point the others were almost rolling off their seats laughing. "And finally the physical pain, a face frozen by the cold air and muscles I didn't even know I had complaining at me. Look…" I walked round my living room to let them see how laboured each step was.

"Don't worry about the muscle ache," said Jo. "In no time at all your muscles will be primed and raring to go."

"Maybe my muscles will get with the programme but I'm not sure about my nerves. The lesson was only on the tiny practice slope and it terrified me. The big run opposite us looked absolutely daunting. Are you sure this is the right sport for me?"

"Yes!" They all chorused.

"I'm not convinced you guys are the loyal friends I thought you were."

"I'll prove you wrong right now and bring through our teas and coffees, save your muscles the journey," said Jo. The rest of the group joined in the laughter.

Jo handed me my mug, and I savoured the warmth of it nestled in my hands. Munching through the biscuits, the group all relaxed back in their seats enjoying my tale of woe from the ski lesson.

"The crowning moment was when the ski instructor decided I was his special project and singled me out to help me down. I got more one-to-one time with him than anyone else!"

"But you enjoyed it, right?" said Jo.

"I'm choosing to remain positive and say there may be the opportunity for enjoyment at some point. But for now I reserve all judgement."

Again the others burst out laughing. "Oh Kirsty," said Carol. "Once we're in France, surrounded by mountains and the vibes in the resort you'll love it."

In the warm glow of my living room, surrounded by my best friends and laughter it was easy to make light of my first ski lesson and gloss over the fact there had been another panic attack this morning.

"Are you and Scott going to come on holiday with us, Jennifer?" asked Jo.

"I've not had a chance to talk to him about it yet. He just arrived home tonight as it was time for me to come here. But I'd love to come with you. Have you booked it yet?"

"Not yet. We're checking a few options and then will hopefully book it by the weekend. But we can leave it a bit longer if there's a chance you'll come."

"Scott's working most evenings this week. I'll get back to you over the weekend."

"How did you enjoy last night, Jennifer? Did everyone fall in love with your interior design?" I was nervous at turning the conversation to Paul's salon but it would be rude not to ask Jennifer how the décor was received.

"I think so. I'm fairly pleased with it. There are a few items I'm still looking for but I realise I need to draw a line under it and move on. I need to learn how to budget and manage timings better. But the experience has taught me lots."

"Fairly pleased?" questioned Jo. "Kirsty, you should see the place. It looked amazing! One of the most stylish salons I've ever seen. I can't wait to get my first haircut there.

"You're very kind, Jo." Jennifer looked a little embarrassed at the compliment. "Kirsty, I think I told you I was looking into Interior Design courses. Well, I've now signed up for a ten-week evening course starting at the end of January."

"That's brilliant, Jennifer. You must be so excited."

"Excited and a little nervous. I'm sure I'll be the oldest person there and what if I can't keep up? It's been a while since I was last in academia."

"For starters," I said. "I'm pretty sure you get quite a mixed age range at evening courses. And secondly, it's a ten-week course, you're not going to be expected to write massive essays or put in a tonne of studying. This course will be perfect for you."

"Here's hoping. Anyway, shall we get started on our Bible study for the evening? As you know I'm a big Christmas fan. And as it's now December, I thought we could start looking at aspects of the Christmas story. It's a story we're very familiar with which unfortunately means we can lose how special it is. But let's pray we learn something new about the Christmas story this December."

I have very mixed feelings about Christmas. I certainly don't get excited about it the way Jennifer does. Or for that matter the way almost everyone else seems to enthuse about it.

"Tonight," continued Jennifer, "I'd like us to read the story of when the angels appear to the shepherds. This is my favourite part. Jo, can you read Luke chapter two, verses one to twenty-one for us?"

"Of course," replied Jo, as she then proceeded to read the passage Jennifer had mentioned.

"Thanks, Jo. I want us to hone in on verse ten: '*But the angel said to them, 'Do not be afraid. I bring you good news that will cause great joy for all the people.'*' This is a season meant to bring great joy to everyone. The birth of Jesus is the start of the good news story for all of us. Christmas is a wonderful time, a time when people are more generous and more aware of others. Let's read this verse every day and remember that Christmas represents good news and joy for everyone."

I considered Jennifer's words as I made another round of tea and coffee for our post-study chat. In many ways tonight had been the healing balm I needed. Telling silly stories with my friends had banished the lingering fear of panic attacks. Being with these amazing women is always my safe place. But Jennifer's talk of joy unsettled me. It was okay for Jennifer to feel happy about Christmas. She has a lovely house and the perfect family. I'm just hoping to survive Christmas. Work has its challenges. I'll be spending Christmas with my family, not always the most joyful of places. And being away means there is zero chance of anything happening with Paul at Christmas. Maybe joy is just an elusive dream for me.

Paul

This was it! Day one of The Smith Salon. Brian, Trish and myself had stayed late last night to clean up after the launch event, ensuring everything was ready for the start of business this morning. It was nice having the place to myself for a little while. I connected my phone to the music system and played my worship playlist, praying for the salon and the clients that would come through our door. It was a risky and unknown venture to start my own business and yet the peace was almost palpable.

A few minutes later, Brian arrived. The faith Brian and Trish have put in me is unnerving but I'm very grateful for them. Being on a journey with people is way more rewarding than going it alone.

"Is your first appointment someone new or someone you already know?" I asked Brian, as he grabbed himself a coffee.

"First up is one of my friends. Then the next appointment is with someone I met at last night's opening."

"Exactly the same for me," I replied. "It's good to have a familiar client to start with. I almost feel like today is my first day as a hairdresser."

"I know what you mean. The turnout last night was encouraging but we need that to equate to new clients. So far it seems to have led to new bookings."

Our appointment books were a mixture of friends, clients who followed us from ByDesign, and new clients. We were still trying to figure out how to assign new clients. The easiest way was to have a rolling schedule, keeping a tally to ensure even distribution of bookings.

Our first appointments arrived, and we officially started The Smith Salon. My first client, Stacy, was a friend from the gym. She enthused about the salon and how great the place looked. We quickly settled into the familiar routine of chatting as I worked on her hair. Talking about the gym, the depressing weather and Stacy's plans for the rest of the day. It was refreshingly familiar and by the time I waved her off, The Smith Salon felt like home.

The day flew by. I had gaps along the way but I was okay with that. It would be unrealistic to expect a full schedule from the first day. Today had been a good mix of clients, old and new, and time to appreciate the thrill of the new salon. My last appointment was with another new client. Or so I thought.

At half past four Matt walked in the door.

"Hi, I have an appointment with Paul," he joked as I met him at the reception desk. I looked at him in confusion and then realised the name in the schedule was an anagram of Matt's name.

"Very good," I said. "Now your behaviour over the last few weeks makes sense. I couldn't understand why you kept coming up with excuses whenever I offered to cut your hair at the flat."

"The freebies are over for me now. Need to support my mate in his new business."

I led Matt over to my workstation and got started on his hair.

"How's your first day been?" asked Matt, as he settled himself down in the chair.

"It's been an encouraging start. I've had some new clients and some of my old ByDesign clients. So far so good."

"How has it been for you guys?" Matt shouted over to Brian and Trish, both of whom were cleaning up their workstations.

"Exciting," said Trish. "Great working atmosphere, and the décor is amazing. A vast improvement on ByDesign."

"I'm relieved we got some brand new clients today," added Brian.

"You're a talented team in a stylish setting, I'm sure this place is going to be a great success."

I appreciated Matt's words of encouragement to Trish and Brian. It was good for them to hear it from someone other than me.

"I'm going to take Paul out for burgers and beer as his first day treat. Do you guys want to come too? My treat."

"That would have been great, but I've already got plans, thanks Matt," replied Trish.

"I can't make it either," said Brian. "But thanks for the offer."

Matt chatted a bit longer with Trish and Brian while I cleaned up my workstation. After they left I set about sweeping and cleaning the floor.

"Look at you being all domesticated," joked Matt.

"Now that you've seen I can do it here you'll be expecting me to mop our kitchen floor." Matt always gives me a hard time for my lack of tidiness in our flat. He has a point.

"One day when we start making money I'll treat myself to hiring a cleaner to come in and give the place a good clean. But for now, I need to be cautious."

"Are you worried about money?"

"Of course. It's a risky thing to start up my own business. Today I have the excitement of starting a new thing. Opening a salon in December is perfect timing because it's one of the busiest months for salons, but what will happen in January when we get one of the quietest months?"

"You'll keep going because you know things will get better. And if those credit card bills drag you down, you know I'll help."

"I'm not going to borrow money from you. You've got your own responsibilities."

"Well, the offer is always there."

Knowing people were supporting and encouraging me had enabled me to get this far. But the salon had to prove itself as a viable business. And I had to prove that I could do it.

Jennifer

Birthday weekend! I love birthdays. I love the anticipation and the excitement of it all. And this year Scott has been uncharacteristically skilled at keeping my birthday festivities secret.

The first surprise of the night was that he came back home rather than meeting me in town. We left on our date to the sound of the girls laughing at some terrible joke my mum had just told them.

Our taxi dropped us off at one of our favourite restaurants. Upon entering, the most amazing aromas immediately surrounded us. My stomach gurgled in anticipation, hopefully not loud enough for anyone else to hear. The waiter guided us to a table for two at the side of the restaurant. The soft music and romantic lighting further tingling my senses with anticipation. Over the delicate bubbles of our champagne we made our food choices.

"Thank you, Scott. This is all so perfect."

He leaned over the table and kissed me. "You deserve it. I'm sorry I've been working so late recently. So I wanted to let you know you are definitely not forgotten."

I smiled, determined not to allow my annoyance at his work hours blot our romantic night out. "So, is it just dinner?" I asked, before my thoughts could run off on the wrong direction. "Or are there other plans for the evening?"

"There might be something else," he teased. "But you need to wait until after dessert to find out what."

Over dinner our conversation was light and fun. The poke of annoyance had been banished and I was able to enjoy our child-free time. As Scott became more animated telling me about the last rugby match he had watched, I enjoyed the sight of the man before me. He looked so dashing in his grey suit and burgundy shirt. His hair, increasingly peppered with grey, was looking very smart after a visit to The Smith Salon. And, every so often I caught the musky scent of his aftershave. Annoyances easily infiltrate into the monotony of the day-to-day, but I need moments like this to banish those thoughts and appreciate the person I get to do life with.

"Thanks for dinner," I said as we enjoyed our post-dinner coffees. The yummy flavours of dinner still playing in my mouth.

"So are you ready for your next surprise?" I nodded my agreement. "We're going to meet Ben and Tara for this next part."

"How on earth did you manage to get Tara to keep this from me?"

Ben and Tara have been our pastors at ChurchX for three years. As soon as we met Scott and myself and Ben and Tara instantly became friends. When they arrived, the church was lacking direction and wasn't sure of its focus. Ben brought in some much-needed structure, and Tara added a big dose of fun. Ministries were rejuvenated under their leadership and the congregation became more engaged. And somehow in the process they didn't make it about them but pointed to Jesus.

I was excited they would be part of my night out.

Once we finished our coffees, Scott led the way to Bath Street. Several basement bars and restaurants occupied both sides of the street. We stopped at the aptly named UnderGround. The chalkboard on the street informed passers-by that part of tonight's musical line-up was Scott Nicol, one of my favourite artists.

The warmth of the bar greeted us as soon as we stepped in from the chilly December air. Ben and Tara had already secured a table for us near the music area. They stood up and greeted us with friendly hugs. This was turning out to be the perfect birthday weekend.

"How's your week been?" asked Tara as we sipped on our gins.

"It's been busy. It was Paul's salon opening on Tuesday night."

"How was it? I was so disappointed I wasn't able to make it. I'll need to book an appointment and check it out."

"You should. He'll appreciate the business."

"And I can't wait to see your handy work."

"It was lovely seeing it all come together and thankfully it was more or less ready for the opening. There are still a few wee things I want to change, but it's pretty much done."

"And how are you feeling about the evening course?"

"I'm excited. But I'm also wondering how I'm going to balance setting up my own business with being a mum. The house is a mess and I've not been there for the girls the way I should have been over the last few weeks."

"Oh motherhood," sighed Tara. "The place where there is always guilt."

"So true. And I think I'm feeling extra doses of that guilt this week."

"Don't get bogged down by the guilt, Jennifer. I know that's easier said than done. But we do the best we can and offer it all in prayer. Find the right balance for you and don't worry about what anyone else says. You're a good mum, your girls are lucky to have someone who loves them and invests in them so unconditionally."

"Thanks. Maybe keep reminding me of that."

Before we could chat further the bar manager switched on the mic and welcomed us to the bar. "Tonight we're privileged to have a great line-up for you. First up we've got Angela Smith. Angela can regularly be heard busking on Buchanan Street. Then we've got UnderGround's very own Nick Carter. We're letting him out from the bar to wow you with a set of covers and a couple of his own songs. Then we'll be finishing up with Ayrshire's Scott Nicol. Scott will have you all up on your feet dancing and singing along."

We all clapped and cheered.

"Have a great night everyone," continued the manager. "Now, give a great big UnderGround welcome to Angela Smith."

Again we all cheered.

Angela took her place behind the mic, guitar in hand. She looked so young and her guitar seemed to drown her. But as soon as she started singing, a powerful voice filled the room and had us all paying attention. Twenty minutes later she bowed to thunderous applause.

"This is a great venue," enthused Tara.

"I love it here," I replied. "We don't come nearly as often as I'd like. But I guess that makes it more of a treat."

Ben and Scott went to the bar to get another round of drinks. I glanced over and watched my husband walk over to where Scott Nicol was sitting. We have met Scott Nicol once or twice before but I don't think he would remember us. What were they talking about? My Scott pointed over at me then went to join Ben at the bar. What was he up to?

Next up was Nick, the bartender. He wasn't as good as Angela, but he put on a good show, and with the staff cheering him on he had plenty of support to encourage him.

After another quick break, it was time for Scott Nicol to take to the floor. "Good evening, everyone," he called out as he adjusted his mic.

"I've been asked to give a special shout-out to Jennifer." As he spoke, he looked over to where I was sitting. "Jennifer! Happy birthday. This first song is for you."

And with that, he went into a song called December Rose. I'd never heard it before. Glancing over at my Scott, I mouthed my 'thank you'. I swayed along and closed my eyes taking in the beautiful lyrics of the song. We all cheered as the song came to an end.

"Happy birthday, Jennifer. That was for you, December Rose," announced Scott Nicol. As he went on to the next song, my Scott presented me with a single red rose with a note saying, 'to my December rose'. I was touched by how much effort Scott had put into my birthday celebration.

Scott Nicol finished to a standing ovation. As promised he had given a great set of songs and had us all singing and clapping along with him. Before we left, he came over to wish me a happy birthday again and thanked us for coming out.

I picked up my December Rose and walked out of UnderGround hand-in-hand with my wonderful husband. Scott works too much, leaving me alone more evenings than I considered acceptable. But he also has an amazing gift for romantic gestures. Tonight I would bask in the delight of that gift.

JENNIFER

The next morning I was woken up at seven o'clock with three girls bouncing on my bed. For some reason, children that struggle to get out of bed for school are able to get up early at weekends.

"Happy birthday, mum," they chorused. "Are we having a special breakfast for you?"

Scott groaned from somewhere under the duvet as the three girls continued bouncing on top of me.

"Right you terrible three," he shouted. Amid the girls' screams of excitement and carry-on, he bundled them up within the duvet, folding it over them. "If you want a special breakfast, you need to come and help make it." He set them free from the duvet and chased them out of our room.

"You wanting to get some more sleep?" he asked.

"Do you really think that's an option?" I replied. "Although it might be nice to stay in bed for a bit and read."

"Okay, I'll bring you a coffee and then get started on breakfast."

In the silence of my room, I glanced over at my bedside table. Leaning over, I picked my December Rose from its vase. Holding it up to my nose, I savoured the sweet aroma and smiled at the memories of last night.

I wasn't sure what Scott had planned for today. But I was up for whatever activities my family came up with. I had raced around the house all day Wednesday and Thursday to ensure it was clean and tidy. My poor house had been somewhat neglected with all the work I had put into Paul's salon. Under a normal weekend schedule, I would still have been doing some cleaning. But maybe it was time for a weekend off.

A few minutes later, Scott returned with my coffee and the girls in tow. "We've been chatting and have finalised our plans for today," announced Scott. "First of all, me and the girls are going to pop out to buy fresh muffins for breakfast."

The girls cheered as I rubbed my stomach to signal my approval.

"Then, even though it's your birthday, we're fairly certain you'll be okay with us putting up the outside Christmas lights today."

"I approve. It's time to get those lights up."

"Then tonight," concluded Scott, "Kirsty and the girls and Paul and Matt are coming over for pizza."

"That all sounds wonderful. Thank you so much, my fabulous family."

"What about mum's presents?" Chloe asked Scott.

"You girls can give her your present when we come back with the muffins. And I'll give mum her present at dinner time."

"I am intrigued!" It was another example of the time and thought Scott was putting into my birthday. I couldn't wait for tonight to find out what it was.

The day passed in a haze of family cosiness. After lunch we trooped outside to put up the Christmas lights. Or more accurately Scott scrambled up ladders to attach the lights to gutters and trees as the girls and I instructed him on the correct positioning. With the lights all set in their rightful place it was time for hot chocolate and marshmallows. Our house felt extra cosy after the chill of the December afternoon. The girls giggled and joked around as we made up our hot chocolate. As it was my birthday, I got to choose the Christmas movie. We clambered onto the sofa, covered up in blankets and hugged our hot chocolate and each other as the feel-good movie began. This was my perfect place.

But even in the perfect setting, my peace was ruffled by a twang of guilt about the hours I'd put in to finish Paul's salon. I'd relied on my parents and other mums to pick the girls up from school over the last few weeks. And when I was home I'd spent time sourcing products for the salon. Tara had told me not to feel guilty, but it's not something you can flick off and on. Now wasn't the time to fall into a spiral of guilt. Today was time to enjoy precious moments with the girls and Scott.

Kirsty

The warmth of a thousand sparkling fairy lights welcomed us as the taxi pulled up to Jennifer's house. The lights wrapped around their porch and on the trees in their front garden. It looked magical. This is a house where Christmas is enjoyed.

"Your lights look amazing," enthused Jo, as Scott opened the door to us.

"Well thank you," replied Scott. "I'm sure Jennifer will buy more before we get to Christmas. There seems to be more and more each year."

"You can't deny your designer wife does have a good eye for such things," I said, and laughed at Scott's expression. He knew he was outnumbered.

We took off our coats and made our way into the kitchen. Amy, Emma and Chloe came down to join us. I love these girls, although it was funny watching Amy. She had reached the age of fashion awareness and she would sneak glances at us to assess what we were wearing. Jo's shoe collection always draws her attention. At just over five foot, Jo loves her high heels and has the biggest shoe and boot collection of anyone I know. Amy now matched Jo in shoe size and height which brought even more fascination from Amy.

While Amy obsessed over our boots, Emma hesitated at the side of the room and Chloe was all about the carry-on. When the doorbell rang again signalling the arrival of Paul and Matt, Chloe squealed with excitement and raced to the door to tackle the boys. Paul and Matt had barely crossed the threshold before Chloe was throwing herself at them, demanding attention and tickles.

"Right you," growled Matt, as he scooped her up and held her upside down. Her squeals of delight filled the house.

I glanced over at Paul. Thankfully, he was chatting with Scott and didn't notice me looking. Every time I see Paul I'm thrown into utter confusion. He really does seem like one of the good guys, plus he's incredibly hot and yet I'm terrified of what happens next. I never know how to act around him.

Jo came over. "Talk to him."

"What?"

"Don't play innocent. Go and talk to Paul. Ask him about the salon."

Jo is probably right, but I didn't want to leave the safety of my seat. Thankfully, Scott came to my rescue by calling us all together. "While we wait for the pizza to arrive, I'd like to wish Jennifer the happiest of birthdays."

We all raised our glasses and joined together to say happy birthday to Jennifer.

"I haven't given Jennifer her present yet," continued Scott. "I needed all of you here because it affects you too."

We all glanced round at each other wondering what Scott's gift would be.

Scott looked to Jennifer. "First of all the apology. This year your present is for your birthday and your Christmas. But hopefully you'll forgive me." Jennifer laughed at Scott's comment. "I overheard the girls inviting us on their ski holiday. So I spoke to Lynn and Matt about it. Checked my work schedule. And asked your mum and dad if they could look after the girls. Then booked us on the ski holiday with the rest of this grouping."

"Oh my goodness," screamed Jennifer, jumping up from the settee to hug Scott. "That's amazing. Thank you so much."

"Although it is a bit of a selfish gift because I get to enjoy it too." He kept his arm around her waist and looked down and winked at her.

"That's not fair!" sulked Chloe. "I want to go too."

"We'll do a family ski holiday another year," Scott reassured her.

"Now," he continued, looking round the rest of us. "The reason this involves all of you, apart from the fact you now have the two of us tagging along, is that I've booked the accommodation. I hope you don't mind but I've opted for a serviced chalet."

"No way!" exclaimed Paul. "That's amazing! But it's too much, mate."

"Not at all. Let's enjoy the holiday with the perfect space to hang out together."

After the pizza arrived, we settled in the living room with our food and Scott put up images of the chalet on the TV.

"Wow! That looks amazing. A hot tub too! This is the best birthday present ever. Thank you," grinned Jennifer.

"I might go as far as to say that I'm looking forward to the holiday now," I said.

"How was the ski lesson?" Matt asked.

"Not great. I think I fell over more than I stayed upright. I'm not optimistic about my current or future skiing ability."

"You'll be great. In no time at all you'll be skiing like a pro," enthused Jo, "You'll love it."

"You do remember who you're talking to here? We're going on holiday to take part in a sport known for injuries. It's like my worst nightmare."

"Where's that competitive spirit of yours?" asked Jo.

"I've no idea. Even it's scared to make an appearance when it comes to skiing."

"Well we'll all need to take extra care of you," said Paul.

The room went quiet, awkward glances flashing around. I'm not sure when the awkwardness started with me and Paul. But judging by the silence in the room, the others were all aware of it too.

"I think the chalet looks amazing," said Matt, breaking the tension. "I'm even more annoyed that I need to leave early now."

"Me too," sighed Jo. "It's such a pain the schools only get a long weekend. It's no use for ski holidays."

Paul glanced over to me. "I'd love to be there for the whole week too. But at least we get to be with you for a few days."

"Yep, you poor teachers and new business owners," said Lynn. "We'll think of you back at work while we're enjoying our post-ski drinks in the hot tub."

"Lynn! You're so mean," said Carol. "We'll miss you all. It's a shame we can't all be there for the entire week."

As we continued eating our pizza, the rest of the group shared stories from ski holidays past. Scott left the images of the chalet up on their TV. It looked amazing.

Once the pizza was finished, people started moving around more. As soon as Jo left my side, Paul came and sat beside me. He looked so good in his jeans and polo-shirt. The short sleeves emphasising his muscly arms. And as if that wasn't enough, his aftershave was sending my senses into overdrive.

"What do you think of the chalet?" he asked.

"It looks beautiful. I'm definitely looking forward to the holiday more now."

Before he had the chance to say anything further an energy-filled Chloe threw herself onto Paul. He hadn't seen her coming and seemed momentarily winded by the landing. I tried not to giggle, but couldn't stop myself. Unaware, or uncaring, about the impact she'd just had, Chloe slid off his knee and squeezed in between us.

"Kirsty, did you see all our Christmas lights outside?"

"I did. They look magical," I replied to my little friend, as Paul regained his composure.

"Next weekend we're going to get our Christmas tree," she continued. "Do you think we'll get spiders on our tree?"

"I don't know," I replied.

"I hope we do. Luke in my class said that when you get a real Christmas tree, you also get nests of spiders in your tree. I think that would be amazing. But I don't think mum would like it. Would you like to have spiders in your tree?" she asked.

She barely gave me time to answer before she was off talking about spiders in Christmas trees again. Paul looked over and smiled at me. How could we have moments like this and still be battling awkwardness?

"You smell lovely," continued Chloe, apparently moving on from the Christmas tree monologue. "You smell so lovely, you smell like diamonds."

"Wow!" I replied. "I smell like diamonds? And what do diamonds smell like?"

"I just said," she replied, in her five-year-old exasperation of adults. "Like you."

"Okay. Well, thank you."

"I think she smells like diamonds too," replied Paul, and gave me the most enticing look. My defences melted in his presence. But even under the glow of his smile I was still battling confusion. How can I be so hopeful about a relationship with Paul and yet have so many fears about it? Was I the one in danger of sabotaging any hope of a relationship?

Paul was back to tickling Chloe. I took the distraction as an opportunity to glance over at him. There was a lot to appreciate about this man. The part of me that longed for a relationship with him was gaining ground. Maybe there was more to look forward to in our snowboots and sunglasses holiday than just a hot tub.

Jennifer

The next morning I arrived at church full of the joys of a fun weekend and the promise of a wonderful ski holiday. Scott had excelled himself and relieved some of the niggles about his current work load.

Before we had even sat down, Tara pulled me to the side. "Jennifer, are you free next week?"

I nodded my agreement.

"Would you be able to help us out? We've got a couple of Advent sessions in the local primary school. Evelyn was going to be helping us. But she texted me this morning to let me know she's down with a terrible cold and won't be able to help."

"What do you need me to do?"

"We're going to let the children dress up and get them to act out the nativity. I know they might be doing a nativity play already, but this gives them space to think about it and have fun with it. You don't need to prepare anything, we just need enough people to help with the children."

"Yes, that will be fine. What days are you there?"

"Tuesday and Thursday mornings. Can you help with both of them?"

"Yes, no problem."

"Thank you so much. We'll get everything gathered together. Can you meet us here about nine o'clock and we'll go over to the school together?"

I was happy to help. But it was another thing to add to my extensive December to-do list.

We settled in our seats, ready for church to begin. Each Sunday of Advent the leaders select children to go on stage to help light the next candle. I say help, but it really amounts to the children standing next to whichever church leader is actually lighting the candle. Today it's the turn of my girls to help. Amy, Emma and Chloe stood next to Tara as she lit the second candle of Advent. Amy was playing it cool, Emma looked on shyly and Chloe couldn't stand still.

With the candle lit it was time for my favourite part of church - singing. I love music, the way it reaches deep within and touches my soul. Throughout the year the worship band lead us in the latest choruses but with Advent it's all about the classic Christmas carols. The carols spoke of Silent Nights, Angels, Shepherds and Jesus and brought their familiar comfort of hope and peace.

As we sat down after the last song, the children filed out to their kids' church rooms and Ben stood up to preach. "This morning we'll be reading from Luke chapter two. *'Glory to God in the highest heaven and on earth peace to those on whom his favour rests.'*"

When it comes to the Christmas story, the angels and the shepherds catch my imagination. I can imagine being one of the shepherds and all the emotions they must have gone through - from the mundane to fear to amazement and then worship.

My imaginings were brought to an abrupt end when Chloe's name flashed up on the screen behind Ben. Our church has this system to alert parents if their kids need them during kids' church. Scott went to check on Chloe.

I appreciated Scott going to check, but it left me wondering what the issue was. A few minutes later he came back alone, which was a good sign. "She's fine," he whispered, "just bumped her knee on a desk and started crying. I think she's overly tired. It didn't seem that big an issue."

Scott's attention returned to Ben. But now that I had been disturbed my thoughts spiralled into a million and one distractions. Once again I questioned how plausible it was to start my own business with a young family. I know lots of other women do it every day, but could I? I thought of Sarah, one of the mums I've known for years through various parenting and school connections. A few weeks ago she and her husband started couple's counselling in a bid to save their marriage. It's been a few weeks since we've spoken. I should text her and arrange to get together. What else did I need to do this week? Well, there are the school activities Tara asked me to help with. Plus, we'll pick our Christmas tree next weekend, which means putting up our decorations, so I'll need to give the downstairs a thorough clean. Chloe's school nativity play is the last week of term, so I need to make sure she's got everything she needs for that. And I need to get all those Christmas cards written and posted. And how could I forget, the Christmas Fayre at school? As head of the PTA, I still have a long to-do list for the Fayre. Tomorrow's school run would be the perfect time to get more helpers. And I needed to meet with the assistant-head to confirm final arrangements with the school.

People around me stood up to sing one more carol. I had missed Ben's sermon! Did I really have that many distractions in my life? I would make time to listen to Ben's sermon tomorrow morning in the stillness of a quiet house.

***

After the school run the following morning, I settled down in my living room determined to listen to Ben's sermon from yesterday. I needed some time out from the rushing around of parenting, housework, PTA and all the other tasks that come my way. I switched on the lights to ward off the dullness of the December morning and snuggled into my settee, coffee in hand. Opening up the church's website on my phone, I searched for the link to yesterday's sermon.

"This morning we'll be reading from Luke chapter two. *'Glory to God in the highest heaven and on earth peace to those on whom his favour rests.'*" But once again my thoughts wandered, and I zoned out from Ben's message.

"This is ridiculous!" I shrieked at the empty room. I stopped the playback and opened the notes app on my phone, making a list of the things that were filling my mind. I would get some of these distractions ticked off my list then settle down to listen to Ben.

I sent a text to Sarah to begin the conversation about when we would meet up. Next up, I cleaned the windows in the living room and gave it a vacuum and dust. There! That should be enough to be able to concentrate on Ben's message.

Once again, I sat down to listen. "This morning we'll be reading from Luke chapter two. *'Glory to God in the highest heaven and on earth peace to those on whom his favour rests.'*"

As Ben's sermon continued, I could feel my attention drift again. Why was this so difficult? I paused the playback and looked around the room. On the table beside me was a notepad. I'm forever buying new notepads and this was my latest purchase, a beautiful green and red geometric design adorned the front, perfect for Christmas time. I picked up my notepad and a pencil and started doodling. The action helped to settle my mind and concentrate on Ben's words. The irony of a sermon on peace was not lost on me.

By the time I got to the end of the sermon, I felt calmer and a flicker of peace warmed my soul. Turning to a new page in my notepad I started sketching. I tried to imagine what it would look like in the stable at Jesus' birth? We have our warm, fuzzy Christmas card images but what was the reality? When I was a kid one of my friends lived on a farm. My memories of their cattle sheds were not warm and fuzzy. It was not a place for a baby's birth. The smells, the noise, the drafts – none of it was conducive to a baby being born. Could I capture some of that reality in a sketch? The stable was a place of obscurity but it was a place where anyone was welcome. A place to come and be.

Somewhere during my sketching, I fell asleep. I'm not sure how long I slept, but when I woke I felt rested and at peace. My nativity sketch lay beside me on the couch. It wasn't finished it but it drew me in. I would make sure I finished the sketch before Christmas. It felt important.

PAUL

"How was last week for you?" It was our first business meeting of The Smith Salon and probably the most excited I've ever been about a meeting. Scott had suggested we had weekly business meetings and to make them a priority from the start.

Over coffee and muffins, Brian, Trish and myself chatted about our first week of business. Trish took a selfie of us with our coffees to post on our social media. Champion of social media is just one of the talents she brings to the salon. We all had a good opening week. Our schedules hadn't been full, but it was a good, healthy start and encouraged us all.

While we were still discussing our highlights from the previous week, the mail arrived. As Brian and Trish continued with their tales, I stood to the side and opened the envelopes. Each one an invoice, some for work carried out on the salon and some for hair products. They were a reminder not to get carried away with our initial success.

We had to make money from our business. We had to pay off our debts.

"You okay?" asked Trish. "Bad news?"

"It's fine, just invoices. But thankfully we've got off to an impressive start." I was still optimistic about the salon. We could make this work. But I didn't want to put any burden on Brian and Trish. After all, it was my name above the door. The responsibility was mine. We had set up the business as mine with Brian and Trish renting their workstations from me. The theory behind this set up was we were all responsible for ourselves but the reality was I still felt responsible for them and their profit levels.

Before either of them could ask anything more, Jennifer arrived, arms full of boxes.

"Hey everyone," she said, "I've got another couple of boxes in the car. Would someone like to pop out and bring them in for me?"

"I'll get them," replied Brian. "What is all this anyway?"

"What is missing from the salon?"

We looked at her with blank expressions.

"Christmas, of course! We didn't want the salon to be Christmas-themed for opening night, but now it's time to get these decorations up."

"Jennifer!" I exclaimed. "You are too much."

"Not at all. Every salon needs Christmas cheer. Plus when I saw all these decorations in navy and silver I just couldn't resist."

Jennifer opened the boxes to reveal beautiful decorations in colours that matched our salon. I hadn't even considered Christmas decorations. I was glad Jennifer was on it.

"And this is especially for you," she declared, as she handed me a gift box and a card.

Inside the gift box were four navy baubles. One had 'hope', one 'love', one 'joy' and one 'peace' written in silver calligraphy. I picked up the baubles with 'hope' and 'peace' written on them. It was a timely reminder. Those invoices had rattled me, but here was a reminder that hope and peace surrounded me. 'Joy' was a daily feeling with the new salon. And as for 'love', my thoughts turned to Kirsty. I hung the baubles from the top of my workstation mirror.

The Christmas card depicted a manger scene and the text inside said 'love came down at Christmas'. Jennifer had written a message, 'Paul, every success on your first Christmas at The Smith Salon. In the busyness of this season and with your new business remember that God's hope, love, joy and peace are always surrounding you.' I taped the card to the top of my mirror. The cards and baubles would keep me focussed on the things that mattered.

However, the bills had me doubting the wisdom of going on holiday so soon after starting my own business. As the others busied about the salon, Brian and Trish getting ready for their first clients and Jennifer setting up the decorations, I looked again at the baubles. 'Love' stood out and my thoughts returned to Kirsty. Things had felt strange at the weekend. It was as if she had erected a wall to keep me away. Knowing women had always been my superpower but with Kirsty I was floundering. Was it me? Was it her? Whatever it was it didn't put me off wanting to know her more. Wanting to kiss her. The last few weeks had been non-stop getting the salon ready and the next few weeks would be busy with Christmas bookings but hopefully the new year would bring new possibilities.

My thoughts returned to the night I told Kirsty I wanted to be with her in the future. We had spent the afternoon karting. Her first drive round was tentative but her competitive spirit soon showed up and she was getting faster with each lap. Matt and I had encouraged her to report Gary to her HR department. Her face was so expressive you could almost see the decision-making process as she walked through it. I was so proud of her when she made the decision to confront the situation. It was a brave step to take.

Kirsty had the potential to be a brave, strong person. But for some reason she kept retreating and trying to hide. I wanted to know why. The thoughts of Kirsty dispelled my money worries. A long weekend in the French Alps would be worth every penny to be with Kirsty. I couldn't wait.

KIRSTY

Friday morning started with a department meeting. However, without the leadership of a department manager, the meeting dragged on. Irene and Angela, the other section head, were competing to lead the meeting. I willed them to bring things to a close.

"As well as department business we have fun items to discuss," said Angela, as she wrapped up her section's update. "Both of which are happening next Friday. First of all, the PR department will be going along to several children's Christmas parties taking place at the various sports centres in the city. We will pick one of you to represent our department."

A chorus of 'Oooo's' ran around the room. "And the second thing," continued Angela, "is our Christmas night out."

Everyone else cheered. "We can stop work at three o'clock next Friday. That will give us time to get ready here and get a drink on the way to the hotel for the party night." Excited chatter circled the room. Everywhere I went people were embracing the Christmas party season. It was a sentiment that passed me by.

We had booked our party night months ago and had all been contributing five pounds a week since then to cover the cost of the dinner and the first few rounds of drinks. With everything else that had been going on, I'd forgotten all about it. It was another thing to dread in the run-up to Christmas.

On Wednesday night Jennifer told us a couple of new girls will start coming to our house group in January. Our group started intentionally small in August to provide space for new people who wanted to join a house group. The two new girls were both students. Jennifer suggested we invite them on a pre-Christmas social to enable us all to get to know each other. We discussed various options before we settled on an evening of a pre-theatre dinner followed by the cinema to see the latest Christmas chick-flick. The small group night out was way more appealing than the work night out.

All these social events made me realise I needed to book an appointment with Paul to get my hair tidied up for the festive season. Jo, Lynn and Carol had all made appointments when they were at Paul's opening night last week. It was silly to exist in this strange uncertainty of whether we would date or not. The very least I could do was be a friend and support his business. After all, we would be going on holiday together in a few months, we owed it to everyone else to get along without any tension.

Irene brought my attention back to the meeting with a final announcement. "And finally, to keep you all in the loop, HR are interviewing candidates for our new head of department next week." She glanced over at me as she gave the announcement. Not helpful.

"I don't have any details. And I have no idea when the new manager will be starting as it will depend on the notice period from their current job."

As we filtered from the meeting room, I overheard some of my co-workers speculating once again as to why Gary had left so abruptly. I was relieved that no one knew I was the reason. And yet, I still felt like everyone knew. Maybe it was only me that had labelled me as 'that girl'. But how long would it be before someone found out? There would be no stopping such gold-dust gossip. Once again I considered the option of looking for a job elsewhere.

***

There was no lazy Saturday morning for me this week. Jennifer had invited me to spend the day with them and help them pick their Christmas tree. I wrapped up and got the bus further into the suburbs of the South Side of Glasgow. When I arrived the girls were in the midst of getting layered up and shouting for help to locate missing gloves, scarves and boots. Eventually, we made it out to the car and Jennifer drove us to the Christmas tree farm. We ordered a batch of hot chocolates from a booth at the farm entrance then wandered around looking at trees.

The smell of pine conjured up memories of home. As with everything to do with my home, it brought a mix of emotions. I love the fresh smell of pine, the reminder of the beauty of the Argyll forests. But it also reminds me of the family arguments around our choice of Christmas tree. Arguments that only got worse when my brother James started working for the Forestry Commission because then he believed he was the only one able to make an informed choice. I was dreading going back home for Christmas. Why had I agreed to go? Hanging out with Jennifer and her family was so much more fun than being anywhere near my family. With Jennifer's family, Christmas is fun and all about family togetherness, with my family it's just another setting for arguments.

It seemed like everything in the approach to Christmas was causing me stress and anxiety this year. What was going on?

Amy came over and stood beside me, hugging her hot chocolate. "Do you like picking Christmas trees?" she asked.

What could I tell her? She didn't need to hear about the negatives of my family and choosing Christmas trees. I was hoping today would help replace the negative memories with a positive one, memories of a family who could spend time together without it spiralling into disagreements. "I'm looking forward to helping you guys pick your tree. Which ones do you like?" I asked, as we wandered along the lines of trees.

"I'm not sure. It's so hard to tell when they are here. A tree's a tree. They all look pretty similar to me."

"You're probably right." I smiled as we continued looking at the trees, sipping our hot chocolate. We had all been instructed to pick our favourite tree and then we'd draw straws to determine the winner. I'm not sure what Scott and Jennifer will do if Chloe is the winner. As we drove over, she whispered to me that she was going to pick the biggest tree she could find. Between her quest for the biggest tree and her fascination with spider nests, I tried not to laugh out loud at the thought of what Chloe's search would entail.

After a bit, Scott got us all back together. "Has everyone picked their favourite?" he asked.

We all nodded. Jennifer produced a bag with lollipop sticks, one name per stick. She jumbled them up and Scott picked one.

"Kirsty," he announced, holding out my stick for all to see. I suspect they somehow rigged the choosing process. Although I didn't spot how they did it. "So which tree did you pick?" asked Scott.

"This way," I said, signalling for them to follow me. "I've picked an eight foot Fraser Fir. It's a good size for your living room, it's nice and even and the perfect Christmas tree shape."

"I bow to your expert knowledge," joked Scott.

What a difference with this family compared to my own. My mum or dad would have found fault with my choice, whereas Scott and Jennifer didn't just accept my choice but congratulated me on it. Maybe there could be joy at Christmas.

We spent our afternoon decorating the tree and then the house. Christmas music and laughter surrounded us as we worked. I thought scenes like this only happened in Christmas movies.

After dinner Jennifer and I relaxed on the couch, wine in hand, gazing at the twinkling lights of the Christmas tree.

"I love that smell," said Jennifer, as she took a deep breath inhaling the aroma of pine.

"I do like it, but it also brings up a bunch of unhappy memories for me. I can't believe I'm going back to Lochcala for Christmas. I wish I had the courage to stand up to my parents and tell them I'm staying in Glasgow."

"Is it as bad as all that?"

"I don't know. I keep questioning it. You know the weird relationship I have with my family. There's always a comfort about home, even with all the crazy dynamics within my family. But the longer I'm in Glasgow the less inclined I am to go back and I'm becoming increasingly aware of the issues. It's not that they go out of their way to be mean to me or anything." I paused to take a sip of my wine, looking longingly at Jennifer's tree.

"With three brothers, I always felt like an outsider in the family. And in our small house, I was the only one with my own room, I know most kids long for that, but it was another thing that made me feel out of the loop with the boys and their 'insider jokes'. And the boys resent me for that room because mum insists it's still my room for when I move back home!"

"I know it's hard," sympathised Jennifer. "Sometimes our views of our childhoods can be a bit skewed. Try going with an open mind. At least you're only there for a few days. And remember, I'm only a phone call away if you need to talk anytime."

"Thanks. I guess being with you guys today just showed me how families can be. And it's a stark contrast to mine. When you spoke about the joy of Christmas on Wednesday, it sounded like such a foreign concept. I look at your family and joy makes sense, especially with how much you all get into Christmas. The sound of laughter fills your home. But my family isn't like that. I'm not sure how much joy will be waiting for me in Lochcala."

"What if you are the joy carrier?"

"What do you mean?"

"It's not about what others offer us but what we can give to them. See, that's the thing with Christmas. There is joy, but that joy is in seeing Jesus and being aware of other people. Maybe this Christmas you can share joy with your family. We're all offered joy, but it's up to us to choose to accept it."

"You make it sound so straightforward. Christmas movies make it all come together magically. But this is real life. And this is my family. Plus," I paused, not sure how Jennifer would respond, "I'm struggling with my faith."

"In what way?"

"I don't know that I can explain it so well. But after the whole Gary thing, I feel so vulnerable and when I'm at church, the sermons seem irrelevant to what I'm going through."

"Do you know something?"

I shook my head.

"It's okay to feel that way. It's okay to question and evaluate what's going on. And it's also okay to not have all the answers. Sometimes it's about clinging on to a thread of hope. You never know, maybe there will be a Christmas miracle in Lochcala this year."

Jennifer has an amazing gift of making everything sound okay. But why would this Christmas be any different from previous ones? I was struggling to see any glimmer of hope or joy in the coming weeks.

Kirsty

"But the angel said to them, 'Do not be afraid, I bring you good news that will cause great joy for all the people.'"

The Bible verse Ben had just read had me sitting up and paying attention. Jennifer had encouraged us to read this verse every day in December. But this morning it was triggering a memory that I'd missed before. What was it? As he continued his sermon, I wracked my brain to try to think what it was. And suddenly it came to me. Jo had shared a Bible verse with me a few months ago that spoke of love driving out fear. At the time it had been a lifeline as I dealt with the Gary situation. But some of that fear had crept back into my life. Are memories harder to deal with than actual events? Could joy replace my anxiety and fear?

"What do you think of when you think about joy, especially in relation to Christmas?" continued Ben. "Do you think of a cute Christmas card picture of the nativity scene? Do you picture the perfect family around the perfect Christmas tree, in all their social media finery? Is your joy in the presents? Or maybe it's the joy of good food and parties."

I was curious where Ben was taking this.

"That birth stable wasn't perfect. It wasn't a clean, sanitary, draft-free place to give birth. Did Mary feel fear at having to give birth to her first baby in such conditions? We don't know. But we are told she 'treasured up all these things and pondered them in her heart'. An angel had told her that Jesus was the Son of God. The shepherds told everyone they met about the angels and Jesus' birth. There's a miracle right there – a group of men excited about the birth of a baby." A ripple of laughter circulated the church. "Joy surrounded the birth. A joy that had nothing to do with the conditions but everything to do with who that baby was."

Ben had me thinking. Did I have the wrong attitude to joy? Was I confusing it with happiness? But more to the point had I missed the deeper meaning in Christmas? There was so much I dreaded about Christmas, especially this year. But Ben's sermon of a less than perfect setting for Jesus' birth offered so much more hope than a perfect setting offered. Could I experience joy this Christmas regardless of my circumstances?

After church, Jo and I went back to my flat to spend the afternoon together.

Jo bounced down on my settee and flicked through a magazine. "What do you want to do?"

"I don't know. Watch a Christmas movie?"

"Good idea. But I need to ask, are these the only Christmas decorations you have?" She looked around my living room with an expression of disgust at my meagre strands of tinsel.

"Yes. I confess my desk at work has more decorations than my living room. But I spend more time at work than home, and I'll be in Lochcala for Christmas."

"Grab your coat and bag. We need to remedy this bah-humbug flat before we can watch a Christmas movie. And it might help brighten you up a bit too."

"What do you mean?"

"Your smile has been lacking these last few weeks. What's wrong?"

"I don't know. I feel flat. I guess after all the work stuff my emotions don't know what to do with themselves. I just need to get this year over and done with and start over next year."

"I get that. But don't miss the joy Christmas can bring."

As Jo navigated her car along the busy roads, I thought over what she had said. Between Jo, Jennifer's chat of yesterday and Ben's sermon of this morning I was beginning to feel I was being ganged up on. Was joy attainable after the last few weeks? According to Ben, Jennifer and Jo, it was.

The homeware store was a sensory overload. Colourful decorations hung from the industrial ceiling. Christmas tunes blasted out of a hidden sound system. The heat in the store was at odds with the cold, grey December day. I didn't even know where to start. "Okay," said Jo, grabbing my arm, "let's have some fun."

We made our way to the aisles that were full of Christmas adornments. "How great would this look in your flat," said Jo, as she stood next to a five foot singing Moose! The sight of Jo standing next to a Christmas decoration that was almost as tall as her had me in giggles.

"You could have this rather than a tree – hang some baubles from its antlers and wrap tinsel rounds its neck."

"You seem keen on it. Maybe you should get it for your flat. It would be good company for you."

"Do you know what? I am going to get it. It's so fun."

"But where will you store if for eleven months of the year?"

"That's easy," replied Jo. "I'll call him Ed the Moose and as the months go by, I'll decorate him to match the season!"

Watching Jo trying to lift the five foot decoration into the trolley had me in giggles again. "A little help, please," she said. "And at least get his little brother. Look they come in small, medium and large."

I picked up a small one to please Jo, but it wasn't enough. "If you're only going to buy the small one, then you need to buy more. Or what about one of the penguins or a husky?" A penguin made its way into the trolley with the Moose. Shopping with Jo could be an expensive outing.

Back at my flat, Jo gave the cuddly Christmas toys pride of place on the TV unit. We decorated the living room to the tunes of Christmas. The room had been through a major transformation this autumn when Jennifer had taken it upon herself to revamp it. It looked amazing compared to the previous mismatch look of my living room. And now with these decorations, it was further brightened up.

"Now we can watch a Christmas movie," declared Jo.

"Okay, you were right," I admitted. "It looks so much better and I feel better too."

"Yeah! So which movie do you want to watch?"

Armed with obscene quantities of popcorn, we flicked through the Christmas channels and picked a feel-good Hallmark Christmas movie. The plot was predictable but sweet. Of course, it ended with the boy and girl getting together for Christmas. There would be no such fairy-tale Christmas for me. Paul was busy with the salon and I was bound for Lochcala. Today had been so much fun with Jo, but could I discover joy this Christmas?

Jennifer

I checked my watch again. Willing the bus to go faster. Why had I decided to clean the kitchen floor before coming into town? This morning was my slot to get into the city centre and finish my Christmas shopping. Plus I'd arranged to meet Tara for lunch, so my time was limited.

Last week had passed in a blur. After my restful sleep on the Monday it had gone back to full-on busy. There had been the school visits with church on the Tuesday and Thursday. On Friday I'd cleaned the house in preparation for the Christmas tree and decorations. Which had left Wednesday as my day of final planning for the Christmas Fayre. In the evenings, as we'd watched TV, I'd finished writing the Christmas cards.

I had hoped coming into town on a Monday morning would provide me with a nice and quiet shopping experience. But it seemed other frantic shoppers had the same idea. The shops were already busy by the time I got in. Perhaps there were no quiet shopping days in December. I felt a surge of panic that I wouldn't get around the shops on my list before it was time to meet Tara. In record time, I purchased the remaining items for the girls. A quick check of my watch told me I only had ten minutes until my lunch appointment. I dashed into an outdoor shops to look for something for Scott. Hopefully,

I'd find some wee gift that would be perfect for our ski holiday. Almost sprinting, I got to the ski department, my eyes darting about from display to display trying to source something fun and useful. Ski socks – boring but a necessity. I grabbed a couple of pairs. As I stood in line waiting to pay, I noticed some items on the counter display. They had mini clip-on torches. I got one for each person in our group. As well as some more gadgets for Scott. I paid for my purchases at noon on the dot. A quick dash and I'd be at the café with Tara, just a few minutes late.

When I arrived at the café, loaded down with shopping bags, Tara was already seated with a glass of juice in front of her.

"Sorry," I said, as I flopped down in the chair opposite her. "How long have you been waiting?"

"Don't worry about it. I was early. Plus I've been enjoying some people-watching time."

There was plenty of scope for people-watching here. Somehow the café achieved an intimate appeal even though it opened out to the shopping centre. Every table was occupied, shopping bags loitering around the table legs. A school choir was singing Christmas carols nearby, and all around was the buzz of conversations. We ordered our lunch and relaxed into easy conversation as we waited for our soup to arrive.

"How are the girls? Bouncing about with excitement?"

"Chloe is, of course. Emma is excited in her own quiet way. And Amy is playing it cool. I'm not sure where we're at in the Santa journey with her. But that's a discussion for after Christmas."

"It's always a tricky one. You want to give them as long as possible and not be the one to ruin the belief but you also need to catch them before they say anything to their younger siblings."

"Exactly. But I'm fairly confident she knows enough to keep it to herself."

"What are your plans for Christmas day?" asked Tara.

"We'll have my parents over for Christmas dinner and marvel at how quickly the girls can tear through their presents. I want to fully enjoy the holiday. I think next year could be quite a pivotal year for me so I want to relax and enjoy every moment of the holiday."

Over soup, Tara filled me in on her plans for Christmas and her excitement at having her boys back home for the holidays. We parted ways, satisfied on soup and good company. This time as I walked along the busy city centre streets I noticed the beauty of the Christmas decorations, both in the shop windows and on the street. One advantage of our dull December days is the dark backdrop it provides for Christmas lights.

However, as soon as I was on the bus home, my mind started racing again, churning over all that was still to be achieved before Christmas. With the bus stopped for a red light, I glanced out the window and noticed a sign at the church across the road. The sign spoke of 'peace to all mankind'. My sketch! I'd completely forgotten all about it. I'd do some more work on it when I got home.

As I opened my front door, my phone rang. I slammed the door shut behind me, dropped all my bags and riffled through my bag trying to locate my mobile, worried it was a call from school. It was school. But thankfully not about the girls. It was the assistant-head teacher with some questions about the Christmas Fayre. I shuffled out of my coat and grabbed a pencil and pad to take some notes. It was all coming together, there were just a few things to be followed up on.

While it was all fresh in my mind, I called other mums to make the final arrangements for stalls and emailed the shopping list to the dad who had volunteered to do the cash'n'carry run. I sat down with a satisfied sigh. The Christmas Fayre was organised and catered for with days to spare. I checked my watch. It was almost time to go for the girls. But first I had to hide all the presents I'd left abandoned at the front door. Hopefully, I'd bought enough wrapping paper in last year's January sales to wrap everything. Nice, environmentally friendly brown paper for the grown-ups, bright red Santa paper for the girls' Santa presents and cute reindeers for their presents from us.

At the school playground, I had a further chat with the mums I'd called earlier. In-person chats ensured there was no miscommunication. When I took on the position of PTA chair I'd been excited at the challenge it brought. I'd even had plans for extra PTA activities but how quickly I'd settled for the usual fund raisers and dropped all my additional plans. And now that I was considering my future as an interior designer my time wasn't as free as it had been when I'd taken on the role. I would stay with it until the end of the academic year and then step down.

As soon as we got home from school, it was the frenzied pace of homework, early dinner then the mum-taxi to get Amy to football practice and Emma to keyboard lesson. I could never decide if it was easier to go back home for a short time or face shops with Chloe on Monday nights. However, I'd had my fill of shops for the rest of the month. So tonight, it was back home for half an hour before collecting the girls. Then it was bedtime. Chloe's bedtime story was first up, a calming story to settle her down. I was reading through a chapter book with Emma, she would read a page then I would read a page. With Amy it wasn't about reading together, it was more of a catch up on the day and making sure she was okay. Sometimes the bedtime routine ran smoothly, other nights one of the girls would have some big question or a school-day drama that needed to be talked through. Anything from trying to decide if a favourite pencil had been stolen or simply mislaid, to worries over what a teacher or classmate had said.

By the time I settled the three of them, I was exhausted. I made myself a mug of tea and took it to bed. Too tired to read I flicked through a magazine. Scott was still at work. He had promised that if he worked late tonight, he would be able to clear a good amount of work from his desk. I had my doubts.

Switching off my light, I suddenly remembered I hadn't done any more of my nativity sketch. Hopefully tomorrow…

Paul

Using my pen as a drum stick, I tapped to the beat of the music playing through the salon speakers. My morning was dragging by. Quiet days were inevitable, but I thought it would be January before we hit this level of quietness. I'd had one client all morning, but she had been in a rush so it was a quick appointment. Thankfully my day would end on a high. Kirsty was finally coming in for an appointment and I couldn't wait to show her The Smith Salon.

I looked round the salon, desperate for something to do. But the place was spotless and the paperwork was up to date. I picked up my mobile and scrolled through my apps, looking for something to amuse me. I stopped at the Bible App.

The other night Matt recommended a couple of Apps - the Bible App and Bible In One Year. I had downloaded both Apps immediately, always desperate to learn all I can about my new faith. I planned to leave the Bible In One Year until the first of January, it made sense to start it with the new year. Matt had mentioned study plans on the Bible App, so I had a look through those. I could complete a couple of Christmas reading plans between now and Christmas. It would be interesting to find out what the Bible actually said compared to my memories of the Christmas story from primary school nativity plays. I found one that incorporated music and Bible notes. In the quietness of the salon I listened to the four brief sessions. Again the focus was on hope, love, joy and peace.

I just finished it as Brain arrived. “Good to see you, mate. It’s been too quiet in here this morning.”

He walked over and checked his planner. “I’ve got a booking in half an hour and then nothing till early evening. And Trish has only got two bookings too.”

“I’m bored. Do you mind if I pop out for a bit?”

“Go for it. And feel free to bring back some donuts.”

I laughed and walked out into the icy wind. I pulled my coat up round my neck, planning to walk to the nearby park, but it was colder than I realised so I merely walked to the next street and my favourite café. I settled into a leather armchair, enjoying the warmth of the café and the smell of freshly baked donuts, as I flicked through a glossy magazine that was all about Glasgow. The centre pages contained a big feature on ByDesign. Several pictures showcased my old colleagues looking happy and showing off all the glamour of the salon. Had I made the right decision?

But then I turned the page and saw a picture of Si, the manager at ByDesign. The photo was obviously staged, making Si look important and the caption underneath claimed he was one of Glasgow’s top stylists. That one photo was all I needed to reassure me we had made the right decision.

I returned to The Smith Salon armed with a bag of donuts and a renewed confidence in our business.

***

"Wow!" exclaimed Kirsty, as she walked into the salon a few hours later. "This place is amazing."

"I'm glad you like it."

"You must be so proud of how it's all come together," she enthused.

"We are. And we've been quite busy since we opened, so we've got plenty to be hopeful about." I held my hand out for Kirsty's coat. "Let me take your coat and I'll meet you at the sinks for your hair wash and head massage."

As I began shampooing Kirsty's hair, I realised I'd never done this before. When she came to ByDesign, I had an assistant who did the hair washing. But in my own salon, it was my job. As the scent of coconut filled the air I slowly massaged in the shampoo, enjoying the intimacy of the moment. I took my time, not even wanting the sound of talking to interrupt us. The atmosphere sparked with possibilities.

It would be so easy to ask her out right now, but didn't we both need more time? Every time I see her I'm confused about what to do. Maybe I should just ask her out. But in the salon with other people wasn't the right time or place. Asking Kirsty out had to be perfect. I needed to show her how serious I was about her.

I kept to the safe conversations of our plans for the next few weeks and the run-up to Christmas.

"I've got my office night out tomorrow night," she stated. "It's part of the reason I came for my haircut tonight. But I'm not looking forward to it."

"I can imagine a work night out would be difficult for you." Should I reference Gary or would that bring up too many painful memories for her?

"I'm not sure whether or not I'll go."

"Why don't you go for at least part of the evening? Gary's not going to be there. You're safe."

"My head knows that but my nerves are still on flight mode when it comes to work. But let's not talk about that anymore."

While I dried Kirsty's hair, Brian and Trish finished up with their last clients, cleaned up their workstations, and left. It was just me and Kirsty. The first time we had been on our own for weeks.

The drone of the hairdryer curtailed the opportunity for conversation, but even without words the atmosphere was charged. We were on our own. Should I ask her out now? Normally asking someone out in a work setting wasn't romantic, but the salon looks amazing. I could put on some more romantic music, dim the lights a bit…

"You don't need to bother with straighteners," said Kirsty, interrupting my thoughts.

"What?" I said, taken off guard.

"You don't need to straighten my hair. I'll be putting it up tomorrow for the night out."

"Are you sure? It's all part of the service. I'm in no rush."

"No, honestly, it's fine. You've stayed late enough to accommodate me. And to be honest I'm feeling quite tired and I have a busy day tomorrow with work."

"Okay. Let me do one final check and then you'll be good to go." As I ran my fingers through her hair, checking her lengths and the ends, the air had gone flat, no longer buzzing with possibilities.

As I watched Kirsty walk out of the salon, I was left questioning what had happened. Today had been a bad business day and a bad relationship day. I looked in the mirror, the Christmas baubles from Jennifer were hanging to the side reminding me of hope, love, joy and peace. None of those words describe how I feel right now!

Kirsty

The next morning I was still annoyed with the way I'd left things with Paul. It had all been going so well and then suddenly it seemed we were on the cusp of something happening. And I got scared. Why? Why was the thing I wanted scaring me so much?

My day with PR would be a welcome distraction from work and Paul. I'm almost certain Irene made sure I was the one selected to accompany the PR department to the children's parties, but I'm not going to complain about escaping the office for the day. Especially as it gave me the perfect excuse to get out of the Christmas night out.

I met up with Dave at the PR department. "Hey, Kirsty?" he checked, as he juggled a pile of folders.

"Yep, I'm your tag along for the day."

"Great. Hey, do you know why it's getting harder to buy Advent calendars?"

I stared at him. What on earth was he talking about?

"Because their days are numbered." He walked away laughing to himself, or maybe that should be at himself. I wasn't sure whether or not I should follow him.

He came back out from his office, now folder-free and wearing his jacket. "Why is it always so cold during Christmas?" He didn't bother waiting for an answer this time, instead coming straight out with the punchline. "Because it is Decembrrrrrrr."

His jokes were so bad they made me laugh. I looked around the department with envy. My department was a step ahead of most of the other council departments but this place was in a league of its own. There was carpet, instead of carpet tiles. The walls were a rich deep-green. Pictures of newspaper articles and awards adorned the walls of the corridor, each one in matching gold-coloured frames with a picture light shining down on it.

"Okay, let's get going on our fun day out, Kirsty. We'll meet up with Rick, our photographer, at the first of the three sports halls we'll be visiting today. Rick will take lots of photos at each location and I'll be taking notes to write up articles for newspapers and our intranet."

"That all sounds good. Do you want me to do anything?"

"I'll get some quotes from you for the articles, so if anything comes to mind throughout the day keep a note of it. Otherwise enjoy the day."

As we walked out to Dave's car I felt a surge of panic, thinking of the times I'd been alone with Gary in his car. But as soon as I opened the door to Dave's car I felt the unease subside. Where Gary's car had been all high-end and immaculate, Dave's seven-seater screamed family man. There were empty crisp packets on the floors surrounded by crumbs. And several toy dinosaurs took pride of place on the child seats of the middle row. And if all that wasn't reassuring enough his bad jokes and crazy banter quickly put me at ease. This man was not trying to impress anyone. My body relaxed as my heightened senses relaxed from their flight mode.

We met Rick at the main entrance of the hall and Dave gave him last-minute pointers and instructions as we made our way into the games hall. There was a massive Christmas tree in one corner, decked in a stunning display of red and gold. Along from the tree, a row of tables were laid out with party plates and cups. Around the walls were balloons, streamers and tinsel. A bouncy castle was inflating in the middle of the hall.

Shortly after we arrived the doors swung open and thirty children from the local nursery came running in, each one of them heading for the bouncy castle. The nursery teachers dashed in front of them and blocked the entrance to the castle. They gave instructions to the kids about what the morning would involve and how the bouncy castle time would be managed.

Rick checked photography consent with the nursery teachers, then began taking pictures of the pre-schoolers running about and having fun. He came sauntering over to where I stood with Dave. "I've got a great idea for a photo. Why don't you go into the bouncy castle with some of the kids?"

Before I could explain to him why that wouldn't be a good idea Dave agreed with his suggestion and grabbed my arm, dragging me over to the dreaded bouncy castle. I was already cringing at all the potential ways this could go wrong.

"Okay," shouted Rick, "I want all you kids to bounce Dave and Kirsty about."

The children all started laughing and jumped with even more enthusiasm. Dave was immediately joining in and jumping with them. I marvelled at his confidence to throw himself into his work, literally! If I didn't join in, I would look like a boring grown-up. "Do you want me to help you bounce?" asked a cute little girl in a pretty little red party dress.

"I would love you to help me," I replied. She started giggling as she took my hands and began bouncing up and down beside me. I jumped in time with her and we giggled together.

"That's great," shouted Rick, as he turned to look for other photo opportunities.

"Stay and play with us," said my new little friend.

"I'll bounce a bit more, but I'm not as good at this as you are."

"Everyone's good at bouncing," replied the girl. And with that, we were bouncing again. More children joined us. In no time at all, I was exhausted. Who knew being on a bouncy castle was such an intense workout?

With the children all settling to their snacks, we said our goodbyes. At the next sports hall, we arrived at the same time as Santa Claus. Rick ran in so he could get photos of Santa entering the hall. We came in behind Santa to the sound of screaming children. The kids all ran up to Santa, each one shouting his name and trying to get his attention. The nursery teachers had to work hard to make themselves heard and regain control of their class. The décor in this hall was basic compared to the last place but Santa provided lots of photo opportunities for Rick. Thankfully ones that didn't involve me being on a bouncy castle again.

By the time we got to the third sports centre, I was exhausted. I had a new respect for nursery teachers and their ability to deal with so many children. Thankfully, we arrived before the children and had a few minutes to take in our setting. This time the Christmas tree was decorated in gold and silver. I stood beside it and gazed at the beauty of it. Below the branches were some Santa-sacks with lots of boxes wrapped in colourful paper. I knelt down to inspect the presents. Each one was made out to a different person. I guessed they were for the party. But the name tags didn't just have a name they also said what the child was good at. 'To Benjamin, the king of jigsaws.' 'To Sophie, the queen of dressing-up.'

How lovely for these children. Little notes to show they were noticed and cared for. I couldn't wait to meet this nursery and their teachers. The children entered the hall holding hands. Some of them looked shy, some started running over to the tree.

This nursery was using the space to have party games. I was getting more comfortable at taking part and interacting with the children. Dave and I stood with them in a circle as we played a game of Bear in the Honeypot. When I was picked to sneak in behind the Bear, I heard a camera click. I'd completely forgotten about Rick. I groaned at the thought of my picture being seen in the office. My groan had given me away allowing the current Bear to get out. Now I was the Bear in the Honeypot.

After the games, it was time for Santa to hand out the presents. Rick snapped a few more photos and we left.

"What did you think?" asked Dave, as he drove us back to the office.

"It was a lovely day, and each party felt so different to the other ones."

"Yep, I've got lots of stories from each party. I'll need to type up my notes as soon as I get back to my desk so I don't forget. Can you email me some thoughts from the parties and I'll include something from you too? It'll probably be Monday before I get anything from Rick, so I'll make Monday your deadline too."

"I dread to think what some of those photos will look like," I said, and laughed at the memory of the bouncy castle.

"I'm glad you've enjoyed your day. You seemed kind of quiet and reticent this morning but look at you now - laughing and enjoying life."

I smiled at Dave's observation. He was easy company and his non-stop 'dad jokes' had me laughing and groaning in equal measure. I thought over the three parties we had experienced today. The kids threw themselves into them at full speed and took every ounce of fun from them. Between being surrounded by children enjoying their Christmas parties and Dave's fun company, my body had absorbed joy from its surroundings. It hadn't been a conscious choice, it was like some mystical osmosis. As Dave drove along the damp streets of Glasgow to our office, I relaxed into the comfort of joy.

Work had been a strange and horrible place over the last few months. Some days I was desperate to escape to a new work environment but other days the familiarity of the council kept my thoughts grounded. Being with Dave today bolstered my thoughts about transferring to a new department in the council. It would offer all the advantage of the familiar but with a fresh challenge. I wonder how often jobs come up in the PR department? Maybe I should have a chat with Dave in the new year.

"You guys have got your department night out tonight, haven't you?" asked Dave, interrupting my thoughts.

"Yes. We're allowed to finish at three this afternoon. So I'll be getting back to my desk to check email then it's the weekend for us."

"Have a fun night out."

"I will, thanks." I had planned to skip tonight's office party. But today had done wonders for my outlook. It had awakened Christmas joy in me and it felt good. Why should I hide away and miss out on life?

Thankfully, I had brought my party outfit to work. I wanted people to think I intended to go on the night out but then I would pull out at the last minute due to tiredness from the day, or a headache, or some feigned excuse. But now I was looking forward to a night out with my colleagues.

The department was as full of excitement as those children's Christmas parties. Rather than keeping a distance, I joined in the chat. It felt as if I'd been offered a gift of joy today, showing me that it was there for the taking. My last work night out ended badly, but if I skipped this one Gary was still winning. I didn't need to stay out long, it was joining in that was important.

As I got changed, I thought about the verse: '*But the angel said to them, 'Do not be afraid, I bring you good news that will cause great joy for all the people*.'' Today I was choosing joy over fear.

PAUL

Tara stood up to preach. "This morning I want to share my favourite Bible verse with you. '*And they will call him Immanuel (which means 'God is with us')*'. These wonderful words are in the first chapter of the gospel of Matthew. Just think on those words 'God with us'. The Christmas story is full of God's love for us. The whole point of Christmas is that it heralds the start of Jesus' life on earth. God with us."

As Tara continued to preach, I closed my eyes and absorbed her words. The concept of Jesus' love for me had been a new thing to grasp, but it made sense and I had willingly accepted it. But how did I share that love with others, especially Kirsty? I had to get it right with Kirsty.

Hours after church, my mind was still full of questions and I wasn't sure what it all meant. The questions had me restless and I needed to workout. When I worked at ByDesign I'd been on a reasonable salary that paid all my bills and allowed for the fun things in life, like gym membership. But as a new business owner I had to curb some of that spending. I had cancelled my gym membership, and I was now running the pavements instead of the treadmill. Matt would join me on runs sometimes, but for today I needed to get out on my own and run.

With no real destination in my mind, I hit play on my workout playlist and started running. It had taken me a week or two to get used to running along streets instead of the treadmill. Now that I was used to it, I couldn't imagine going back to the gym. Even on a grey, drizzly day like today it was still good to get outside and enjoy the fresh air. And thanks to the number of parks in Glasgow you could always incorporate some traffic-free areas into your run. I ran along the footpath beside the River Clyde, keeping away from the busyness of the city centre, and made my way to Glasgow Green.

Once in the park, I relaxed into a steady pace, no longer needing to adjust my pace to cross roads or avoid people. I opted for one of the shorter park loops then began the run back home. As I ran, I thought of Kirsty. When she was at the salon, I had come so close to asking her out. But was it the right time? I was far too busy with the salon and I'm sure she still needs time. But for today, I could dream. Going on a ski holiday together offered so much potential. I could imagine encouraging her with her skiing, being the one to teach her how to ski. We would have so much fun together, especially based in a luxury chalet complete with hot tub… maybe best not to think about the hot tub too much!

I turned my thoughts to the salon. This coming week would be busy. The thought of the salon energised me and motivated me for the final push home. Matt wasn't in the flat when I got back. I stripped off my wet, muddy running gear in the bathroom and went straight to the hot shower. My skin complained as the hot water hit the cold, red areas of my thighs and chest. You didn't get this kind of invigoration from running on a treadmill.

Standing enjoying the steam, my body finally appreciating the hot water, my mind went back to Tara's words of this morning about love. My run had quieted my mind and I could think over the sermon without my thoughts wandering to Kirsty. Much as I enjoyed thinking about her, I wanted to think about what Tara had said. I thought my childhood of nativity plays and school assemblies had taught me all I needed to know about the Christmas story. But familiarity didn't equate to knowledge. There was still much to learn, and I was excited to learn.

***

One area I thought I knew inside out was hairdressing. But our busiest day in the salon highlighted how much I had to learn.

It was the week leading up to Christmas. Our diaries were almost full and we'd even decided to open on the Monday to take full advantage of the demand. Much as I enjoy more relaxed appointment times, clients wanted in and out as quickly as possible on Christmas week, everyone rushing about trying to finish all the last-minute chores and shopping.

My first appointment was with a new client. I always enjoy getting to know people, especially new clients. Paula was a student, treating herself to a good haircut for the holidays. Turns out she's also a runner so our conversation centred on running routes in the South Side.

I'm still getting familiar with the area so it was helpful to get local knowledge. It occurred to me how much time I was now spending in the South Side of Glasgow. It was home to my salon, Kirsty lived between here and the City Centre and Scott and Jennifer lived slightly further out.

The next appointment was with a client who had followed me from ByDesign. The City Centre location of ByDesign had suited Ann as she worked in town three days a week. But our new salon was equally convenient for her days at home. For Ann, it was an easy choice to follow me to The Smith Salon.

My third client of the morning was another new client. However, I was running late and as she waited she constantly checked her watch and tapped her fingers on her chair. I was ready for my challenge appointment. The one where you work extra hard to brighten someone's day. But it wasn't as easy as I'd hoped. She complained about the noise, the heat and how long she'd been waiting. Our little salon was full and the noise levels were rising – Trish was washing her client's hair and the sound of conversation and running water filled that part of the salon. Brian's hairdryer sounded like it was on overdrive as he styled a client's hair. The salon was heating up with all the hot water and hair dryers and straighteners. But what could you do about noise and heat in such a small space? I had no idea. By the time the client left I hadn't been able to make her smile. I doubt I'll see her again. For me that's a failure.

By some miracle, Brian, Trish and I all had half an hour between appointments before the lunchtime rush.

"How has your morning been?" I asked them both.

"Good," they replied.

"I can't believe I'm going to say this. But I'm actually missing ByDesign today!"

"No!" said Trish. "How can you say that? This place is amazing and we're so busy this week. It's exactly what we need."

"But I think that's what is stressing me out. At ByDesign we had receptionists and juniors to assist us. But now we need to do it all and I'm running behind time. Plus, everyone who comes in is busy and clock watching. What can we do to help people feel more relaxed?"

"It's a shame we don't have someone who can help us this week with dealing with the phone, drinks and sweeping up the floor between appointments," commented Trish.

"That's a really good point. And you've reminded me that I forgot to offer any of my clients a drink this morning," I confessed.

"Have you got any students at your church who would be up for helping us this week?" asked Brian. "We could pay them with a free haircut."

"That's a great idea. I'll ask Jennifer. She seems to know everyone." I took out my phone and sent a quick text to Jennifer.

Before my brief lunch break was over she replied, 'There are 2 students about to join my house group. Do you want me to ask if they'd be interested?'

"Jennifer's on it guys. She's already got a couple of students in mind. I've said to ask them both and we'll see if one or both of them are interested."

Getting to know Scott and Jennifer had been a God send. Between the help with opening the salon and guiding me in my faith this couple had become key players in my life. How could I ever thank them for everything they did for me?

Jennifer

Tears of laughter were rolling down my cheek. The school nativity play was coming to its conclusion. Thankfully the laughter had nothing to do with Chloe, who had been cast as one of the sheep. Rather, it was due to Mary and one of the angels arguing over who was going to look after baby Jesus. I guess the angel wasn't happy that she hadn't been given the coveted role of Mary. But let's be honest, these are the things we hope to see in nativity plays.

Chloe performed her little sheep dance beautifully. Although now that she'd had a dancing part in a school play she was asking to go to dancing classes.

As the play ended, a sadness settled on me. This was the last year any of my girls would be part of the nativity scene. Chloe still had a couple of years of being involved but that would be narrating and singing. Parenting! A constant yo-yo between 'the first' and 'the last' experiences.

When I got home, I let out a sigh of relief, I could tick the school events off my December to-do list. Nativity play. Done. Christmas Fayre. Done. The Christmas Fayre had gone well last Friday. It had been well attended with lots of money raised for the school. For many parents it was the perfect opportunity to clear their homes of toys, books and DVDs that their children no longer used. The resulting donations worked well for the younger children come Fayre day. But there wasn't much to entice the older kids. For them the Fayre was about helping at the stalls and getting their parents to buy the Christmas decorations they'd made in class or buying raffle tickets for the enormous basket of chocolate. It had been a success but also a lot of work.

Making myself a cup of tea, I had a vague thought that I was missing something in amongst all the events. I love the excitement and the busyness of Christmas, but I didn't want to miss out on the peace of Christmas by being overly busy with so many different things.

And then I remembered the nativity sketch I'd started. I still hadn't done anything more to it. As I walked through to the living room to get my notepad, my phone pinged with a text message from Paul, asking if I knew any students who would be willing to help in the salon this week. I contacted Elsie and Jane to ask if either of them would like to help. They both said yes. I made a group chat with the girls and Paul and left them to sort it out between them.

My focus returned to my sketch, but this time Scott called me on my mobile to tell me he had finally received the information they needed from a client to finish off their accounts for the year end and that he would need to work late. My emotions were feeling frazzled, and I probably didn't end the call as graciously as I should have.

We had planned to spend tonight wrapping the girls' presents, but if Scott was going to be late, I would be as well starting now. The sketch all forgotten about again, I set to work wrapping the presents.

***

By the time I got to Wednesday my busy week took another hit. I had planned my week out to the minute to ensure that everything was taken care of and sorted for the holidays. However, my planning did not take into account a sick child. I got the call from school at lunchtime to inform me that Amy wasn't feeling well and needed to be collected from the office. When I picked her up, she was running a temperature and her face was flushed. A childhood illnesses can be anything from a twenty-four-hour bug to something more serious, but even if it was a twenty-four-hour bug, there would be no point in her going back to school with the end of term just two days away.

I would like to say my first thought was compassion for my daughter, but I confess my thoughts went to the impact on my to-do list. Although, by the time I got Amy home I could tell she really wasn't feeling well and needed some cuddle time on the couch. I spent the rest of my afternoon watching Narnia and trying to encourage Amy to keep drinking her water. When it was time to get Emma and Chloe from school, I did something I'd never done before and left Amy home alone while I drove along to school to collect the girls. For the duration of the journey, guilt and anxiety gnawed at me. I felt such relief when I got back home that we all got into our pjs, brought our duvets downstairs and watched a family Christmas movie.

With only a few days till Christmas, I was struggling to feel the peace the shepherds were told about. Between Scott working late, as usual, and having a sick child at home, I wondered again if I was taking on too much with the Interior Design course. Would my dream become a reality?

Kirsty

The mist hung low around Ben Lomond and the Loch was dark and still in the greyness of late December. As I gazed out of the bus, taking me along the familiar roads back to Lochcala, my expectations felts as bleak as the surrounding scenery.

I settled into the familiarity of the journey. Roads that were full of tourists and campervans in the summer were now deserted. The atmosphere of the hills varied greatly between the seasons, from lush greenery in the summer to the yellowish-brown of withered grass and ferns of winter.

As the bus pulled into Lochgilphead, we passed my old high school. So many people have happy memories of high school. But not me. Being one of the taller girls at school I stood out far too much for my liking. My high school experience equated to years of awkwardness and trying to work out who I was. I'm still trying to figure that out.

For the remainder of the journey I put my ear pods on and listened to my Christmas playlist – otherwise known as Christmas songs Jennifer had recommended. I felt my soul lift with the words of love, joy, peace and hope contained in the songs. I looked at the Bible App on my phone, *'Do not be afraid. I bring you good news that will cause great joy for all the people'.* Could I experience joy with my family this Christmas?

I arrived at the family home mid-afternoon. "Mum! I'm home," I shouted as I entered the kitchen. If you're family you don't use the front door of the house, you walk round to the back of the house and enter via the kitchen door. I've no idea why. It's just what we do.

The dim afternoon light and the musty smell of a dark room reminded my senses I was home. The kitchen was the place my mum spent her days. An old Aga range heated the room, a thread-bare carpet covered the middle of the floor, too small to cover the entire floor space. Next to the Aga was an old, worn, wing-backed armchair that mum would use for her daytime cups of tea and naps. Kitchen cupboards with chipped Formica ran from the sink to the Aga and a large farmhouse table filled the middle of the room. Neighbouring families had invested in their houses and had designers in to modernise their homes. But not my mum. The house was like a time capsule.

"Take your bags up to your room and I'll put the kettle on," instructed mum. No hugs, no big welcome, just instruction.

I trudged to my room, through the living room, every bit as old-fashioned and familiar as the kitchen and up the stairs to my tiny bedroom. The single bed and mismatched furniture filled the little room. However, my room had one amazing redeeming feature: the view.

Rather than unpack my bags, I sat them on the bed and walked over to gaze out the window. The hills around the village were shrouded in mist, robbing the area of precious light. Even on a clear day light is limited in winter. People like Jennifer used the short days to make their houses feel extra cosy and welcoming. But mum thought such things were frivolous. My family home was lost in a by-gone era, no cosy memories here. My gaze shifted from the mist-covered hills to the harbour outside my window. The tide was in and the boats were bobbing about on rhythmic waves. The shops dotted around the harbour looked warm and inviting, a mixture of food, hardware and tourist shops. It was a tranquil and ruggedly beautiful setting. My heart lifted with the calming scene outside my window.

A small yacht came gliding into the harbour. I watched as the owner manoeuvred it expertly to its mooring place. How many times in the past had I looked at those boats and longed to sail off on an adventure? But, even though we live so close to the harbour, we've never owned one of those boats. I'd been out a couple of times when friends of mum and dad had taken us out. One time for a picnic on one of the uninhabited islands and another time for a tour of the coastline until mum had complained about feeling sea-sick and brought our trip to a premature end. My only other escape on the water was the year I'd asked all my relatives for money for my birthday and then paid to do kayaking lessons. I had loved those lessons.

"Kirsty, what are you doing?" shouted up mum. "Your tea is ready."

Back in the kitchen, mum was sitting at the table. A pot of stewed tea accompanied by a plate of plain biscuits sitting in front of her. I knew there were boxes of homemade baking in the pantry, but the treats were for company.

"Why don't you have any Christmas decorations up?" I asked.

"We've all been far too busy to put up decorations."

"Why don't I put some up once I've finished my tea?"

"If you want," replied mum.

"What time will dad and the boys be getting home?" I asked, trying to move the conversation along.

"Their usual time I expect."

I took a sip of tea. I tried not to grimace at how stewed it was. I'd need to remember to volunteer to make the tea from now on.

"You know your brothers are making a good life for themselves here. Do you not think it's time you were moving back too? Glasgow was okay for your student days but for settling down you can't beat Lochcala."

I didn't bother saying anything. Mum says the same thing every time I'm home and fairly often in our weekly phone calls. My brothers might be happy making their home here but Glasgow is my home now. It amazes me they all still live at home. Although, why would they leave the good thing they have here? Mum is old-fashioned in many things, like believing that the woman should have the man's dinner on the table for when he comes home from work. It's ridiculous! And the boys are happy to take advantage.

People assume I'm the spoiled one of the family being the only girl. But it's quite the opposite.

Andrew, the oldest, is one of the local police officers, like dad. Every time I come back to Lochcala he has a different girlfriend. I've no idea how he manages it, it's not like it's that populated an area. Although, he does take advantage of the influx of seasonal workers in the busy tourist months. James works for the forestry commission. He's been with his girlfriend, Aileen, for quite a few years now. We're all waiting for news of their engagement, but it seems my brothers are not the most motivated of men. And then there's Craig, he works for one of the local fish farms. I thought he might be the one to break free, but he's not showing any signs of moving out soon either.

If nothing else I would have expected the cramped sleeping quarters would have encouraged the boys to move out. But a few years ago Andrew did a rough loft conversion and claimed it as his bedroom. It feels temporary to me, but I guess he likes it well enough. James and Craig still share their old bedroom. Poor Craig! And in amongst these arrangements, my old bedroom remains unused unless I come home. I had expected one of the boys to claim it. But Craig told me mum wants it left as my room to try to encourage me to move back home.

"Guess who I met at the post office this week?" Mum had a habit of suddenly switching conversations, you had to pay attention to keep up. I shrugged my shoulders.

"Mary."

"Who?" I needed some clarity on who she was referring to.

"Mary Ramsay! You know Iain's mum."

Even after all these years, I still blushed at the mention of his name.

"Iain is home for Christmas this year. She was asking if you'd be home too."

"Why?"

"Maybe Iain wants to see you."

"Why would he want to see me? It's not like we were friends at school."

"You were in primary."

My mum's memory amazes me at times. She can't seem to retain me constantly telling her that I'm happy in Glasgow, but she can remember kids I was at primary school with.

"That's true. But in high school, he hung out with a bunch of kids from other villages and barely spoke to me."

"I'm sure that's not the case at all. Maybe I'll invite them over. He would be a nice boy for you."

I could cry!

When we were in primary school, Iain and I had played together a lot. He lived round the other side of the harbour, I can see their house from my bedroom window. But once we got to high school, he immediately got into the popular group. My parents had a rule that I couldn't date until I was seventeen. It was just one more reason for me to be in a group far removed from Iain's group. I liked him from afar, knowing that he would never be interested in me. However, in my daydreams, I made-believe that he liked me and he would pick me over all the other girls in the school. Somehow these silly fantasies still had me blushing.

"Mum, I'm only here for a few days, can't we just do our own thing? A nice quiet family Christmas would be lovely."

"I'm only trying to help," sulked mum.

I stood up and took our tea cups over to the sink. "I'll get started on those Christmas decorations now," I offered, glad of the excuse to get away from this awkward conversation.

It didn't take long to put up the meagre Christmas decorations. Jo had expressed her disgust at how few decorations I had for my flat, but compared to this I had a profusion of colourful adornments. You would think with a brother working in the Forestry Commission there would be a lovely big tree in the living room, but somewhere along the years the beautiful pine trees had been replaced by the most insignificant artificial tree mum could find. A few baubles and a string of no-longer working lights were the only items in the decorations box.

I checked my watch. There was enough time to pop down to the ironmongers to see if they had any lights and decorations for sale.

The shop was stacked full of a staggering range of products. I didn't even know what some of the things were for. And how often did someone need to buy a replacement stainless steel tea-set? Although it is the kind of thing my mum likes. The Christmas decorations, what was left of them, were located near the cash desk. I got the last box of tree lights and a few decorations to put up in my bedroom. I smiled at the little reindeer that carried a banner with the word 'joy' on it. It would be a good reminder for me. In addition, I got a jolly little outdoor Santa Claus to sit at our front door. Mum will probably think it's tacky, but if ever a house needed cheering up, it was mum and dad's.

I made my way to the door, battling between trying to bag my purchases and return my debit card to my purse when I bumped into someone entering the shop.

"I'm sorry," I said, before even looking up.

"Kirsty?"
I looked up into the smiling face of Iain Ramsay.

Paul

Our Christmas Eve gift was a busy salon. We had full schedules for the entire day. Trish had stopped off at the local supermarket to stock our kitchen with sandwiches, fruit, yoghurt and juice in an attempt to get us through the day fuelled on healthy food.

It was invigorating having a jam-packed day. And, thanks to Jennifer, we'd had Elsie and Jane helping us this week. They had picked up their duties quickly and complemented our little team. I enjoyed hearing their easy interactions with the customers. They even took over our social media, posting fun captions and behind the scene videos.

Today they went above and beyond, taking over the music playlist and persuading some clients to sing along with them to popular Christmas tunes. And where there were breaks in the singing there was laughter. Everyone was in the Christmas spirit and ready to party.

The girls had been happy to work for a free haircut, but thankfully most clients had rewarded them with generous tips. I was going to miss Elsie and Jane, they had injected their youthful energy into the salon just when it was needed.

When the last traces of hair were swept from the floor and the sinks were left sparkling clean, we all collapsed into chairs and let out a long sigh of relief. "Great team effort this week, everyone. And Elsie and Jane, you've been fabulous. Thank you so much."

"You're welcome," chorused the girls.

"I'm going to take Brian and Trish out for a celebratory drink. Will you join us?"

"Yes! We're coming."

We locked up the salon and made our way to the local pub. I got the first round of beers. "Cheers," we chorused as we chinked our bottles.

"December has been good," enthused Trish.

"It has," I replied. "And today was lots of fun."

"It was perfect," said Brian. "Here's to The Smith Salon."

As we clinked our beer bottles, there was an excitement and anticipation for our future. This past week had been exhausting, but a good kind of exhaustion that made me happy. Over our beers we laughed about various incidents from the past week. And Elsie and Jane giggled over some of their 'behind the scene' footage. It had been fun having a bigger team for a few days.

"You up for another beer?" asked Trish.

"Absolutely," I replied. Over another round of beers, we chatted about our plans for Christmas. We had a few days off before another burst of busyness to take us up to Hogmanay.

"We'll need to go now," said Elsie. "We've got the watchnight service at church tonight and have a few last-minute things to do before then."

"What's a watchnight service?" asked Brian.

"It's a short service that goes over midnight from Christmas Eve into Christmas morning. It's pretty short but is the perfect way to start Christmas."

"I'll see you both there," I replied. As Elsie and Jane stood up, I looked to Brian and Trish. "Do you guys want to come too?"

"I'm not sure that I'm church material," replied Trish.

"They don't just let certain people in, Trish. Church is for everyone. And if anyone tells you you're not welcome in a church, they're wrong. Come back to mine, we'll get takeaway and you can come with Matt and me."

"Okay, I'm up for giving it a go. You going to come too, Brian?"

"Why not?"

"Brilliant!" said Elsie. "We'll see you all later."

We stopped off for a Chinese takeaway and went back to my flat. Already a few days into his holidays, Matt had the flat cleaner and tidier than I'd seen it in a while. Apart from my room, of course, which was still a mess. I had a quiet morning tomorrow, maybe I'd deal with it then. After tonight's service, Matt was going to drive over to his parents' house. His parents live about half an hour away in a neighbouring town, but they enjoy having their family all together for Christmas morning.

By the time we finished dinner, we were almost asleep. It would have been easy to stay on the couch, relaxing and enjoying the company, but the draw of my first Christmas Eve service motivated me to get up. We got to ChurchX just before the start of the service. There had been a family service earlier in the evening leaving this service to the students and child-free adults. Instead of the regular rows of seats, the church had been transformed into a more intimate set up. Circles of seats faced into an area currently occupied by the worship band. Fairy lights had been strung above us and tinsel adorned the mic stands and drums and keyboard.

"Not what I was expecting," whispered Trish.

As I looked for four seats together, Elsie came over. "Hey guys, we've kept you some seats beside us."

I directed our little group to the seats Elsie had pointed out. I waved over to Carol and Lynn who were already seated on the other side of the circle. The band finished their background playing and Josh strummed his guitar and welcomed us all to the service. He led the band through some familiar carols, but to a higher tempo than they would normally be played to. It was fun to sing familiar songs differently.

A sheet of paper on our seat had the words of the carols and the Bible references that Ben would be preaching from. Normally the lyrics are on the big screens, but for tonight there was no screen.

The band finished their set with, 'O Little Town of Bethlehem'. It was a popular carol that I'd heard many times in the past, even without being a churchgoer. But tonight it caught me. It had everything we needed to know about Christmas.

The band sat in their seats and Ben stood up. "I feel like I should be on a revolving platform so I can see you all. But don't worry I'll keep moving about to see you all." With a mic clipped to his shirt, Ben walked around the circle, just like he promised. "The Christmas story," started Ben. "It's a story we're probably all very familiar with." My thoughts drifted away from Ben's preaching back to the words of O Little Town of Bethlehem.

The words spoke of peace, love and hope. Somehow when I asked Jesus into my life, I didn't think about the Christmas story. I just thought of him as a man. But Jesus was born. He was a boy. He was a teenager. He didn't materialise as a man, he experienced life as a child too. He knew what it meant to be human. The carol spoke of stillness and peace, almost as if Heaven paused in wonder and awe before the baby. I closed my eyes and thought of that stillness.

As Ben continued to speak, I read through the words of the carol again. The last few weeks had been frantic but tonight there was time to stop and think. '*While mortals sleep, the angels keep their watch of wondering love.*' As I thought on the words, I realised love covered the whole of the Christmas story. But it wasn't the slushy love we talk about and see in movies. It was much deeper than that. It was perfect love. And that perfect love didn't require the perfect setting. There is nothing romantic and perfect about a stable, yet it's where the miracle took place. My understanding of Christmas was being transformed from nativity plays to a realisation that it was all about Jesus and God's love.

The service ended with another couple of upbeat carols from the band. We shuffled outside at the end of the service. After a full-on day, and week, we were all too tired to hang about for coffee and mince pies. I was so lost in my own thoughts I didn't even ask Brian or Trish if they enjoyed the service.

Matt dropped me off at the flat before driving over to his parent's house. I was glad of having the flat to myself for a couple of days. I needed some thinking time.

JENNIFER

In the glow of early morning sunshine I sat with my girls on either side, eating breakfast and watching a Christmas movie. Thankfully Amy's illness turned out be nothing more than a random twenty-four-hour bug and she was back to her normal self. The Christmas tree glittered in the corner, the fresh smell of pine still filling the room. All the stress and rushing about of the last few months forgotten as I treasured the love, joy and peace around me.

At mid-day, Sarah and Kevin arrived laden down with Christmas gifts for all of us and treats for our afternoon together. After lunch the girls and Kevin all ran upstairs to play, leaving Sarah and myself space to talk.

"I think it's too late to salvage our marriage," said Sarah. "I'm not sure that the marriage counselling offered us much hope but at least we can say we tried."

I walked round to the other side of the breakfast bar and hugged her. "Oh, Sarah, I'm so sorry."

"The best we can do now is split as amicably as possible. It's damage limitation. Making sure Kevin doesn't get dragged into our arguments and that we do what's best for him."

"And what's James saying about it?"

"For once we agree."

"So what happens next and what will you do tomorrow?"

"I guess tomorrow is our last family Christmas."

As I gave her another hug, she started sobbing in my arms. For weeks she had been quite blasé about the issues in her marriage but the toll was heavy on her.

"How do I do this?" she asked. "How do I put on a Christmas that means something?"

"I don't know. Can I do anything to help?"

"I don't think so."

"Do you want to come over tomorrow?"

"That's so lovely of you to ask," said Sarah, sniffing through her tears. "But we need to be the ones to make this work. To make one final combined effort for Kevin."

"Does Kevin know?"

"I don't know. We don't want to say anything to him till after the holidays. He'll get spoiled like crazy tomorrow as we both try to overcompensate for the last few months."

"Why don't you come over and have dinner with us on Boxing Day?"

"That would be lovely. Thank you. Are you sure you want to have us? We might bring down the joy of your home."

I smiled at my friend. "There's no limit on joy, Sarah. We're here for you and we want to do whatever we can to help you. Whether you and James decided to stay together or separate, the next few months will be hard. You need to have time and space and I'll do whatever I can to help."

Sarah sniffed and tried to smile. I handed her a tissue and squeezed her hand. "Why don't I make us another coffee and we'll enjoy some of those chocolates you brought while we watch the cheesiest Christmas movie we can fine." As the movie started, I silently prayed for Sarah, James and Kevin, prayers for love, joy, peace and hope to wrap around their home this Christmas.

***

Christmas Eve is one of my favourite days. A day full of excitement, anticipation and family traditions. One of those traditions is the family Christmas Eve service. The kids' leaders pulled off an amazing feat by putting on a nativity play that included lines for every child and songs that the children sang with lots of enthusiasm. There were moments of laughter and, for me, crying at points.

And now, we were back home. The girls were tucked up in bed. Despite the protests they weren't tired and wanted to stay up to see Santa, they were now sleeping peacefully. Leaving Scott and me some much appreciated time together. Snuggled up on the settee we sat with our drinks and snacks and watched our favourite Christmas movie. Our only light sources were the fire, fairy lights and candles. It was so cosy, a perfect moment of calm.

By the time we got halfway through the movie, Scott was snoring gently beside me. I looked around at him and smiled. He had only stopped working today and had been putting in a lot of extra hours over the last few weeks. At the start of the year Scott had taken on a new partner, assuring me it would mean fewer hours for him. However, it didn't take him long to resort to his habit of working too much. His long hours annoyed me but I could appreciate his motivation was to provide for us. And after my conversation with Sarah, I was more appreciative of Scott than ever. I continued watching the film as he slept. As it drew to its happy conclusion, Scott was still snoring.

I poured myself another glass of wine and enjoyed the cosy glow from our fire. It was only an aesthetic thing but it certainly added to the atmosphere, especially accompanied by the twinkling fairy lights on the Christmas tree.

In the stillness of the moment, I stretched and sighed. Everything was organised. As I looked around, I noticed my notepad on the lamp table. I'd forgotten all about my nativity sketch. How could I be so forgetful? I switched on the lamp and flicked through the notepad. I looked at the sketch, it blurred as my eyes welled up with tears. Emma had completed it. She had taken my rough sketch and developed it in her own style. The childish drawing captured the simplicity of the nativity.

In the comfort and stillness of my living room, the sketch transported me to the first Christmas in all its noisy starkness. The stable isn't a cosy place, but it's a place that anyone can approach. It's a place to come and be yourself. And, in that place there is peace.

CHRISTMAS

Jennifer

"Mum! Dad! Wake-up! It's Christmas!" shouted three very excited girls.

Scott pulled the duvet over our heads. "Do you think if we ignore them they'll let us sleep for another hour?" asked Scott.

"Dad! Get up now!" shouted Chloe.

The girls worked together to drag the duvet away from us and immediately jumped onto the bed and bounced up and down chanting "Christmas! Christmas!"

"Come on!" said Chloe, grabbing my hand to pull me out of the bed. "I want to see what Santa got me."

"Not so fast," I replied, and grabbed Chloe onto the bed to tickle her. "Your dad has to go downstairs and make sure Santa has left before we can go down."

"Go now, dad," encouraged Emma.

With exaggerated groans, Scott got out of bed and went downstairs.

"Who is the most excited?" I asked.

"Me!" chorused the three girls.

"You can come down now," shouted Scott.

"Me first! I want to see your faces as you open your gifts." I ran downstairs with the girls scampering right behind me.

In a whirlwind, the girls ripped open their packages. Amy's pile was the smallest now she had grown away from toys, but from the look on her face, clothes and phone accessories were perfect. Emma jumped up and down with her new Lego Friends sets and Chloe was already ripping into the bright pink Barbie boxes.

Scott and I had agreed on no Christmas presents for each other as we have the ski holiday in February. But we had still bought each other gifts with the holiday in mind. Although the ski socks and mini torch I'd bought Scott seemed rather insignificant compared to the gorgeous snowboots and sunglasses he'd bought me. The snowboots were grey with fake-fur edging and bright turquoise laces, inside the light grey fleece promised to keep my toes cosy whenever I was out in the snow. And the black sunglasses had fabulous turquoise frames that matched my snowboots.

When the presents were all opened, I organised breakfast. Breakfast on Christmas morning is always a buffet-style offering that we can all pick at throughout the morning, everyone too excited and busy to sit down to breakfast. I laid out croissants and mini muffins and fruit juice on the breakfast bar in the kitchen and made coffee for Scott and myself.

Before it was time to get busy making Christmas lunch, we grabbed a little oasis of calm in the living room with our coffees and croissants and watched the girls delve into their presents. I snuggled into Scott and enjoyed the wonder of the moment.

My parents would be arriving within the next hour or so. Scott's parents were going to his brother's for Christmas this year. Cooking Christmas dinner used to be a major stress for me but a few years ago I discovered the joy and ease of oven-ready Christmas dinners and ever since then the stress of Christmas Day had all but gone. Now I could enjoy the aromas floating through from the kitchen and all I had to do was keep an eye on the timer.

As we all sat around the table, ready to begin our meal, dad stood up to do his traditional Bible read and prayer of thanks. "'*And there were shepherds living out in the fields nearby, keeping watch over their flocks at night. An angel of the Lord appeared to them, and the glory of the Lord shone around them, and they were terrified. But the angel said to them, 'Do not be afraid. I bring you good news that will cause great joy for all the people. Today in the town of David a Saviour has been born to you; he is the Messiah, the Lord. This will be a sign to you: You will find a baby wrapped in cloths and lying in a manger.' Suddenly a great company of the heavenly host appeared with the angel, praising God and saying, "Glory to God in the highest heaven, and on earth peace to those on whom his favour rests.*" Father, we thank you for Christmas. A day of joy and a day to celebrate. Thank you for this food and for this family, in Jesus' name."

"Amen," we all said in closing.

"Okay, everyone," I said. "Dig in." Every year dad reads the same verses from the gospel of Luke. The familiarity of the words meant they could be easily glossed over. But somehow today, I paid more attention. *Peace to those on whom his favour rests.'* In the busyness of Christmas Day that peace was wrapping around me and bringing me comfort. December had been its usual manic self but over the last twenty-four hours, the peace of the season has filled me. I'm not sure what next year will bring in terms of balancing studying, working and family but where there is peace I'll soak it in. I smiled as I looked around the table, thankful for my family and all that we have.

Kirsty

The sound of banging cupboard doors woke me up. I pulled the covers over my head, this didn't bode well. I could picture mum in the kitchen stressing about the cooking. Would she have enough food? What if she burnt something and undercooked something else? You would think she'd appreciate the offer of help but she liked to be the martyr and do it all herself. Dad and the boys would be oblivious and would spend the morning talking about fishing or forestry or some other dull subject.

I checked the website for the village church to see if they had a Christmas Day service. They did. It started at ten o'clock. What a perfect opportunity to get out of the house.

A blanket of warmth greeted me as I entered the old stone church. Christmas decorations draped along the walls and a large tree glistened in tinsel and lights beside the pulpit. There was a smattering of people throughout the small church. Some I recognised, some I didn't. Six children sat in the front pew, unable to sit still with all the excitement. The minister of my youth had retired several years ago, and the post had been filled by a much younger woman.

Away In A Manger started off the service, the familiar song catching the attention of the children. Next up was Silent Night. The old, familiar Christmas carols wrapped themselves around me and brought their peace.

"I'm going to do an uncharacteristically short sermon this morning," joked the minister. "Because I know there are some little people here who are desperate to get playing with their amazing toys. Hold up your toys and let everyone see them," encouraged the minister.

I smiled as eager little faces beamed with delight at being the centre of attention and showing off their new treasures. This minister was much more kid-friendly than the previous guy.

"I'm only going to read you one verse from the Bible this morning, from Luke chapter two verse ten. '*But the angel said to them, "Do not be afraid. I bring you good news that will cause great joy for all the people.*"' Good news can be scarce at times. We switch on the TV to watch the news and the headlines are all negative, full of fear and troubles. We pick up our newspapers or the news apps on our phones and again we are met with fear and trouble. But the gospels bring us Jesus and good news. Good news takes away fear and brings joy."

There was that verse again and its message of joy. It was certainly being talked about a lot this year. This morning it was a timely reminder. In a house full of stress and tension was it possible to feel joy? A glimmer of hope was flickering in my soul.

However, as soon as I entered my house that joy was snuffed out. Mum was fretting about in the kitchen and the boys were winding each other up. I sat next to dad on the couch. My dad is the quietest one in the family, we could sit in perfect silence, neither of us feeling the need to talk. Left to ourselves we were able to enjoy each other's company. But in this household that rarely happened.

After a tense family dinner, with mum still fretting about the food and my brothers throwing jokes and sarcasm at everyone, James stood up. "I've got an announcement," he declared, "I'm going to be moving out next week and moving in with Aileen."

I glanced over to mum. It was impossible to read her face. Had she already known or was it a surprise to her too? Although her lack of reaction suggested she already knew. I wondered if I was the only one it was news to.

"Well it's not ideal," said mum, "But it's nice to have at least one of you partnered off. I wish you were getting married first though."

"You need to get with the times, mum, this is how everyone does it now."

"Not everyone," I replied, without thinking.

"Oh here we go, little miss goody-two-shoes," sneered James. "Did you say a prayer for all us sinners when you were at church?"

"Leave your sister alone," interjected my dad. I smiled at him.

"I'll make a start with the dishes," I said.

"I'll come and help you," replied Craig.

I know you shouldn't have favourites within your family, but Craig is my favourite brother. Although, it's not like my parents bother with the rule of not having favourites. Andrew is my dad's favourite, it's not just because Andrew followed dad's lead and joined the police, the two of them were always close. James is mum's favourite, as witnessed in how she reacted to his news about moving in with Aileen. If anyone else had made such an announcement, she would have had plenty to say. Which left me and Craig to fend for ourselves. Maybe it's also easier with Craig because he is younger than me and didn't give me a hard time my whole childhood the way Andrew and James did.

Growing up there were more rules for me than the boys, such as the awful no-dating rule. The boys had no age limit and could date as young as they pleased. I had a tighter curfew than the boys too. The only saving grace was that mum didn't expect me to wait on them the way she did. Thank goodness.

"Don't let them get to you," said Craig, as he dried the dishes.

"Are they like this all the time or do they store it up for when I'm home?"

"No, it's all the time."

"It's like a time-warp! Every time I'm here they come out with the same old guff."

"I know. But I'm glad you're here. Nice to have some conversation that doesn't solely revolve around Lochcala."

"Why do you stay? Don't you want to escape?"

"My options are more limited than yours. Fish farming tends to be restricted to similar places."

"I suppose that's true. Well, anytime you want to have some fun in Glasgow come down and stay with me. You know you're always welcome."

As I continued to wash the dishes, I imagined Craig coming down to stay with me for a few days and introducing him to Paul. Thinking of Paul brought a smile to my lips and a spark of joy to my heart.

Paul

The only thing scheduled for today was Christmas dinner with my mum and sister. Which gave me till mid-afternoon to enjoy some alone time in the flat. Initially, I'd been planning on a morning of PlayStation fun but after last night, I wanted to read the Christmas story again. I made myself a coffee then went back to bed and opened the Bible app on my phone. I read through the first couple of chapters of Matthew and Luke. The words brought a different meaning now that I thought about them in terms of God's love. It was a strange love that meant his son was born in a stable instead of a safe place. Why? It was a strange love that announced the birth first of all to shepherds. Why? I always seemed to end up with so many questions, but I was hungry to know more.

I searched on YouTube to find O Little Town of Bethlehem. The search provided a list of artists and choirs with their versions of the song. I clicked play on a couple before I got to one by Matt Redman. This was it. This version had a different chorus to it that connected with my thoughts: '*The glory of Christmas is the story of His love.*' I put it on my playlist and set it to repeat.

The words of the song were reaching out to me, but I couldn't figure out what they were telling me. Was it about my faith journey? Was it about Kirsty? Or both? I wanted to know, but the answer was alluding me. I continued listening to the song as I got ready, hoping the answer would come to me.

The restaurant was exactly as you would expect on Christmas Day. Christmas tunes playing in the background, noisy groups of people in paper hats celebrating the day in style, tables full of Christmas crackers and more food than anyone could eat. I glanced around to see if mum or Lauren were already seated, but as usual I was the first to arrive. It wasn't long before they joined me.

"How was your journey up?" I asked Lauren, as we settled at our table.

"The usual joy of battling through security and the Heathrow crowds. Glasgow is much more pleasant in comparison."

"You still enjoying it down there?" I asked, as the waiter gave each of us a glass of champagne.

"Yeah, it's fine. I love the nightlife. The job is okay."

Mum picked up her glass. "A toast," she said, "to my wonderful son and daughter and the brave steps they've both taken this year."

"Thanks, mum," said Lauren, and kissed her on the cheek. "You know we're just following the example you set us."

My dad walked out on us when I was six. I have some vague memories of him taking Lauren and me out a few times, but his visits became less and less frequent until finally, he stopped coming. I don't even know if he ever gave mum any money in child support. She's fiercely independent, so it's not the kind of thing she would discuss with us. When dad left, she got a job as a secretary in a legal firm and has been there ever since. It's quite a big legal company, so she's been able to move up admin ranks and has done well for herself. She doesn't complain and works hard. There were times she wasn't able to come to things at school when we were kids, but we knew why.

Lauren filled us in on her life in London as we ate our starters. It was clear she was having fun in a new city. I've always felt comfortable around women, even in the awkward puberty years, and these two women are the reason.

"So tell me all about your new salon," said Lauren.

"You need to come and see it. My friend Jennifer decorated it and it looks great."

"That's a brilliant idea. I could do with a haircut, how about I come in next week?"

Over our main course, I told them about the salon and how it was going.

"And how's that love life of yours?" teased Lauren.

"Working out a bit differently this year. I've taken a break from all the dating. There's a girl at church that I like. Her name is Kirsty, but she's been through a bit of an ordeal lately so I want to give her time before asking her out. Plus I'm trying to figure stuff out too and get the salon up and running."

"Sounds like you're making excuses," concluded mum.

"I see it more as trying to be sensible and make the right decision for Kirsty and for me."

"And how do you think she sees it?" asked Lauren.

"I don't know. Probably the same way. I told her a couple of months ago that I'd like to date her in the future once I've got stuff sorted."

"Paul!" chided mum. "The poor girl is probably desperate for you to take the lead and ask her out."

"Or at the very least talk to her about where you stand," added Lauren.

"Are you sure?"

"Yes!" They both replied at the same time.

"But the salon is still so new," I continued. "How can I give Kirsty the attention she deserves if my mind is constantly distracted by how busy my appointment diary is, or how I'm going to move money around to pay some supplier or other?"

"I didn't realise you were so caring," teased Lauren.

"It's good you're thinking of Kirsty. But maybe you should tell her this instead of leaving her hanging. Girls like to know where they stand," advised mum.

"Have you at least been hanging out together?" asked Lauren.

"Yes, we're part of a group of friends. Although we haven't seen so much of each other recently. And any time we are together there are always other people with us."

"Well, maybe start with just being friends," said my mum. "It sounds like that's what she needs most right now. And that's what you need too."

The waiter came and cleared away our main course dishes, thankfully breaking our conversation. Things were getting too intense. Of course I wanted to be friends with Kirsty and then date her. But mum and Lauren were right, I had been making excuses and putting things off. Life was easier when you could slot it into different compartments.

However, for now it was time to turn the conversation elsewhere. The other person I hadn't spent enough time with recently was my mum. It was an unintentional thing, but I realised it was weeks since I'd last went to visit her. "What's the latest with you, mum?" I asked. "Have you found a new dad for us yet?" It had almost become a tradition to tease mum about us getting a new dad. Only today she wasn't laughing it off the way she usually did. Lauren and I exchanged glances.

"I can't believe you're dating and Paul's not. Tell all…"

"It's nothing serious, at least I don't think it is yet. It's a man I met at the gym."

"No way!" I laughed. "Can you believe it Lauren, our mum hooking up at the gym?"

"Well at least we know he takes care of himself. Tell us more, mum."

As we enjoyed our desserts, mum filled us in on this new man in her life. After dad left, she had never seemed interested in dating. She always told us her life was full between us and work, and I guess that was the case. It was nice to see her looking out for herself.

"Here's to mum and Alex," I said, raising my glass. Lauren raised her glass too.

I love my family.

Kirsty

Things took an unexpected turn in Lochcala. After bumping into Iain Ramsay on Christmas Eve we crossed paths again on Boxing Day. Christmas Eve had been nothing more than pleasantries. But on Boxing Day Iain happily launched into conversation. As soon as he realised we were both travelling to Glasgow today, he offered to drive me home. He hadn't accepted my reply that I already had my bus ticket and now here I was preparing to get in a car with Iain Ramsay for the two-and-a-half-hour trip to Glasgow.

Once again I was getting into an expensive car with a good-looking guy. Teenage me would be loving every second of this. Present day me was flattered but also fearful. What if it all triggered another panic attack? I took a few deep breaths and settled myself on the soft leather seat.

"Why don't we stop for coffee part way down?" suggested Iain.

"If you have time. I don't want to slow down your journey." After dropping me off in Glasgow, Iain would be driving on down to London. It was a long drive but in the luxury of his car I understood his reason for driving.

Iain's electric car glided silently from Lochcala, passing our old primary school as we left the village. "Do you remember Mrs McDougal?" he asked. I laughed at the memory. "She was something else, wasn't she? Do you remember the day she brought her dog to school and it got into the school kitchen and started eating our lunches?"

"I'd forgotten all about that," I said. "It was hilarious. Although I remember a lot of tears as kids thought it meant no lunch." With childhood memories replacing my fear, I relaxed. Maybe this wouldn't be so bad.

"And do you remember our adventures after school," Iain continued. "Climbing trees and walking the long way home from school."

"It was fun." I glanced over at Iain. As we laughed about our childhood adventures, I felt that old familiar flutter I used to get around him. But were those flutters just about our youth or did I still have feelings for Iain?

"Do you remember all the outdoor activities we got to do in primary seven? I loved that we got to try out water sports. We really were blessed to live in this area." The warmth of happy childhood memories filled the car as we laughed and chatted the whole way to Lochgilphead.

However, as soon as our old high school came into view, the conversation turned. "But how much better was high school?" asked Iain. "So many great memories from there?"

I smiled. How could I reply? Did he even remember me in high school? Of course Iain had fun memories of high school days, he excelled at everything at high school.

Iain didn't wait for my reply, for the next hour he provided story after story of his time at high school – the grades he achieved, the sports he was involved in and the girls he dated. I didn't need the reminder of how much our lives diverged from primary school to secondary school. We had very different experiences from the same building. As he spoke I gazed out the window, at least I could enjoy the comfort of these expensive seats and the grandeur of the hills we drove beside. Unlike my journey of a few days ago, it was now sunny and bright. The hills took on a golden hue rather than the drab colouring of cloudy days. Tufts of clouds dotted the sky, allowing unobscured sun rays to stream through the window and add to my comfort.

Iain's car came to a silent stop in the car park of a loch side hotel. A table by the window offered us uninterrupted views of loch and hillside and the nearby crackling flames of a wood burner ensured we would be warm. A waiter brought us coffees and scones. The coffee was non-descript, but the scones were perfect – warm, light and so delicious. Thankfully I had the scones and views to appreciate, Iain's non-stop discourse about high school had been replaced with a monologue on how successful he was in his job. I confess I zoned out. Where was the fun boy I used to climb trees with?

The remainder of the drive down contained more Iain stories. I can't believe I was so infatuated with this guy when I was a teenager. What a waste of time and emotions. As we passed the turning for the Erskine Bridge and entered the edges of Glasgow, Iain finally asked about my life in Glasgow. I only gave the briefest of answers, knowing he wasn't really interested in what I had to say.

"How often do you go out partying?" he asked.

"Not much. I enjoy going out for dinner with my friends."

"If I'd known I'd be driving you home, I would have stayed over in Glasgow and taken you out."

My stomach started clenching and my heart beat sped up. I looked out the window and distracted myself by naming colours and counting to ten in my head. It wouldn't be long till I was in the safety of my flat. Away from Iain and his assumptions. Away from the memories of Gary. What was it with guys and their expectation that any woman was theirs?

We were ten minutes away from my flat. The distraction techniques were becoming less effective. I was moments away from a full-on panic attack. Iain was completely oblivious as he continued his stories of his party lifestyle in London. His ceaseless talking was adding to my stress. *'God! Help me,'* I prayed. I needed a way out of this. I needed a miracle.

I opened the window, hoping a blast of cold air would help. Iain glanced over. "Sorry, I just needed a bit of air," I said. Before he could reply my phone started ringing. I grabbed it out of my bag and checked the caller ID, smiling at my friend's name on the screen. "Hey Jo, I'll be home in ten minutes. Where are you?"

"Are you okay," she asked. A car offers no privacy for a phone call, I would need to play this carefully.

"I'm good. Glad to be back in Glasgow."

"I got back an hour ago. You want to meet up for lunch?"

"That would be perfect. Why don't we meet at mine?"

"Okay, I'll be over in an hour."

Iain glanced over at me again. "That was Jo, my best friend," I offered by way of explanation. Not that he'd asked, of course.

A few minutes later we arrived at my flat. Iain jumped out of his car to retrieve my bag from the boot. I know I should have been polite and invited him in for a coffee but I'd had enough of Iain Ramsay's company. "Thanks so much for the lift, Iain. It's been really great to catch up again," I lied.

"It's been good to see you again too. Next time I'm up in Glasgow for business I'll be in touch."

Iain Ramsay kissed me on the cheek then returned to the luxury of his car. As the car disappeared from view, the last feeling of panic disappeared too.

HOGMANAY

Kirsty

Hogmanay. New Year's Eve. Thirty-first of December. Whatever you call it, it's party night in Scotland.

The pressure is on to get yourself to a good party for the bells. And a ceilidh, in my opinion, is the perfect way to welcome the New Year. What can be better than fun, fast paced dancing with your friends?

We had arranged to meet at a pub around the corner from the ceilidh venue. The pub was bursting at the seams, full of revellers out to enjoy the last night of the year. By the time I got a round of beers in Matt and Paul arrived. It was the first time I'd seen Paul since my pre-Christmas haircut. We exchanged awkward smiles then turned our attention to the group. However, between the noise of the music playing over the sound system and the levels of conversation and laughter, it was difficult to hear one another. Our group moved to the side of the pub in the hope of being able to hear each other, but there was no respite from the decibels. Paul stood across from me. I could see him glancing my way but conversation was impossible.

Jo checked her watch and motioned that it was time for us to leave. As we walked out of the pub, we all pulled our coats around us trying to protect ourselves from the ever-increasing wind and rain. Lynn tried putting her umbrella up, but it immediately blew inside out and broke.

By the time we got to the hall, Paul was beside me. Away from the noisy pub and sheltered from the rising storm, conversation was possible. "How was your Christmas?" he asked.

"It was okay, thanks. Being back home is never stress free, but it wasn't too bad. How about you?"

"It was great. I had the flat to myself as Matt was at his folks. The only thing I did on Christmas day was meet up with my mum and sister for lunch."

"That sounds very civilised."

"It was. My sister, Lauren, transferred down to London with her work a few months ago and this is the first time she's been back in Glasgow since she moved. It was fun to catch up."

"Are you close with your sister?"

"Yeah, I guess so. I mean we don't talk much, but when we're together, we can have a laugh."

"You're so lucky," I sighed.

"Right. All those brothers."

"And don't forget the mum and dad!"

"Was it all a bit full-on?"

"Like I said, it could have been worse. But at least I get Hogmanay in Glasgow with my friends."

"I'm glad about that. I'm looking forward to seeing the New Year in with you."

The smile he wrapped the sentence up in melted my heart. In moments like this I can imagine being Paul's girlfriend. I can imagine it all working out perfectly. But I've been wrong so often in the past. Can I really trust my instincts now?

Jennifer

We arrived at the church hall uncharacteristically early. We knew the ceilidh was sold out and were keen to grab ourselves a table for the night. As we entered the hall Chloe tugged at my hand, excited at the prospect of being with friends and staying up until midnight. We spotted Ben and Tara and sat with them. Tara informed me the band were a young grouping from one of the other churches. With an accordion, violin, keyboards and drum it promised to be a good ceilidh.

"How has your week been?" asked Tara.

"It's been lovely. We've had a fairly quiet week since Christmas. Days spent with walks in the park and playing the new board games. And of course, eating far too much and binge-watching movies and box sets. It's nice to get out tonight for some socialising and high-energy activity."

"That sounds very similar to our week," replied Tara. "It's been lovely having the boys all under one roof again and catching up."

"Are the boys here?" I asked, as I glanced around the hall. Tara and Ben are about ten years older than us and having had their family soon after getting married, their three sons were now at university stage, either living away at university or living the student life from home. They weren't quite at the empty nest stage of life but were able to live free of the school run and school holiday restrictions.

"No. They're out with their friends. I don't think they want to spend Hogmanay with their parents anymore."

"Parenting seems to be years of being overwhelmed and then years of wondering where it all went."

"Yep. That sounds about right," replied Tara, and then smiled. "But let's not get too down about it. How are you feeling about your course now that we're approaching the new year?"

"Optimistic. December was frantic but on Christmas Eve I experienced a wonderful wave of peace and since then I've been able to slow down and relax about the future. I need to learn to take things one stage at a time."

"It's important to take the rest phases whenever they present themselves. We all get far too busy."

"I also prayed for a Bible verse for this year."

"That's a great thing to do. What did you get?"

I smiled as I replied, "Luke chapter two, verse fourteen. A Christmas verse for the entire year! '*Glory to God in the highest heaven and on earth peace to those on whom his favour rests.*'"

"Well, the Christmas story is not just for Christmas! We relegate the verses and songs to a few weeks of the year, why not carry it with us the whole year?"

"I like that way of looking at it," I replied.

Chloe came running over to me and threw herself onto my knee. "Mum, can I get money for juice?"

"Of course you can." I gave her some money and she shot off again.

"She has so much energy," commented Tara.

"That's one way of putting it. I'm hoping my mum and dad will have the energy to look after them when we go on our ski holiday. Especially as the girls won't be in school the whole week."

"I'm sure they'll love every minute of it."

"I am excited about our ski holiday. I wish you and Ben could come with us."

"I wish we were coming too. It's so unfortunate that it's the same week as the leadership conference."

"Well, at least you and Ben are still getting away together."

"That's true. But I think a full-on leadership conference schedule may offer less relaxing times than a ski holiday. Especially a ski holiday with a hot tub."

"I'm just looking forward to being with younger people and having conversations that don't revolve around how to fill a dishwasher and best snacks for school pack-lunches."

"Yes, the fun conversations of parenthood. Just be grateful you've passed the point of discussing nappy content."

We both laughed. My friendship with Kirsty and the girls is great and we have lots of fun times together but Tara gets me in a way the younger girls don't. I'm grateful for the range of friendships I have in my life.

Paul

Mum and Lauren's words were playing in my head as I walked into the hall with Kirsty. They were right. I had to speak to her and make sure she understood I still wanted to go out with her, but that I needed a bit more time to get the salon properly set up. I wanted to be able to focus on her without constantly studying sales figures and marketing techniques. But it looked like Hogmanay wasn't the night for such discussion, everywhere was too noisy for conversation. The pub had been full of revellers, outside had been stormy and the hall was getting noisier as more and more people arrived and the band carried out their sound check. Best to leave discussions about our future for another night and enjoy the party. Here's hoping there will be enough men to dance with Jo, Lynn and Carol leaving me time to dance with Kirsty, but not too many men that I lose out on dancing with her.

"We'll get the night started with a Gay Gordons," shouted the guy on the keyboard.

"Shall we?" I asked Kirsty. As we walked on to the dance floor, I had my arm round her narrow waist. She looked amazing in her tartan mini-skirt and fitted top. "It's been a while since I was last at a ceilidh," I confessed to Kirsty. "I hope I remember how to do all the dances."

"It'll all come back to you. Plus, with this dance there are more steps for the girls than the guys. Just watch the couple in front, and hope they know what they're doing."

Thankfully the keyboard player also took on the role of the caller and walked us through the dance before they started playing. The walk-through triggered memories of social dancing from school and I began to feel more confident that I would get at least some of the steps correct. The music struck up and we were off. I got a few steps wrong the first time through but then I had it. My favourite part of the dance was the waltz at the end of each phase when I could hold Kirsty close to me. Her frame felt so fragile in my arms.

By the time the dance finished, we were breathing hard and laughing. The tension of earlier replaced with friendship. We sat back at the table to get a drink and catch our breath. Kirsty's eyes sparkled with laughter and her cheeks were flushed with dancing. I didn't want to wait any longer to ask her out. There would always be a reason to put it off, especially with the salon still in its fledgling stage. Maybe tonight did offer the perfect setting. Dancing together up to the bells. Then as the clock struck midnight, it would be the perfect opportunity to hold her in my arms and kiss her. That would be my moment to ask her to be my girlfriend.

The next few dances came and went, a Canadian Barn Dance with Lynn and The Military Two-Step with Carol. The first reel of the night was a Dashing White Sergeant. It's a long time since I was last at a ceilidh but I remember the reels being the most fun.

"One man with two women, or one woman with two men for this dance," shouted out the caller. I grabbed Kirsty and Carol for it. Once again we walked through the dance to help us learn the steps. The high-energy reel had us going quickly right from the start. After going around for a count of sixteen we split into our row of three to spin round with each other, one at a time. Kirsty and I faced each other and did a side-to-side step then spun, then I did the same with Carol, then back to spin with Kirsty, then back to spin with Carol then another spin each. Now I remembered. This was the dance that you didn't want to be in the middle of your line of three.

By the third time through I was beginning to wish I'd worked out a bit more during the holidays, especially as Kirsty and Carol seemed to be getting faster and faster. With my next spin with Kirsty, I tripped over my feet and fell over. I immediately jumped back up to continue the dance and hoped no one had noticed. Kirsty was doubled over laughing and couldn't continue the dance from laughing so much.

This wasn't how I'd hoped to bring fun to her night. With the tension between us now completely gone, midnight couldn't come quickly enough.

Jennifer

The Christmas holidays had been exactly the break Scott and I needed. Time away from work. No running around and adhering to schedules. Instead we enjoyed time together as a family watching TV and playing games. Tonight had given us the perfect excuse to come out and party. I watched Scott as he danced with each of the girls, laughing together as they twirled.

As he finished his dance with Emma, I claimed him for the next dance, the graceful Pride Of Erin waltz. It wasn't one of better known dances, so only a few of us took to the floor. We glided through each of the sections of the dance, Scott drawing me close to him when it was time to waltz. The scent of his aftershave, the touch of his hand, the closeness of his body and his whispers in my ear had me looking forward to getting home.

Kirsty

I was having so much fun. The ceilidh band was fantastic. The dancing was high energy and a perfect release from all my worries. My nerves at seeing Paul had evaporated. Especially after his fall at the Dashing White Sergeant.

After another couple of dances, the caller announced an Orcadian Strip the Willow would take us to The Bells.

I looked over to Paul. This is my favourite dance of all and I wanted to dance it with him, especially as it would take us to midnight. I wanted to be with Paul for the midnight moment. He smiled over and nodded his head to the dance floor. I nodded my agreement.

With an Orcadian Strip the Willow, the men stand in a line down the hall with their partners across from them. The top couple will twirl with each other for a count of sixteen before making their way down the line. Meaning I would spin with Paul, going out to spin with the next man in the line, back to Paul, out to the second man in the line, back to Paul, and so on. The key thing with this dance is to go as fast as possible and make sure someone catches you before you fall. Amazingly, we made it the entire way down the line without falling. After we completed our final spin, we stood breathless in each other's arms, neither of us wanting the moment to end. We had to separate back to our lines to make space for the next couple. But even once we were apart we continued to gaze at each other.

Midnight was only a few minutes away.

Paul

I couldn't take my eyes off Kirsty. We were both breathless and laughing from the fun of the dance. I had seen the way other men looked at her, trying to build up the courage to ask her to dance. Jealousy had flickered with each guy I watched her dancing with.

Midnight was ticking ever closer. The perfect opportunity to take Kirsty in my arms and kiss her.

Suddenly, the lights went out and the music faded. The musicians stopped playing. We all stood still. Was this the countdown to midnight? I pulled my phone out and switched on the torch function, as did others. I made my way over to Kirsty and put my arm around her.

"Sorry everyone," shouted the caller of the band. "The power has gone. If people can stay where they are we'll try to find out what's happening."

After a few minutes, someone announced a tree had come down on a power line down the lane from the church causing the power outage. The storm that had been gathering force as we made our way to the ceilidh had brought our evening to a premature end and ruined my plans.

We were instructed to return to our tables and then the hall would be vacated table by table. I guided Kirsty back to our table to collect our belongings. As we shuffled out of the hall, the sound of fireworks could be heard near and far. We had missed The Bells! A power cut had stolen our midnight kiss!

Outside Scott shouted, "Happy New Year everyone!"

The rest of the group joined in with his celebration. I cheered and hugged with them all but my celebrations were only surface level. As we walked away from the hall,

I glanced over to Kirsty, she smiled. Was that a look of disappointment on her face too?

Jo

1 January

(Kirsty gave me this beautiful, sparkly journal as part of my Christmas present. Journaling is one of my goals for this year, so here's hoping I follow through with it and commit to putting my thoughts on paper.)

The year certainly started with a bang at last night's Hogmanay ceilidh. A power cut brought it to a hasty conclusion before we even got to the bells. It was so funny. At least we got in some good dancing before we lost the power. Although Paul and Kirsty looked a bit put out by it all going wrong.

So here we are! A new year with new hopes and dreams and possibilities stretching ahead of us. It's so exciting to look out to a new year and wonder. There are some specific things I'm thinking through for the year ahead:

Work. This is my second year of teaching. And I'm beginning to sense the rhythm of it all and feel I'm getting to grips with the planning and the marking. Dealing with the behaviour of certain classes can still be a challenge but I'm learning the tricks. I'll keep going as is until the summer then see what I can volunteer to help with. It's time to raise my profile and think about my career path. It's not that I'm bored with teaching Geography, I still love it, but I want to know what my future options are too.

Church. Now that work is settling into a routine, it's time to volunteer for something at church. What are my options there? Perhaps I should chat with Ben and Tara and see what they suggest. It definitely will not involve anything to do with music. Nor will I get involved in any of the kid/youth things. I love working with kids at school but I think to also do youth stuff at church would be too exhausting.

Holidays. I'm so excited we're going snowboarding in a few weeks. And so grateful to Scott and Jennifer for taking care of the cost to upgrade us to luxury. It would be good to get a summer holiday too. But we'll get the winter holiday in first before I start planning for the summer.

Relationships. Over the last few months I've been spending time with Matt, he's a great guy with a strong faith. I think I'm starting to like him as more than just a friend. I wonder if there is the potential for something to happen between us…

Father, thank you for this New Year. Thank you for new possibilities. Thank you for work, for church, for holidays and for friendships.

Thank you, Father.

Amen

Kirsty

As the ski pull jerked me up the final few metres, the slope looked more and more terrifying. And it wasn't just the height of the slope that had my nerves on high alert, the slope was busier than ever. Parents treating their children to one last day of fun before the new school term and couples out for end of holiday dates. The ice-climbing wall and the sledging area were also bustling with people. And, overlooking the snowy activities, the restaurant and bar were full of customers enjoying the entertainment value of observing those of us down below in the chill. There were too many people around to witness my non-existent skiing ability.

By some miracle, I removed myself from the pull and shuffled over to the rest of my ski class. As I shivered in fearful anticipation, I wondered if I was the only scared person here. My senses were on high alert as I waited my turn to go down the slope. The sound of laughter surrounded me, affirming my belief that I was the only one who was scared. Even the swooshing sound of the skis mocked me. Why had I agreed to this?

'Please God, don't let me break any bones on the way down. Help me get down without causing a scene.'

And then it was my turn. The last run had comprised two teenagers who took off at breakneck speed. Their fearlessness only heightened my nerves. But I think the instructor sensed that he'd left the least confident till last. "Now ladies, we're going to take this nice and easy. Follow my lines and we'll get down no problem. You've skied down from the halfway point, so you can do this."

I admired his optimism! I wasn't sure my legs would be able to move.

The other woman pushed off slowly and followed the instructor. I had to do this. I couldn't stand here at the top forever. 'Stop overthinking,' I instructed myself.

I closed my eyes and pushed off from my standing position. No! I had to keep my eyes open. I opened my eyes, I was doing it. I was moving. All was going well. I kept my sight fixed on the instructor and followed the lines he used. We used the width of the slope, going from side to side, in long sweeping turns.

However, as we got partway down, my attention diverted from my instructor to the restaurant. Behind its big windows, people were eating dinner and watching the activities on the slope. As my eyes darted back to the slope, I panicked and floundered. I couldn't get my skis to turn to follow the instructor. I collapsed in a heap, unable to get up. My legs and skis were twisted together as if they were attempting some strange yoga position. To add to my misery, the teenagers from my lesson came zooming down beside me, making it all look so easy. The instructor shouted directions as to how to untangle myself, but I couldn't work out what he meant. Thankfully some fellow skiers stopped and helped me get back to an upright position.

This lesson was doing nothing to convince me of my aptitude for skiing!

"Come on, Kirsty," shouted the instructor. "Follow the line to me and let's get down to the bottom." I didn't want to. I wanted to go home. But I'd never hear the end of it from everyone else if I quit.

"Well done, both of you," he said as we finished our first run. "Now, back up and get in another couple of runs. I'm here to help and give more advice as needed."

As I held on to the ski pull, I once again had negative thoughts about Lynn!

Somehow I made it to the end of the lesson with no broken bones. But there would be aching muscles and bruises. I could already feel a bruise forming at my hip from one of my falls. I longed to be home and in my bath, soaking in the soothing bubbles. However, I had arranged to meet Jo after my lesson to complete my holiday shopping. The girls had clubbed together and bought me a beautiful pair of black, fluffy snowboots and new black sunglasses for the holiday but I still needed a ski jacket and trousers.

As I made my way from the slope, I heard my name being called. However, when I looked up to the viewing platform, I didn't just see Jo – Lynn, Carol, Matt and Paul were waving down to me too. How much of my lesson had they seen?

"Come up here once you're changed," shouted Jo.

I gave her a thumbs up and went in to change.

By the time I got upstairs to the bar, they had a claimed a table. I pushed my way through to them, past groups of similar-aged people laughing and chatting.

"There she is," said Jo, as I sat down with them.

"What can I get you to drink?" asked Paul.

"I'd love a hot chocolate," I replied.

Paul walked off to the bar to get my drink. Would it be rude of me to put my head on the table and rest?

"Great job with your lesson," encouraged Jo.

"Are you kidding? How much of it did you see?"

"We got here about half an hour ago. So long enough to see that you're doing well."

"It doesn't feel like it. I'm guessing you missed my spectacular fall near the start of the lesson then?"

"We missed it, you'll be glad to know. But you're doing really well. It takes time."

"I am grateful for your optimism," I said, and leaned in to hug her.

Paul interrupted our hug with a big mug of hot chocolate, complete with whipped cream and little marshmallows. And, a great big slice of carrot cake. As he put my treats in front of me he placed his hand on my shoulder. The heat from his touch sent the final shivers of cold from my body.

"Wow. That looks amazing. Thank you so much, Paul." He rewarded me with a stunning smile. My stomach did a somersault. If only I could enjoy my time with Paul. But every time I see him I flip between hopeful and scared. The skiing holiday was looking equally dangerous for my heart as well as my bones!

Jo, Matt and Paul started a discussion on snowboarding, telling of adventures they'd each had in the past. With nothing to add to the conversation I devoured my cake and hot chocolate, the calorie hit doing wonders for my energy levels. The warmth of the bar and my friends were also working their magic.

"I can't wait to be snowboarding again," said Matt.

"It's going to be so good," replied Jo. "Have you been to Val Thorens before, Matt?"

"Years ago, I don't remember much about it except that it had some great black slopes."

"We need to get a few of those in," said Paul.

I lifted my head from the table. "You lot are going to be having so much fun and I'll be stuck in ski lessons all by myself." I hadn't meant to sound so huffy but I was tired and sore from my lesson.

"Why don't I do the lesson with you?" offered Carol. "I'm guessing I'm the least accomplished out of the rest of us, so it probably wouldn't do me any harm to do some lessons again."

"Are you sure?" I asked.

"Of course, no problem at all."

The new arrangement settled some of my concerns for the holiday. "Thank you so much Carol. I really appreciate it." It would be fun to hang out with Carol, she's so easy going.

"Okay, let's get to the shops," said Lynn. "And get that holiday shopping done."

"Just don't get any high heeled snowboots," said Paul, and laughed.

We sighed and walked away from Paul and Matt.

I had asked my family to give me money for Christmas so I could buy my ski jacket and trousers. Mum had said they would buy my jacket, but that was not a purchase I wanted my mum to make. I would be relying on my friends to guide me in my purchasing decisions.

The girls made a few suggestions on jackets and trousers and after trying a few on, I made my decision. I wandered around the ski and snowboarding store, no clue if I had everything I needed, or if there was some other bit of equipment I should buy.

"Help me, Jo," I sighed. "Should I be getting myself anything else for the holiday?"

"Have you got thermals yet?"

"Nope."

"Then I would recommend getting a couple of thermal tops and trousers. Have you got a buff?"

"Nope."

"Okay, get a couple of those too."

"This is all sounding expensive, Jo,"

"Don't worry that's you sorted now. And best of all you already have the essentials for the holiday."

"I do?"

"Of course. You've already got the snowboots and sunglasses!"

KIRSTY

I felt no thrill in getting back to work after the New Year break. A year of mundane work stretched before me. Granted, my negative thoughts could be down to an extreme version of the Monday Morning Blues. The Christmas holidays were over. I was still single. And, I had no clue what to do about my job.

There was no point getting to work early, everyone would push their flexi-time to the last possible second. However, despite my decision to aim for a later start, I was still up early and ready for work. I decided to get my usual bus and stop for coffee on the way. Should I go to Chocolate and Vanilla? It used to be my oasis of calm from work, but it was yet another thing that was tainted by Gary. At first I had been flattered that he noticed it was my favourite coffee shop and sought me out there. But now it was just another place that was contaminated by his actions.

Starting my work year with a panic attack wasn't what I wanted. I opted for one of the coffee chains a few streets away from my office. The atmosphere and coffee couldn't match Chocolate and Vanilla, but at least there were no memories or panic attacks here.

Just after nine o'clock I walked into a quiet office. The decorations that brightened the office in December were all gone. A pile of Christmas cards sat on the corner of my desk, I must have forgotten to put them in the recycling bin.

The top card caught my attention. 'Joy to the World'. The phrase jarred against my lethargy. Joy was part of December - getting excited for Christmas, surrounded by sparkly lights and happy people. However, on a cold, dark, sleeting morning in January was it still possible to feel joy? But wasn't that the point of those Advent sermons? Hope, love, joy and peace were gifts for the entire year. Some glimmers of joy had surprised me during my dreaded stay in Lochcala, so who knows, maybe you can experience joy in a cold, grey January.

By lunchtime, I still hadn't shaken my mood. I was restless and couldn't think what to do with my lunch break. Shopping was out of the question. Every penny was accounted for until I paid off the ski holiday. Which also meant no coffee shop treats at lunchtimes. It was too cold to simply walk about town. The only option left was to spend my lunchtime in the staff break-room.

A few colleagues were sitting in groups of two or three, low tables offered a smattering of out-of-date magazines full of gossip and quick fixes. I sat on my own with my coffee and my book, thankfully I'd remembered to bring the latest novel I was reading. Just as I was losing myself in the story, I heard the dreaded words, "Did you to find out why Gary left?"

I didn't want to glance up, fearing it would give me away. Pretending that I was still reading, I listened to the conversation. Terrified that my name was about to be spoken.

"No! I was talking to Beth in HR. Normally she'll give me the gossip on whatever is hot news."

I made a mental note to never confide in Beth.

"But even she's not saying. So I think it must be bad."

"It's such a shame. With Gary, we had some much-needed eye candy."

"I know! It's not the same in the office without him. I wish I could find out what happened."

"I did hear he was working for his fiancée's mum's company. Which wouldn't be that big a deal except that he left so quickly. And especially just after the launch event. There's definitely something more to all this."

I was relieved my name wasn't being mentioned in the rumours about Gary. But how much longer until I was part of these conversations? Would I end up being the focus of the staff-room gossip?

It was time to look for a new job.

My thoughts of moving department were further bolstered when I received an email from PR Dave in the middle of the afternoon. In his usual jocular style, he sent his greetings and attached his article that had featured in the Evening Times in the run-up to Christmas. I'd already seen it, but it was nice of him to send me a copy. Thankfully, the photo they used for the article was from the second party with Santa, the children and Dave and myself. Dave also attached several photos of me from the day, including a couple from the bouncy castle and the Bear in the Honeypot game. Thank goodness none of these shots had been in the paper.

On a complete whim, I replied, telling him how much I'd enjoyed the day and asked if there were any potential job opportunities in his department. I hit send before I could overthink it or talk myself out of my unusually bold move. After all, he had included a couple of my observations in his article, so hopefully, that meant I was PR department material. But as soon as I hit send I went into double guessing mode and completely regretted my actions.

Paul

This was going to be the best year ever! Last night's trip to the ski centre had been a good night out. Between the ceilidh and last night's fun, it felt like things were in a better place with Kirsty. The way Hogmanay finished still frustrated me, but hopefully the ski holiday would offer the perfect setting. Between now and then it was time for friendship to develop.

However, as I entered the salon I was met with an unwanted sight and all thoughts of Kirsty were pushed away. Over by the sinks, a puddle of water was forming, I went to investigate. Water was slowly dripping out of a join in the pipes. When the plumber fitted our sinks, he pointed out the valve to turn the water off, but there was so much going on that day I can't remember where it is. I ran around the salon, checking in the toilet and kitchen, but nothing obvious presented itself.

I looked through the contact list on my phone, but I didn't have the plumber's number. A quick call to Jennifer provided his details. He said he would fit me in at some point during the day depending on how his other jobs were going. That wasn't the answer I was hoping for. As I hung up, I realised I hadn't asked him where the valve was to turn off the water. I walked around the salon trying to remember where the valve was, but I had no clue what I was looking for. The best thing for now was to place a tub underneath the offending pipe to catch the drips.

Half an hour later, Jennifer was knocking on the door. "You didn't need to come," I said, as I let her in.

"Don't be silly. Looks like you could do with some help." Jennifer walked over to the sinks and inspected the area around the leak. "We'll need to see how it looks when it dries out. I might need to paint that area," she said, pointing to the wall behind the sink. "Hopefully, the flooring will be okay and there won't be any water damage. Have you not turned off the water?"

"I can't remember where the valve is. Do you know where it is?"

"I think it's in the kitchen," replied Jennifer, as she made her way through to our little kitchen area. "This is it here." She pointed to a turn valve in the cupboard below the sink and turned it ninety degrees.

I sat down with a sigh. "Are you okay?" she asked.

"You don't think about having to deal with water damage when you start your own salon," I replied. "Last week one of our new hairdryers blew a fuse that took out all the plug points. The week before that, Trish left a plastic tray on the radiator in our prep area and it caused a horrible smell for a few days. In all my planning it never occurred to me to consider maintenance issues."

"Isn't that like the adverts you see on the TV for business start-ups? You need to be able to deal with everything. Every job, no matter how much you love it, always has the annoying elements."

"I guess you're right."

"It's something I'll need to be aware of too once I'm doing jobs for people I don't know. I've no idea what has caused this fault. Is it something I'm responsible for? Would clients blame me for damage caused by parts other trades use?"

Jennifer slumped down beside me. Now it was her turn to sigh.

"Sorry, Jennifer," I said, as I put my arm around her shoulders. "I didn't mean to bum you out too."

"But these are the things we need to be aware of and ready for."

"Right, I'm popping next door to get us coffees. And when I come back, we can only talk about happy things," I said.

"Like ski holidays?" she suggested, a big grin replacing the momentary sadness.

***

The next day Brian, Trish and myself had our weekly business and marketing meeting. Thankfully yesterday's leak hadn't caused any serious damage. The plumber appeared late morning and fixed the faulty part. But the experience served as a reminder that we needed to keep plugging away at getting our name out there and getting more bookings coming through. We still had credit card debt to pay off from the renovations and start-up costs. Money for maintenance hadn't been in our budgeting, we had to try to create a safety net as quickly as possible.

Once again I questioned the wisdom of going on holiday this soon after opening. But thoughts of snowboarding and time with Kirsty convinced me it was a good idea.

"We need something that doesn't cost any money," suggested Trish, getting my mind back to business. "What if we get a chalkboard to put outside advertising a discount for walk-in bookings?"

"Or even all January bookings?" I suggested.

"I think it's worth trying," said Brian. "After all, most of the appointments we have booked for this month are with people using their ten percent off code."

"Trish, can you have a look and source a blackboard for us?" I asked. "I know it'll be a cost, but hopefully not too much."

"Sure," she replied.

"Any other ideas?"

"Why don't you contact the community newspaper and see if they'll do a feature on us. I'm sure they'd love to do a piece on our stylish salon. Might be good for Jennifer too," suggested Trish.

"Another great idea. Thanks. I'll give them a call. No harm in asking."

"And I'll post up some pics on the local social media group pages," suggested Trish. "We put up some posts when we opened, but it would be good to remind people we're here."

"Okay, let's do it. I'm sure this place is going to be successful. December is a great month to open, but it's followed by the worst month."

Our meeting was brought to a close by the arrival of Elsie, who was booked in for her free haircut. "Hi everyone, it's so good to see you again," she enthused, as she made her way around to give us all hugs. "Have I interrupted you?"

"No, it's fine," said Brian. "We were having a marketing catch up. Trying to decide what to do to get more business."

"Anything I can help with?"

We filled her in on what we'd been discussing.

"I'll keep sharing anything you put up on social media. Why don't you do some kind of students' night?"

"What do you mean?" asked Brian.

"I'm not sure. We could put on a kind of open evening. Students always like free food so you could do a pizza night or something and then do a chat about being hairdressers or starting your own business or something like that. I'm sure plenty of students would like to hang out with you guys and then they'll all start coming here for their haircuts."

"That sounds like a promising idea," said Brian.

"Tell you what, pay me with another free haircut and I'll organise it for you."

"That seems a lot of work for a free haircut."

"It's more than a free haircut. It helps me with my studies. If I can build up a portfolio of events I've organised, it will stand me in good stead for getting a job when I graduate. I could be your events planner."

I left Brian and Elsie to their conversation and walked through to our kitchen to make us all some coffee. As Brian started washing her hair, I could hear the two of them laughing and chatting together. It really did feel like Elsie was becoming part of our team. I liked that idea. We'd come up with several ideas this morning, only time would tell if any of them would result in new clients. While I was waiting for the coffee machine to perc I fired off a text to Scott and Matt. 'Hey, nothing wrong, but would appreciate prayers for the salon. Some days throw doubts in the path.'

As I sat my coffee mug down at my workstation, I noticed the Christmas baubles that Jennifer had given me. The rest of the decorations had been packed away weeks ago, but somehow I'd known that I would need a constant reminder of God's love, joy, peace and hope over me and the salon.

Even when you're following your dream you still need reassurance and hope.

KIRSTY

Eventually, I made it to the end of the week. A shadow of discontent had been following me all week. The break-room conversation about Gary had unsettled me. But it was more than that. I'd made mistakes with almost every task I'd undertaken at work. I'd been grumpy with everyone at house group on Wednesday night. And with the ski holiday coming up, there was no budget for going out this weekend.

I threw a ready meal into the microwave then picked at the subsequent offering. I poured myself a glass of wine and curled up on my settee, pulling my throw over me. A flick through the TV didn't provide any relief from my mood.

I was on the third flick through of the channels, when the downstairs entry buzzer sounded. Should I ignore it? It was probably someone for one of the other flats anyway. But when it went again I answered. "Hello?"

"Kirsty? It's Paul. Hurry up and open the door it's chucking it down out here."

I buzzed him in. Running through to the living room I grabbed the remnants of my microwave dinner and threw it into the kitchen sink. I stuffed the magazines littering my coffee table in a cupboard. Paul was at my door before I had time to brush my hair and freshen up my makeup.

"Hey, sorry to turn up unannounced but I wondered if you needed some coffee." He held up a couple of takeaway coffee cups and a bag that I assumed held some tasty cake or pastries.

As Paul walked past me into my flat, I smiled. This guy had a habit of knowing the right thing to say and do. Well, apart from all the times he threw me into utter confusion.

"I've got a chocolate muffin or a raspberry and white chocolate muffin. Which one do you want?"

"Raspberry every time." I took it from him and savoured the delicious scent of raspberry. Over coffee and muffins we chatted about our week. He had me laughing with his tale of running around his salon looking for stop valves. I didn't bother telling him about the lows of my week, instead I glossed over my week as an uneventful passage of time.

"So, tell me more about your Christmas in Lochcala. How was it?"

"Ugh! It was as bad as I expected. Although, I guess there were a few points where it was okay. But I'm glad to be back."

"Did you say your brothers all still live at home?"

"Yep. Can you imagine it? Three grown men all cramped into a tiny house. I really don't know how they do it. Although, James has just moved out to live with his girlfriend. But I wish Craig would escape."

"Is that your youngest brother?"

I nodded. "And he's the only one that's nice to me. Andrew and James thrive on being mean to me and mum just wants me to move back and get married." I blushed at the mention of getting married.

"And would getting married be so bad?"

"Don't you start teasing me now!" I could feel my face getting redder. I needed to get this conversation to safer ground. "How was your Christmas?"

"It was good. The salon was busy. And I learned lots about Christmas. I thought I knew the Christmas story from school nativity plays and assemblies but there is so much more to it. There are so many great verses in amongst the story that I had no idea were there."

As Paul shared about his Christmas discoveries his movements became more animated, and there was an intense brightness in his eyes. "And when you really listen to the words of the carols, there is so much hope in those lines. O Little Town of Bethlehem was my favourite one this year. What's your favourite carol?"

"I really enjoyed Joy to the World this year."

"I think I remember that one from school assemblies."

Paul's enthusiasm was infectious and his visit was the highlight of my week. As we continued our conversation about Christmas, there was a reminder of joy. "Did you get much time with your sister when she was home?"

"A bit. But not as much as I would have liked. I was hoping you would get to meet each other, but she only stayed for a few days." Silence followed. Was I the only one feeling the tension between us? I could barely swallow. The allure of his aftershave floated around me. I started picking at a loose thread on the cuff of my top.

"Are you okay?"

I looked up. The colours of his eyes captivated me, the blues and greys dancing together, communicating more than mere words.

"Sorry, I'm just a bit tired. It's been a tough week back in the office."

"I'll leave you to an early night." His goodbye hug gave me the parting comfort I needed.

As I closed the door behind Paul, I sighed. Tonight had been strange. Why was I so terrified of dating Paul when it was what I wanted? I had no idea why he had come over tonight but maybe just maybe it brought us a step closer to being together.

Paul

"How do you view the year ahead of you? With anticipation? With dread? Or maybe you don't give it much thought. Have you set any resolutions or any goals for the year ahead?"

Church. It had become the anchor in my week. And the start of Ben's preach had me wanting to hear more. The past week had been a hard one. The salon had been too quiet.

"I want to read you a verse I read during the week," continued Ben. "'*May the God of hope fill you with all joy and peace as you trust in him, so that you may overflow with hope by the power of the Holy Spirit.*' And those words are from the book of Romans chapter fifteen verse thirteen."

I glanced up to the screen behind Ben where the words were displayed. That one verse seemed to encapsulate so much of what I needed to hear. As soon as I made the decision to start my own salon, there had been peace but in the day-to-day reality of starting a business it was easy to lose peace and worry about the balance sheet.

But even though worry tried to creep in, there were times of hope and joy. Hopefully that peace and joy was for my future with Kirsty too.

After church, Matt, Kirsty, Jo, Lynn and Carol and myself went out for lunch. I wasn't sure if it was my imagination or if Kirsty seemed a bit more relaxed. Over soup and crusty bread we talked about the upcoming ski holiday and our first week back at work.

"My week was so slow," I informed the group. "But yesterday's mail brought a surprise. I've been put forward for an award."

"That's amazing," said Kirsty. "What for?"

"It's for the styling I did last year on the Raincoats & Sunglasses fashion shoot."

Kirsty started giggling. "And you hate raincoats and sunglasses."

"Not as much as I used too." I secretly smiled at the blush that crept up Kirsty's face. "The awards event is at the end of the month. Brian and Trish will be coming with me but I've got a ticket for one more person and I was hoping you would come with me, Kirsty."

Her fading blush burst back into vivid colour as the other girls giggled and nudged each other. "That would be lovely, thank you. I've never been to an awards ceremony before. What's involved?"

"It's at City Hotel. There will be a big dinner, the awards will be given out and then it'll finish with some dancing. The only thing is, it's a Sunday night, will that be okay?"

"No problem. It sounds very sophisticated. I wonder if I'll be able to find a hairdresser for a Sunday appointment."

"I can always check if Brian or Trish have any slots." As we continued to joke about the evening, the others were watching our interaction with interest. Maybe it hadn't been the best idea to ask her in front of everyone. But it wasn't a date. A hairdressing event was not how I imagined my first date with Kirsty. This was about having a friend at my side. The team from ByDesign would be there and I confess I wanted to show off Kirsty as well as The Smith Salon.

It would be fun to go to a prestigious event together. But it wasn't a date.

***

It was Friday night and once again I buzzed Kirsty's door, hoping for another evening of hanging out together. "Raspberry or lemon muffin?" I asked, as she answered the intercom. She giggled and buzzed me in.

"How did the dreaded work go this week?" I asked.

"All very boring and non-eventful. Well until today, when I got trapped in our filing room."

"You know I'm going to need to hear the full story." I settled back in her settee, enjoying my coffee and the company.

She blushed as she began her tale. "I was putting some ring binders up on a high shelf but because I was on my tip-toes, I lost my balance and fell against the shelving unit before I had fully pushed in the binders. Somehow that led to several folders falling down, hitting me as they fell. The binders blocked the door and my arm was so sore I couldn't lift the folders for a few minutes. I then realised I would have to deal with it on my own as no one would be able to get in to help. And then, when I finally got out, no one had even noticed!"

Her laughter was infectious as she finished her account of the filing cupboard. "Well at least you have a highlight from your week. Mine was way more boring in comparison."

"Yes, but your working week doesn't finish until tomorrow, so there is still time."

Our conversation flowed naturally from one topic to another. Neither of us in a rush to bring tonight to an early conclusion. "How are you feeling about the ski holiday?" I asked, unable to cope with the silence.

"I'm not sure, to be honest. I'm so excited about getting away with my favourite people and the chalet looks amazing."

"I've never stayed in a chalet before. I've only ever been in tiny little hotel rooms or hostels. And that hot tub!"

The mention of the hot tub coloured Kirsty's cheek, and she quickly moved the conversation on. "But you all seem to be accomplished skiers while I'm still terrified at the top of the indoor ski slope, which is probably tiny compared to the slopes you're used to."

"I'm not buying it. I was there the first time you went karting. And I heard the stories of previous competitive exploits, like climbing walls and abseiling."

That beautiful blush flushed her cheeks. Mum and Lauren had told me to be honest with Kirsty. But I had no idea how to express my feelings. How can I when I'm still trying to figure it out? Plus, based on our conversations over the last few weeks, she still needs time to get over Gary. And the salon is still at a fragile stage that needs lots of attention.

Maybe this stage is about establishing our friendship. But every time I'm with Kirsty all I want to do is pull her into my arms and kiss those alluring lips.

Jennifer

I slammed the car door behind me and took a few deep breaths before I sped out of my driveway. Scott had promised he would be home in plenty of time for me to get to college but as usual he lost track of time and had just arrived home. I didn't even speak to him as I rushed out the door. How could I set up a business if I couldn't rely on Scott?

My stress levels were at tipping point just leaving my house, never mind trying to decide on the best route or where to park in the city. As I followed the satnav's directions, every traffic light seemed determined to slow me down. I tried to ignore the clock on the centre console but the bright red display was a constant reminder that I was cutting it close.

By the time I parked my car, the rain had started. With no time to search for my umbrella, I had to run to get to the college on time. I entered the building dripping wet and gasping for breath. All I wanted to do was run home and cry. Who was I kidding? The evening course would prove I had no talent and was fooling myself. *'God, help me!'*

'One step at a time,' I told myself. Walking into the college transported me to a different world. Outside was a noisy, busy road. But inside was a bright, modern atrium.

A spark of excitement quickened my steps. What a great place to be a student. There was a coffee shop to one side and reception desks to the other with a staircase straight ahead.

"All evening courses are starting in the lecture theatre, up the stairs and immediately to your left," shouted a bored-looking member of staff.

It felt unbelievably nerve-wracking to enter a lecture theatre again. Especially as my late arrival meant there were no free seats in the theatre and I had to stand at the back. Thankfully it looked like there was quite the age range, at least I wasn't the oldest person taking an evening course.

After several nervous minutes, a man stood up at the lectern. He introduced himself, but I didn't quite catch his name. As he called out each evening course, a member of staff stood at the front to take the class away.

"Interior Design," he continued. "You will go with Eva McBride."

I'm guessing about twenty of us stood up and followed Eva out of the lecture theatre. She led us up another flight of stairs and we came to a more open area. "We're based on the ninth floor. To get beyond this public area, you need to have student cards. I have temporary evening class passes for each of you." She passed the cards around us all. "Now follow me to the lifts and I'll show you where you'll be for the next ten weeks."

Arriving at our classroom, I realised anger and fear were subsiding to excitement. The modern building had me expectant for what lay ahead. Eva explained the content for the coming ten weeks and then got right into it. It looked like we had a lot of material to cover.

My fellow students varied in age from, I would guess, twenty-year-olds to sixty-year-olds, mostly women. The diversity in the room encouraged me that I was in the right place. In terms of introducing ourselves, nothing more was required than saying our names, Eva said there would be plenty of time to get to know each other over the coming weeks. Our mingling time in the middle of class gave us time to inspect the 'tools of the trade' that Eva had laid out for us to look through. We all smiled at each other as we flicked through design magazines and fabric swatches. I spoke to a couple of fellow students, tentatively getting to know new people and hearing stories of the attraction of design.

I couldn't believe how quickly my three-hour class passed. I no longer feared the workload or the learning curve. From just one class I could see the potential for my own business. I couldn't wait to get home to tell Scott all about it.

The house was silent when I arrived home. I expected the girls to be sleeping by now, but there was no sign of Scott downstairs either. I crept up the stairs and into my bedroom. The sight before me melted my heart. Scott was slumped in bed with the three girls tucked in around him. Four sleeping beauties. I tiptoed over to the bed. First up was Chloe, I scooped her up and carried her through to her bed. Next up was Emma, I was just about able to carry her without stumbling. I doubted my ability to carry Amy, so I gently woke her and guided her to her bed. Somehow Scott slept through it all.

Back downstairs I made myself a mug of tea and took my notepad out of my bag. A fresh wave of excitement washed over me as I read through the notes from tonight's class. I couldn't wait to get back to it next Tuesday. With the family sleeping, I took advantage of the quietness to look up the suggested tools of the trade.

On the front page of my notepad I had jotted down the list of items Eva told us interior designers should never be without: a Colour wheel; Wallpaper and paint charts; fabric samples; measuring tapes; design magazines; design software and our portfolios.

During our break-time, while we were looking through Eva's examples, I had noticed that some of the younger students took photos of the various sample books and charts. It seemed like a good idea. I took out my phone and looked through my photos from tonight. I thought I had been doing well with the design magazines and paint charts, but I had so much to learn to turn this into a business.

Eva had given us a list of companies we could get wallpaper, fabric and paint charts from. I would email them in the morning. Tonight's search was about looking at some of the free software packages available for interior design. Eventually, I would invest in a more sophisticated package, but for starting out one of these free packages was perfect. I had no idea how to decide which software to go with so I picked the one on the top of our list. While it was all fresh in my mind, I made a list of tasks for tomorrow.

I leaned my head back on the couch and smiled. '*And on earth peace to those on whom his favour rests.*' Peace and joy surrounded me as I lost myself in the creativity of interior design. For tonight I would ignore the questions and embrace peace and joy.

PAUL

"Your salon is beautiful!" My last client of the day was a woman from Jennifer's evening course. "Jennifer was telling me all about your salon and recommended you as the best hairstylist she knows."

"And did she tell you the décor is all her handiwork?"

"She did say she'd helped, but not that it looked this amazing. I'm feeling a bit intimidated at being in class with her now," said Sophie, gazing around the salon.

Jennifer is outgoing and chatty, but even so, it seemed incredible that these women had only met on Tuesday night and already I had a new client from their meeting. "And what are your hopes from doing the evening class?" I asked.

"Similar to Jennifer. I'm using the evening class to test out if interior design could be a career. I'm currently working in a boring office job. Taking an evening class in something creative brings some fun to my life, and if I don't explore options, I'll be stuck in my dead-end job forever."

"Would you like to start your own company?"

"No. I don't have those kinds of aspirations. I'd be happy to work for someone. I'm not cut out for the stress of being responsible for the client work and my own business."

"Well, it's still impressive that you're taking control and not letting yourself get stuck in a rut."

"Thanks." Sophie paused as she looked round the salon again. "Your salon really is beautiful but you've also created a wonderful relaxed space. Nothing quite like getting a good haircut in a nice setting to relax and unwind."

I appreciated Sophie's compliments. "Why don't I make you another coffee? Relax and enjoy some extra 'me time'?"

"You've got a repeat client with me," Sophie enthused. "Do you have any business cards? I'll hand some out at work."

"That would be great. Thanks so much." As I handed Sophie her second cup of coffee, I also gave her a bundle of business cards.

With the cut and style finished, I waved Sophie off. Another satisfied client. Having clients volunteer to advertise for you was the best advertising you could get. Hopefully, it would lead to more new clients. Just another thing to thank Jennifer for.

Trish and Brian had already left for the night, so I put on some high-energy music and set about cleaning my station and preparing the salon for tomorrow. Looking around the salon I sighed. A big, deep satisfying sigh.

The last few weeks had been quiet. But in their quietness, there had been glimpses of what lay ahead, like the conversation with Sophie tonight. One of my frustrations at ByDesign had been the constant time pressure with appointments. The focus was on profit margins rather than clients. The whole concept sickened me. It dehumanised our clients. The Smith Salon would be different, our clients would have time to chat if that's what they wanted.

A couple of weeks ago a new client had sat in my chair and told me how lonely her Christmas had been. She had no immediate family and her friends had all been away for Christmas. Her appointment was on a Wednesday morning, my quietest time of the week. With no one booked in until the afternoon, I took my time with her cut and style. We chatted about the little things in life and laughed about a comedy box set we'd both seen. She'd left the salon brighter and with an appointment for her next haircut.

I was still new to the South Side and getting familiar with the local cafes. But thinking over the conversation about Christmas Day loneliness, I wondered if there was a café somewhere that opened its doors for people who were alone at Christmas. If there was we could advertise it in the salon and volunteer at it. And if there wasn't I would speak to the local cafes and see if it was something we could put in place for next Christmas.

And last week I'd had a nurse in for a haircut. She had worked Christmas and missed being at home with her children. She was sad to have missed a precious Christmas morning with her children but explained it came with the job. As she was the last client of the morning, I decided to skip my lunch break to give more time to her cut and style. This woman needed time to relax and have someone do something for her.

For the next couple of days, I thought of the nurse. I also thought of Matt and how hard he works as a teacher. Perhaps there was something we could do to treat our public sector workers. It could be a monthly 'nominate a public sector worker' thing, or perhaps it would be easier to work it as a prize draw.

When I got home, Matt was working his way through a pile of marking. "Shall I order pizza?" I asked.

"Sure."

I pulled out my phone and ordered our pizza from one of the many food delivery apps I had on my phone. Maybe we should aim to cook for ourselves a bit more.

Over pizza, I told Matt about my thoughts about Christmas in a local café and the monthly prize draw.

"Those are both great ideas, mate." He grabbed himself another slice of pizza. "Remember a few months ago you thought hairdressing wasn't a worthy enough occupation?"

"Yep, and I can guess where you're going with your comments."

"It's not rocket science. You are making a difference. And with your own place, you're already seeing new ways to help people. Have you spoken to Trish and Brian about either of these ideas?"

"No, I just thought of it as I was cleaning the salon tonight. But with the way we've set up the businesses they don't need to participate if they don't want to. It's up to them if they take part in any of these kind of plans."

"How busy have you been this month?" continued Matt. "Have you had enough clients?"

"It's been okay. We knew it would be a quiet month but we've had some new clients. So that's been encouraging. Sometimes I still pinch myself when I walk into the salon. I'm living my forgotten dream, and it's thanks to you making that comment about me setting up on my own."

"Glad to help in any way I can. And, as if your life isn't exciting enough, we're going snowboarding in a few weeks."

"I can't wait to get to the slopes again. It's been far too long since I last went snowboarding."

"Me too! I went to Aviemore a couple of years ago with a group of friends from church, but it was only for one day. It will be amazing to get a few days in. Just a shame we need to come back early."

"Suits me we are coming back early. It would be good to go for a week, but I can't be away from the salon for that long."

"Look at you being all grown-up and responsible," said Matt, laughing as he cleared away the pizza box.

Sharing a flat with Matt was an example of a small decision that turned out to be life changing. A guy at our gym had introduced us when Matt was looking for a flatmate and I was looking for a new place. What a life-changing decision it had been. I could trace all the good stuff in my life to sharing with Matt. Getting to know Jesus. Meeting Scott and Jennifer. The encouragement to start The Smith Salon. And, of course, Kirsty.

Kirsty

January, in all its boring gloom, was nearly at an end. But this year January was ending on a high. Tonight was Paul's awards event.

"Your hair looks fabulous," said Jo, as she arrived at my flat.

"Thanks. Paul came over this afternoon to work his magic. It's quite fancy, isn't it?"

"So Paul was over this afternoon? And how did that go?"

I hadn't told Jo that Paul had been over the last few Friday evenings. Jo is the least likely to tease me about guys, mostly because she knows how insecure I am about it all, but I wanted to enjoy the time with Paul without any of my friends analysing it. "It was fine. He was in a rush to get back to his place to get ready."

"How was he? Was he nervous?"

"Are you kidding? Have you ever seen Paul nervous? I think I'm the one carrying all the nerves for tonight."

"You'll be fine. Enjoy getting dressed up and going to a fancy event. You can trust Paul."

I hugged my friend. She was right. I could trust Paul.

"Now, let's get your makeup done. Have you decided what dress you're going with tonight?" Jo had volunteered to help with my makeup. I was also grateful for her emotional support.

I held up a black dress and a red dress. "I still can't decide between these two."

"The red one. This isn't a night to blend into the background. Tonight is your night to stand out with Paul."

"But I don't want to stand out. Tonight's about Paul, not me."

"I know you don't want to stand out. But trust me the red dress is the right dress for tonight. And one more bit of advice, don't overthink things and analyse every word that Paul says. You might just be going as friends but you two are on a journey. Enjoy the romance of the build up!"

At six o'clock on the dot, Paul arrived at my door. "Wow! You look amazing!"

"You look rather dashing yourself," I replied, eager to get the attention back on him. He was wearing a fitted black suit and shirt that highlighted his toned muscles. A thrill went through me as he guided me out to the waiting taxi. I couldn't believe I was getting to go to a fancy event with such a handsome guy.

When we arrived at the hotel, I marvelled at the range of hair styles and colours. This certainly wasn't going to be a boring event. Jo had been right about my dress, this was not an event for black dresses. Paul placed his hand on my lower back and guided my through the gathering crowd to the drinks reception. The warmth of his touch sparkled throughout my body.

People kept coming up to Paul to congratulate him on the new salon and on his award nomination. He was clearly well liked and respected by his peers. It was a relief when Brian and Trish joined us, at least now I had someone to talk to when Paul's attention was commandeered by others.

We settled down to our dinner. Representatives from two other Glasgow hair salons were at the same table as us. Paul assumed the role of table host and kept the conversation flowing between hairdressing and small talk. It was nice getting to know Brian and Trish a bit more.

By the time we were served our coffees, a man stood up at the top table and tapped his glass to get everyone's attention. "Thank you all for coming out tonight. We'll get straight to the awards and then we can enjoy the dancing and the bar." A ripple of laughter circulated the room. "We have several award categories tonight, so let's get right into it.

We all held our breath when it came to the photoshoot category. It was between Paul, a woman from Edinburgh and a freelance guy. "And the winner is… Paul Smith." We all stood up and cheered. Paul picked me up and spun me round then kissed me on the cheek. He walked off to the front to collect his award, leaving me reeling from the unexpected celebration. As I clapped and cheered with everyone else, my mind was racing. Several times now Paul had treated me as if I was his girlfriend. What did it all mean? But there was no time to process it now. Tonight was about celebrating Paul.

The awards dragged on endlessly, but finally the last award was handed out. As soon as the band struck their first note, the dance floor filled up. Paul took my hand, "Come on. I want to show you off." Before I knew it we were up and dancing. What had he meant by wanting to show me off?

Paul definitely isn't shy when it comes to dancing. While he moved with confidence, attracting attention, I was out of my comfort zone. I had enjoyed every minute dancing with him at the ceilidh but I had never been comfortable with discos. As Paul revelled in the spotlight I wanted to shrink in the shadows. When the band brought the first tune to an end a sea of well-wishers, mostly women, engulfed us wanting to congratulate Paul.

I excused myself and went to the toilets. While I was washing my hands, a woman came in and stood next to me as she applied more lipstick. "You're with Paul, aren't you?" she asked, as she completed her task.

"Yes, we're friends." I'm not sure why I felt the need to quantify our status.

"Ah! That explains it," she said, placing her lipstick back in her clutch. "You're not really Paul's type."

As I met her stare in the mirror she continued. "I went out with him once. One of the best nights of my life. But everyone knows that with Paul it's one night and then it's over. He's probably been with half the women here." She ran her hands over her hair then walked away. I started shaking. She was right, I wasn't good enough for Paul.

When I came back out I glanced into the hall, Paul's adoring fans still surrounded him. I couldn't compete with these women. They were glamorous and part of Paul's world. The uncertainty of everything came crashing down on me. My breathing started to shallow and my stomach cramped. I had to get out of here. Away from all of this.

Gasping for air, I ran out of the hotel then stood still for a few seconds trying to catch my breath. The cold,

January rain shocked my burning cheeks. Flight mode was still in control but the jolt of cold somehow stopped me from jumping in the nearest taxi and going home. The lights of a late night coffee shop caught my attention. I ran through the rain and entered the café to the stares of the staff. Their stares didn't bother me nearly as much as the sight of all those women around Paul. How could I compete with those women? Why would Paul want to be with me when he could have any woman?

Tears silently rolled down my cheeks and into my coffee as I came up with reason after reason why Paul wouldn't want to be with me.

Someone placed a tissue on the table in front of me. I looked up into the worried eyes of Paul. "What happened?"

What could I say?

Paul reached over and squeezed my hand. "Talk to me."

"Why did you ask me to come with you tonight?" I wasn't sure if I wanted to hear his answer.

"Because I like you and I want to spend time with you."

"But you could be with anyone."

"I don't want to be with anyone else. I want to be with you." He squeezed my hand again, causing me to look at him. The depth of compassion in those beautiful eyes caught my breath. "I'm not leaving you."

I couldn't hold his gaze and looked out the window. "How did you know where to find me?"

"I saw you bolt from the hotel and head over to here. Plus, I know you and coffee shops." He stroked my hands and I risked looking at him again. His smile melted my heart and brought a fresh wave of tears. I hid behind the tissue. He reached over and moved my hands away from my face. "Let me take you home."

"But what about your award?"

"Brian can keep hold of it for me." He stood up and guided me out the door, never letting me go. The taxi ride back to my flat was silent. When we arrived, he asked the taxi driver to wait for him. He walked me up to my door and kissed me on the cheek. "Try to get some sleep." He brushed his thumb across my cheek, turned and walked back down the stairs.

Paul had countered all my fears tonight. But at what cost? Would he want to see me again? I had made such a fool of myself and ruined his special night. Tonight should have been about him not me.

Paul

In the pre-dawn darkness I ran along the deserted streets of Glasgow. After hours of tossing and turning I needed to get out and clear my mind. Since I'd left Kirsty, she was all I could think of. Why is she so down on herself? And how could I convince her that she is amazing?

She looked absolutely stunning last night. I had encouraged her to let me put her hair up. Such beautiful facial features should not be hidden behind a curtain of hair. Her makeup was simple and highlighted her natural beauty. And that dress!

During dinner she had engaged with the conversation and seemed to be enjoying the evening. And when my name was called for the award, I scooped her up and kissed her on the cheek without thinking. I heard her cheers above everyone else's as I collected my award. Things seemed to unravel when the dancing started. I could feel her body stiffen as I led her to the dance floor. And yet at the Hogmanay ceilidh she'd danced every dance with unbridled enthusiasm.

Thankfully, I'd caught sight of her when she came out of the toilets. I've no idea what happened, but she looked lost and scared? It was impossible to get a coherent answer from her. I don't know what she would have done if the coffee shop hadn't been there. At least I'd been able to get her home safely.

Kirsty was a mystery. But that added to her appeal. I wanted to know her more.

As I continued my run beside the River Clyde a light drizzle began to fall. January can be such a depressingly dark, grey month in Glasgow. But soon we would be leaving this greyness behind and flying off to the bright whiteness of the Alps. Snowboarding beckoned. However, I needed this holiday to be about more than snowboarding, it was time to let Kirsty know how I feel. I'd enjoyed the Friday evenings at her flat. It had been good having time together, just the two of us. But every time we are together I want to move things on. I want to kiss her. I want to tell everyone she's my girlfriend.

***

"How did last night go?" asked Matt, as we munched our way through pizza.

"It was great. Won the award for photoshoot styling."

"Well done. But where's your award?"

"Brain's got it. I hope."

"You hope? What happened?"

I filled Matt in on the events of the evening and Kirsty escaping to the café. "What do you think it meant that she ran off?"

"I can't believe you're asking me. You're the expert on women."

"I used to think I was. But I've no idea what's going on with Kirsty."

Rather than reassure me or sympathise with me, Matt burst out laughing. I glared at him, "Why are you laughing. This is serious."

"I know. I'm sorry. But it is kind of amusing seeing you out of your depth with a woman."

"Does it mean something though? Is Kirsty all wrong for me?"

"I think it's more likely that it means she's right for you? The two of you are so into each other but neither of you know what to do about it. Maybe it's time to take that leap of faith into the unknown!"

Kirsty

A night of crying and no sleep, had left me with a blotchy face and red eyes. Even though it was cloudy, I wore my sunglasses. My shield to hide me from the world. However, once I got to work, I would be meeting our new department manager. What a lovely first impression I would make!

As I got on the bus for my morning commute, a quiver of anxiety pulsed through me. My emotions were still raw from last night and the thought of meeting my new manager filled me with dread. *'Please God, don't let me have any panic attacks today.'* I looked out the window and tried to control my breathing. From nowhere the song 'Joy to the World' popped into my mind. Without even thinking, I pulled out my phone and searched for the song. I settled back in my seat, earbuds in place, and on a grey January morning listened to a Christmas song.

Somewhere along the journey, all hints of fear disintegrated and instead, there was joy. As the triumphant words of joy rang in my ear, I smiled at the scenes that flashed before me. Within the bus, my fellow passengers were mostly silent and downcast. Outside people were rushing to work, bin men whistled as they emptied bins, workmen shouted to each other. Nothing changed around me, nothing about my circumstances changed and yet there was joy.

When I arrived at work, Irene came over to check on me. "Are you okay, Kirsty?"

"I am," I replied. She cast me a glance as if she didn't believe me. Irene had been my ally and buffer in the office since the Gary incident. But hopefully, she would see that things were slowly improving and she would let me move on from the overly needy person I'd become.

"It'll be fine," she continued. "He's at HR just now and should be with us in about an hour."

The encounter with Irene knocked my confidence a little and I struggled to settle to my work. Thankfully, my Monday morning work is quite repetitive, so it didn't take me long to lose myself in the mundane. After a while, the chatter of colleagues ceased as a new presence entered the department. I peered over my computer. At the entrance to our area stood an incredibly tall man. I'm guessing he's in his thirties, although I'm not the best judge of ages. With a tailored suit and styled hair, he reminded me too much of Gary and his perfect appearance. But unlike Gary, this man had a warm smile and something about his stance told me he wasn't looking for the adulation that Gary demanded.

"Good morning, everyone," announced Irene. "If we could have your attention. This is Mark Carter our new head of department."

"Good morning. It's an honour to be the manager of this prestigious department and I look forward to working with you. Throughout this week I will meet each of you and learn more about your individual roles. Thank you."

Well, as introductory speeches go it was short and to the point. I relaxed a little. Maybe things would be okay at work.

For the rest of the day I tried to distract myself with work but it was difficult to settle between worrying about the new manager and trying to decide if I should message Paul. I constantly checked my phone in case he contacted me. But why would he? I fired off a text to Jo, asking if she was free for an emergency catch up. She replied immediately saying she'd bring the pizza.

By late afternoon, just as I was watching the clock and counting down to home time, Irene appeared at my desk. "Mark's meeting with your section now. Do you want to be first in?"

"Yes, means I won't have time to get nervous. Will you be in with me?"

"No, he wants to meet everyone individually. I think he's hoping it will highlight any issues with your assistant heads of department."

I couldn't bring myself to laugh at Irene's attempt at a joke.

"Kirsty, you'll be fine. I like him. Go and see for yourself."

With more than a little trepidation, I knocked on Mark's door and entered his office. As I walked towards his desk, I could feel the anxiety rise. This office had too many bad memories for me.

"Sorry, can you remind me of your name again?"

"I'm Kirsty."

"And what are your key roles in the department?"

I told him about my regular duties and some of the ad hoc tasks I'd worked on. I didn't want to tell him about my work on the launch event. What if he knew I was the one who had reported Gary? Or what if by talking about the launch event he joined the dots and realised I was 'that girl'? I tried to control my breathing. I couldn't be a wreck at our first meeting. I prayed for joy and instantly remembered my bus journey and 'Joy to the World'.

If Mark knew anything about Gary and me, he didn't show it. During our conversation, I mentioned I wouldn't be in the office next week as I was going on a ski holiday. At the mention of skiing, our conversation moved completely away from work and Mark asked me questions about my holiday: where we were going; how experienced a skier I was; what the forecast was for our week. And then he mentioned several ski holidays he'd been on and how jealous he was of me getting away to the slopes. I'm beginning to think I'm the only person who's never been skiing before.

My first meeting with Mark was over. I took a deep breath. He seemed friendly enough. He'd asked the right kind of questions but also kept himself detached, except for his ski enthusiasm. And I noticed he wore a wedding ring. I wasn't ready to let my guard down, but the meeting had done enough to chase away some worries.

***

Over pizza, I filled Jo in on everything. I told her about meeting my new manager today. The car journey home with Iain Ramsay. The Friday night coffees with Paul and the disaster of last night.

Jo took a deep breath. "I think you have the least boring life of anyone I know."

"Help me, Jo! I don't know what to do. Should I message Paul?"

"Slow down. Let's take this one step at a time."

"First of all, Iain. Do you see the positive in that one?"

"What positive? The guy was all about himself."

"The positive is not about Iain but in how you feel about him now. You've put to rest your teenage crush. He's no longer a measure of future men. Or the perfect guy you idolised."

"I hadn't thought of it in those terms."

"You met your new manager today. That's another step in leaving behind the ordeal of Gary."

"Here's hoping."

"Which brings us on to Paul."

"How can I face him on holiday?"

Jo held up her hand. "Let me stop you right there. You are not going to over-analyse and worry about what might happen. We're going to think about what did happen. But I think we need some ice-cream."

Delving into a tub of creamy chocolate ice-cream, Jo continued to provide her much-needed insight. "I think Paul's trying to show you he's there for you as a friend. He's got a lot to deal with in setting up the salon and he knows you still need space too. Honestly, I would take it all as a good sign."

"But does it mean he wants to date me or just be friends? Or did I blow it all by running out on him?"

"You said that last night a group of women surrounded him. But did he stay with them when you left? No, he sought you out because he wanted to spend the evening with you. That's not the action of a guy who just wants to be your friend."

It was hard to deny Jo's logic. If only I could be so sure. "How can you see all this so rationally?"

"Because it's a lot easier to be wise with other people's lives than our own, especially when it comes to relationships. Honestly, I think God is preparing you for an amazing future by dealing with your past hurts and insecurities."

I felt a lightness with Jo's words. I was still battling fear but now there was a glimmer of hope. "What do I do now?"

"I don't think you should do anything. Leave the conversations to the ski holiday. You'll have more time then. Why not send him something fun, like a box of craft beers, to say thanks."

"That is a good idea."

I waved Jo off, grateful for my friend's insight. But I was still dreading seeing Paul on Saturday morning.

Jennifer

I was enjoying the familiarity of my Monday morning routine – the girls dropped off at school followed by a race around the downstairs of my house. With high-energy music on, I vacuumed, polished, steam cleaned and tidied. Just as I sat down to enjoy a coffee, the doorbell disturbed my peace. But the interruption brought a very welcome prize. My first delivery of design samples. I tore open the cardboard sleeve and gently removed my new treasure. It was fabric samples. A quick flick through had me eager to study them in detail. I changed my playlist to a 'chill out' compilation and sat back down at the breakfast bar, the glow of the mid-morning sun streaming in through the kitchen window. I ran my fingers over each sample delighting in the colours and textures.

When the mail arrived later, I received some further goodies for my interior design collection. There was one of my new magazine subscriptions and my new digital laser measuring tape. My excitement levels were growing with the new arrivals. I moved through to the family room and curled up in the oversized chair reading the interior design magazine cover to cover.

Receiving the various items today confirmed my love for design and how much I was looking forward to this new venture. However, even in the fun of my new deliveries there were doubts. Scott had been so apologetic about making me late for college last week and promised this week would be different. But would it? And I still had questions as to how to balance family life and work.

On Saturday we would be leaving for our ski holiday. Hopefully the holiday would give us time to talk, really talk. I needed Scott to understand what was at stake. It was time for a change in the Thompson household.

***

"Mum, Mum," shouted Chloe. "Get up! Get up! You have to look outside. Snow!"

I groaned as Chloe tugged at my duvet, desperate to get me out of bed. She dragged me over to my window and pulled back my curtain. I was expecting only a light dusting of snow, but, it was several centimetres thick and it was still snowing. Chloe tugged at my arm. "Can we go out to play?"

"Give me a moment, Chloe." Picking up my phone to check the forecast, I noticed a text from Scott telling me how slow his journey to work had been and asking if I'd heard anything from school.

"I hope school is off," said Chloe. "I want to go sledging and build a snowman."

"I wouldn't get your hopes up," replied Amy, in her big-sister-knows-best voice.

As the girls ate their cereal, I checked the council website. "Girls, you're in luck. The announcement's just been made that your school is closed."

"Yeah!" cheered the girls. "Let's go out and play," shouted Chloe.

The girls ran out to the back garden, eager to build a snowman. In the gradually slowing snowfall, each of the girls rolled their own section. We put the three tiers one on top of the other, smoothing snow in between to hold the snowman in place. The girls sourced the sticks and a hat and scarf to finish him off.

We celebrated our snowman achievement with a round of hot chocolates. "I wish we were going on the ski holiday with you," said Emma, as we sipped our warm drinks.

"It will be strange being away without you. But you'll have lots of fun with granny and grandpa. And once we get back, we can start planning our summer holiday."

By the time we finished our drinks and snacks, the sun was peeking through the clouds. It was time for snowboots and sunglasses and a walk to our local sledging hill. The brightness of the sun reflecting off the white ground and the icy touch of the snow-chilled wind brought back memories of past ski holidays. A thrill of anticipation coursed through me.

The park was busy with children making the most of their extra day off school. Each of the girls waved at children they knew from school, many of whom I recognised. "There's Kevin," pointed Emma, and ran off to join him for sledging races. If Kevin was about, then Sarah must be close by, unless she'd got someone else to take Kevin for her. I looked around and spotted her just as she noticed me too. As the children enjoyed their sledging races, Sarah and I exchanged pleasantries. It wasn't the time or place for deeper conversation. At various points one of the other mums or dad came over to chat.

My rumbling stomach demanded an end to the sledging and the call to lunch. "Okay, you lot. I'm starving! Let's go home and have lunch. Sarah, Kevin do you want to join us?"

"That would be lovely," replied Sarah. "We'll buy some cakes and meet you back at yours."

After a round of cheese toasties, the girls and Kevin all ran upstairs to play. Sarah got out plates for the cakes and perched herself on one of the breakfast bar stools while I made us coffee. As we drank our coffee and made our way through more cakes than we should have, we had a remarkably pleasant chat. Sarah can be a bit full-on and opinionated at times. But this afternoon she was surprisingly mellow and good company.

However, the easy-flowing chat came to an abrupt halt when I started telling her about my Interior Design course and the samples I had received.

"It's time you got out there and made a way for yourself," she started. I sighed quietly, knowing where this conversation, or maybe that should be monologue, was heading. Twenty minutes later she was still waxing lyrical about the joys of working and achieving independence. I couldn't get a word in edge-wise. And, was there even any point? I've told her so often in the past I don't care if other mums work or not, I'm trying to decide what work-home balance looks like for me.

Finally, she stopped long enough to take a bite of her cake. "But take today as an example," I jumped in. "How do you plan your work when you need to take random days off for snow days? Or what if Kevin is sick? I'm trying to work out what it will look like for me – emotionally and in terms of time."

"I just phone work and tell them I can't make it in."

"Which works for you. But I'll be my own boss. I can't tell clients I can't work on their décor because I need to stay home with my girls."

"Of course you can. People understand. You'll be your own boss, Jennifer. It's up to you to establish your own rules. Build-in an extra day or two on all your projects for 'just in case' purposes. If you don't need to use it your clients will be happy you've finished ahead of time."

I was pleasantly surprised at Sarah's helpful wisdom. "Now," she continued, glancing at her watch. "Let's have another coffee and cake before I leave."

JENNIFER

For once I was up and showered before my alarm went off. So unlike me, but then it was the start of our holiday. Racing around the house I took care of all the final bits of packing and the last-minute checks that we had our passports and confirmations of flights, chalet and travel insurance. As the taxi beeped its arrival, we said our goodbyes to the girls and my parents. I was excited but worried about going on holiday without the girls.

Matt and Paul were already waiting for us by the time we got to Glasgow Airport. Kirsty and the others arrived a few minutes later. Check-in and security went smoothly and efficiently, thankfully, leaving us enough time to get coffee and croissants before boarding the plane. There are various elements in an airport that trigger my excitement for the journey – the energy of people rushing about, the bright lights and scents emitting from the duty-free shops and, probably most bizarrely, the smell of airplane air as you enter the plane.

A few hours later we were on the tarmac at Geneva Airport. The thrill of arriving in another country coursed through me. There wasn't much snow at the airport. However, we knew from the resort live cams the slopes of Val Thorens were white and welcoming. We piled into the transfer minibus, excited for the next part of our journey. Our driver acknowledged us with a nod then drove towards the mountains. I'd dozed a little on the flight but I wanted to stay awake and take in all the scenery of our bus journey. The lower-lying ground looked sparse and barren, but as we began our ascent, the snow levels increased and the mountains looked spectacular. Easy-flowing chat meandered through the bus, however, I was content to leave the conversation to others as I took in the surrounding beauty.

Eventually, we pulled into Val Thorens. It seemed a long way to come for just a few days for Jo, Matt and Paul, but they are all young and it was part of the adventure. Val Thorens seemed so busy compared to the sleepy villages we had passed along the way. The driver slowed to a crawl, giving generous time and space to the pedestrians who didn't seem overly concerned whether they walked on the streets or pavements. All around skiers and snowboarders strolled about carrying their skis and boards, the sight of them thrilled me. We were here.

Scott collected our keys from the hotel that owned the chalet and then we were driven the final few metres to our holiday abode. As the bus turned the corner my breath caught. The views were spectacular. In front of us the snow-covered mountains commanded our attention. To the side we could look down to the resort where the ski runs converged and ended.

With great excitement, we all jumped out of the bus and grabbed our bags. Scott led the way to the chalet. We dumped our bags in the hallway and kicked off our snowboots. We opened the door into the living area. It was a large, airy open-plan space. To one side there was a fireplace with comfy-looking couches around it. To the other side was the kitchen and dining area with a smaller seated area. Pine walls and ceiling brought a cosy glow to the room and the large windows showcased the snow-covered mountains. Patio doors directly in front of us led out to a terrace. "Hot tub!" shouted Lynn, as she pointed out to the terrace. We rushed over to see for ourselves.

"This is amazing," I squealed. I hugged Scott. Hopefully we would get some alone time in the hot tub during our stay.

"Let's check out the bedrooms," suggested Jo. We exited by a door to the side of the kitchen and investigated the corridor of bedrooms.

"Who wants which rooms?" I asked.

"You and Scott need to have the fabulous master bedroom," said Kirsty. She and Jo picked the room next to us. Carol and Lynn picked their room then Paul and Matt went with the final room.

"Why don't we unpack, then decide what to do first," I suggested.

"What's to decide?" said Jo. "It's hot tub time!"

"Not so fast," said Scott. "It would be best to get our equipment sorted now, so we're ready in the morning."

We all moaned at Scott's suggestion. Everyone had been eyeing up the hot tub as soon as Lynn had pointed it out, but he was right, it was best to get the boring task done. We got our puffy jackets and snowboots and sunglasses back on then trooped out the chalet. Scott led the way, walking with Paul and Matt, while I followed behind with the girls. The ski hire shop was in the centre of the resort. It looked small and old-fashioned from the outside, and the inside. With the eight of us in the shop, it seemed quite full. However, the staff were lovely and efficient and in no time at all they had us in the correct size boots, skis and snowboards and helmets. The guys all hired helmet cams too.

I walked back to the chalet hand-in-hand, or is that glove-in-glove, with Scott. Darkness was descending and with it an exciting après-ski vibe. It was fun to take in the atmosphere and people watch as we walked.

Back at the chalet, each grouping went to their respective rooms to change into swimming costumes. It wasn't long before I heard footsteps running past our room towards the living area.

"Let's give the younger crowd a bit of time on their own in the hot tub," said Scott, as he pulled me into a hug and kissed me.

Kirsty

"Let's get changed quickly," I said to Jo, grabbing my costume out my case. When we first saw the pictures of the chalet, I loved the idea of the hot tub and indulged in a daydream or two about being in a hot tub with Paul. But now the reality of it was triggering all kinds of insecurities. Paul was going to see me in a swimming costume for the first time – a guy who has been with models in the past. How can I compete with that?

Thankfully, we got to the terrace before anyone else. We lifted back the hot tub cover and Jo switched on the lights and the bubbles. She settled herself in the water with a satisfied sigh as I hung our towels on the nearby hooks. Just as I turned to the hot tub Paul and Matt walked out.

Paul greeted me with a boyish grin. "This is a very welcome addition to our holiday." He cast his gaze over me. With no inhibitions of his own he hung up his towel and went straight into the hot tub. I confess he wasn't the only one gazing. The guy has an actual six-pack!

"Come on, Kirsty," said Jo. My friend's words broke my inability to move, and I quickly made my way in to join her. In my eagerness to get in my foot slipped on the base. Paul caught me. We stood in the middle of the hot tub, neither one breaking away from the moment. A subtle cough from Jo broke the spell. Paul guided me to the seat next to him. My senses were in overdrive as I sat next to one of the hottest guys I know. I didn't know what to say or where to look. But then my thoughts returned to the woman at the awards event and her comment about how many women Paul had been with. Why does being around Paul cause me so much confusion?

As per Jo's suggestion, I had sent him a box of craft beers as a 'thank you' for taking me to his awards event. It was also an apology for the way I had behaved. He had been the perfect gentleman on Sunday night but had I ruined any chance of a relationship? I had spent the week worrying about it. Wondering what he thought of me. He had sent me a text to thank me for the beer and said he was looking forward to the holiday, but was he looking forward to seeing me?

When I arrived at the airport this morning, he hugged me as soon as he saw me. The depth of that hug told me we were still friends. Throughout the journey, Paul and Matt had been larking around and playing tricks on us. His goofiness further confirmed our friendship was safe. But will we ever be more than just friends?

My negative spiral was interrupted by Lynn and Carol as they came running out to join us. "This is amazing!" screamed Lynn.

I was grateful for their arrival. With more of us in the hot tub I was able to speak again. "I can't believe we're in a hot tub in the French Alps."

"Do you think we'll spend more time in here or on the slopes?" asked Jo.

"The slopes," said Matt. "Look at those mountains! It's the ultimate invitation to snowboard." We all laughed at Matt's enthusiasm.

"Why do I get the feeling my life will be in danger snowboarding with you guys?" said Jo, throwing in an exaggerated groan for good measure.

"You're going to have the best snowboarding experience of your life!" replied Matt.

Paul laughed. "Don't worry, Jo. I'm not looking forward to boarding with him either."

Jennifer and Scott were the last of the group to come out. As they climbed into the hot tub we all shuffled around, my leg touched Paul's, it felt strangely intimate when there were so many others with us. We exchanged a glance and Paul rewarded me with a beaming smile. His smile gave me the reassurance I so desperately needed and relieved some of my anxiety.

A lot hinged on the next two days.

Paul

A knock at the terrace door attracted our attention. "Welcome everyone. My name is Mathieu and I am your host for this week. If you have any questions, please do not hesitate to ask. I will serve dinner in half an hour."

"Guess we better get dried off for dinner," said Scott, as he stepped out of the hot tub. Our first hot tub time had been perfect. Sitting next to Kirsty, enjoying the touch of her leg next to mine. I watched her as she left and grabbed her towel. As she looked back, I smiled at her, willing her to understand how amazing she looked. I can't fathom why Kirsty has so many insecurities or why she is so negative about herself. She has the body and looks of a model. Plus, there is never a dull moment with her, which makes her extra fun to be around. I couldn't wait to get time alone with her this weekend.

Dinner was delicious and plentiful. For starters, we had some concoction that involved beetroot and goat's cheese. Our main course was beef teriyaki served with fancy rice and stir-fried vegetables. And then dessert was

French apple tart with vanilla ice-cream. It was a big step up from my usual diet of take-away and oven-ready food.

"Let's have our tea and coffee around the fire," suggested Scott. We all followed him over to the lounge area and collapsed onto the comfy chairs.

"Has anyone decided which slopes to try out tomorrow," asked Scott.

"It's the nursery slope for me," replied Kirsty.

"And me," said Carol, as she smiled over to Kirsty.

"We were thinking of trying out this red slope in the morning," I said, as I picked up a resort map from the coffee table and pointed to the nearest red run.

"Looks good. Are you up for it, Jennifer," asked Scott.

"I'm not sure I can start with a red. I think I'd rather start with a few blue runs."

"I would prefer that too," joined in Lynn.

"Shall we split into two groups then? Those who want to start with blue and those who want to start with red?" I suggested.

"Sounds like a good plan," said Matt.

"I want to start and end this week with Jennifer," continued Scott. "So I'll do the blue run with Jennifer and Lynn, and you guys and Jo can go straight to the red."

I couldn't wait to get out snowboarding again. "What do you say we aim for a black run too, Jo?" Matt asked her.

"Maybe." Jo sounded unusually hesitant as she then turned to the rest of us. "You need to pray for my protection whenever I'm boarding with these two."

"Go, Jo! Show them how it's done," cheered Kirsty.

"I wouldn't be surprised if she's the one showing us up," added Matt.

As Jo laughed, Matt lifted his playing cards from the coffee table. "Now that tomorrow is sorted, who is up for a game of Switch?"

We all groaned but happily joined in the competitive card game. This was going to be a perfect holiday.

Jo

5 February

We're in Val Thorens!!!! I'm so excited.

Our day has been a wonderful day of travel. The sights, the sounds and the smells along the way. Matt and Paul established themselves as the jokers of the group as they carried out their schoolboy pranks throughout the journey. They slipped a couple of sachets of sugar into my coffee when we were at Glasgow airport. I pretended not to notice, but it was foul. I was a bit hacked off with them as my coffee is sacred. But it's impossible to stay mad at Matt and Paul.

The resort is beautiful and the chalet is out of this world. We ran from room to room taking in the cosiness of the chalet and the stunning views. I'm sharing a bedroom with Kirsty, which will give us lots of chances to catch up as we probably won't see much of each other during the day.

Tonight we played Switch after dinner. The card game turned the guys from jokers into competitive card-sharks. Kirsty was the first one out and treated herself by heading out to the amazing hot tub.

And then as other people got out they followed Kirsty's lead and went to join her. Matt and I were the last two playing. We took that to mean we were the winners (even though we knew we were the losers). Paul stayed with us for a little while but got bored and joined the others. Before he left us he suggested we set a timer or we could be playing for hours. I think I might have blushed when Matt said he was happy to keep playing until one of us won, no matter how long it took. I'm not normally a blusher! When I eventually beat Matt, I felt a little bit sad as it had been nice being alone with him and a couple of decks of cards. But my prize for winning was a big hug from him. With our height difference, he completely enveloped me. I'm not complaining about that at all. Plus, while we were in the hot tub this afternoon, I confess I did check him out. Very nice!

Tomorrow I'll be snowboarding with Paul and Matt. I can't wait to get on a snowboard again. It's been a while though, so I hope I don't show myself up, especially in front of Matt. This holiday could be promising in so many ways.

Father, be with us as we ski and snowboard tomorrow. I'm in awe of your creation and I can't wait to see more of this beautiful place.

Thank you, Father.

Amen

Kirsty

The sound of footsteps in the hallway woke me up. For a few seconds I felt disorientated until I remembered where I was. The fear of the ski lessons hit me afresh.

When I entered the kitchen, Mathieu was busy making scrambled eggs. A delicious-looking arrangement of pastries, fruit and yoghurt was spread out on the table as well as cafetieres with coffee and a flask of boiled water for those who wanted something from the tea selection.

"Can I just stay here and eat food and enjoy the chalet?" I asked.

"No," replied Jo. "You're going to get out there and you will have fun in the snow."

Paul wandered through wearing shorts and a t-shirt. Oh great. Just what I needed. A constant reminder of how good he always looks. He poured himself a coffee then started chatting with Mathieu, asking advice on slopes and après-ski activities. As they discussed slopes, Matt joined them, also in shorts and t-shirt. I sat at the dining table munching a croissant, the whole time observing the men in the kitchen. If it wasn't for the confusion filling my poor heart, this would be the perfect way to start the day.

"Morning everyone," greeted Jennifer, as she came into the living area. "Mathieu, this spread looks fantastic. Merci."

"Thank you," he replied. "You need to have good energy to spend your day on the slopes." As he spoke he turned off the hob and scooped the scrambled eggs into a serving dish. "Does anyone need any assistance with deciding where to go today, or how to get anywhere?"

Jennifer looked around the group, "I think we're all fine, thanks."

I glanced at my watch and sighed. Carol, who was sitting next to me, nudged me. "It'll be fine," she said. "Now let's go and have a fun lesson."

Carol and I made our way to the ski school. Despite all my layers I was shivering, but I knew it was fear rather than cold that had me shaking. As we arrived at the school an instructor was organising people into the various groups. When we gave him our names, we were directed to a group to our left. We smiled as we joined the others. No one initiated conversation, which suited me perfectly.

"G'day, everyone," greeted a man in ski school clothing. A slightly chubby Australian ski instructor was not what I was expecting. Maybe the lessons wouldn't be so bad after all. "My name is Chris, and I'll be your ski instructor for this week. And before anyone makes any reference to the fact I'm Australian, yes we do have ski resorts in Australia. Now it's your turn – what's your name and have you skied before."

One by one we introduced ourselves. The group seemed to consist entirely of British people. A few of us had done some lessons in the UK, either indoor ski slopes or dry ski slopes.

"Let's get started. First up. Put on your skis."

Already I felt myself relax. If Chris assumed we had no ability, maybe I would be okay. As he went along the line checking our skis, I took the time to take in our surroundings. The area was getting increasingly busier as skiers and snowboarders arrived to take the chair lifts and gondolas to the various slopes. I imagine today's conditions are perfect for skiing. Crisp snow, beautiful blue skies and barely a breath of wind.

"Okay, now that you've all got your skis on we're going to do some basic balancing. Then we'll take a ride on the magic carpet to the top of the nursery slope and get you skiing." Chris used his stick to point over to the covered travelator. I was relieved we wouldn't have to deal with chair lifts yet. After some stretching and balancing exercises, he led us to the travelator and we shuffled our way on. I wobbled as I made my way onto it but thankfully kept my balance.

Chris instructed us to stand in a line at the top of the nursery slope and demonstrated a snow plough. Our first task was to go down the slope in the snow plough position. As Carol was the most experienced skier, he got her to go first, then I was to follow. Pushing off from the top of the slope, I was finally glad I had taken the lessons before we came. I held my balance and manoeuvred my way down to the bottom. Carol cheered and gave me a high-five as I pulled up beside her. "There you go," she said. "That wasn't so bad was it?"

I smiled. I was too nervous to comment.

The rest of the group joined us. A couple of people had taken a tumble on the way down but were still smiling when Chris came down at the end.

"Okay, everyone back up the magic carpet, and let's do it again."

We completed another couple of snow plough runs before Chris introduced us to turns. With the turns, we all had our falls but somehow here in the resort, it didn't feel like the trauma it had in the indoor ski slope. I couldn't decide if it was because of our laid-back teacher or the buzz of being in an actual ski resort.

By the time we got to the end of our lesson, I was ready to have a break. Carol and I were the first ones back to the chalet. We peeled off our outer layers and collapsed on a settee.

"You looked like you were enjoying yourself out there," remarked Carol.

"I actually did. Thanks for doing the lessons with me. I know I wouldn't have enjoyed it so much if I was alone."

"No problem at all. Besides the rest of our group are a lot better than me. I don't need the pressure of trying to keep up with them."

"Do you think the others will come back for lunch?" I asked.

"I can guarantee it. They'll all be starving. I'm feeling quite hungry myself, but for now, I cannot be bothered getting up from this settee to search for food. Plus look at that view. Let's relax and enjoy it until the others get back."

"I couldn't agree more," I replied. "In fact, I don't want to move again. I feel quite cosy and content sitting here."

By the time Jennifer, Scott and Lynn arrived both Carol and myself were almost asleep. "How did the lesson go?" asked Jennifer.

"Yeah, it went well," I replied. "How was your morning skiing?"

"It was great," said Jennifer. "But I am exhausted. And starving." She immediately got to work in the kitchen pulling out bread and cooked meats. "Do people want hot or cold drinks?"

Lunch wasn't catered, but there was food in the chalet, including the left-overs from breakfast. As we gave our preference for cold drinks, the others arrived. With reluctance, I peeled myself from the settee and moved over to the dining table. Paul and Matt helped Jennifer take the food over to the table. After a morning of outdoor activity, the food tasted extra yummy.

"What's everyone's plans for the rest of the day?" asked Scott.

"Before we plan this afternoon, let's talk about tonight," suggested Paul. "When we were talking to Mathieu earlier, he told us about the toboggan run. It sounds amazing. Six kilometres of sledging!"

"He said the night run was the best one to do," continued Matt. "If we want to go for it, he'll book it and time our meal accordingly. Shall we go tonight?"

"Yes!" said Scott. "That sounds brilliant."

"Okay, I'll text him now and see if he can book us in," said Matt, as he got his phone out and started texting.

By the time we had finished lunch, Matt's phone pinged. "Great," he said, as he glanced at his phone. "We're booked in for tonight at half-past five. Mathieu will have afternoon tea ready for us at four and dinner at seven."

"As we're doing the toboggan run tonight, I'm definitely taking this afternoon off," I said.

"I think I'll join Kirsty and stay here this afternoon," said Jennifer. The men enthused over an afternoon of red and black slopes, and Jo, Lynn and Carol decided to stick to blue slopes for an hour or two. An afternoon with Jennifer offered a rest from skiing and my thoughts of Paul.

JENNIFER

We waved everyone off for their afternoon adventures, then Kirsty and myself snuggled down on the large couch for some relaxing time.

"This is perfect," I said, as we gazed out at the vista. "It is so beautiful."

"So what did you think of your first Alps ski lesson?"

"It actually went okay. I'm feeling quite relieved right now. Our instructor seems fun and I think he'll keep me from getting too down on myself. But I am glad to have the afternoon off and build up to the slope time. How did your morning go?"

"It was fun. But I'm quite rusty when it comes to form. And, dare I admit it, not quite as brave with my speed as I used to be. Like you, I'm quite happy to build up to it. But then that's also a luxury we have over Jo, Matt and Paul."

"It's such a shame they need to leave so early."

"The joys of work commitments." I took a sip of tea and glanced over to Kirsty. "And how are you feeling about Paul?"

She hesitated for a moment before she replied. "I like him, of course. And we've been spending more time together. But I'm constantly wondering if he really is interested in me?"

"Yes!"

"Really?"

"Kirsty, we all see it. We're all rooting for you to get together sooner rather than later so we can move beyond the tension."

"Seriously?"

"Yes!" I'm not sure I should have laughed at Kirsty's hurt expression. But the two of them need to realise this thing between them affects the group. Although, I think the onus is potentially more on Paul to be upfront with her and let her know where he's at. Kirsty's insecurities won't let her believe the best for much longer. Paul's the only one who can give her that hope.

"Enough about me," she continued. "How's your evening course going?"

"I've only had two classes so far. But I'm loving it. During our first class, our teacher told us about some of the tools of the trade. So I ordered swatch catalogues for fabric and wallpaper and paint charts. It's been so much fun studying them. I also ordered some more design magazine subscriptions. And now when I look at the pictures I dream up different combinations of fabric and wallpaper. It's so much fun."

"It sounds like you've found your dream occupation."

"I really hope I have."

We sat in companionable silence for a few more minutes.

"Why don't we indulge in some hot tub time while the others are hard at it on the slopes?" I suggested.

"That sounds like a perfect idea."

The warm, welcoming water did not disappoint. Last night had been magical under the sparkling starlight. The moon lighting up the snowy landscape, enabling us to still enjoy the mountain view. However, the daylight was also incredible. We could hear the faraway chatter of skiers and snowboarders and the squeals of delight from children enjoying their ski-schools. The mountains stood proud and magnificent before us. It was a tough call whether to spend time skiing or in the hot tub.

"Thanks again for all of this," said Kirsty, relaxing in the warm water.

"Stop thanking us. We did it for us too. I have to say we've never done a ski holiday to this level before and my aching little muscles are enjoying having a hot tub on demand."

We both rested our heads back enjoying the view and the hot, bubbly water working its magic.

"How's work going?" I asked, as I got up to press the button to restart the bubbles. "Have you met the new boss yet?"

"He started on Monday and I had a short meeting with him. He seems okay, but obviously, I still have my anxiety about the place. But something encouraging did happen at work, and I can't believe I forgot to tell you earlier. I'd emailed a guy in our PR department a few weeks ago to ask if they had any job openings. He didn't reply, so I assumed it meant they weren't interested. But then I got an email from him on Friday telling me that one of their admin staff had resigned and asking if I wanted to apply."

"That is exciting."

"I know! I mean there's nothing certain. But the fact Dave emailed me makes me hope I could have a chance of getting it. It would be ideal. A fresh start in a new department but still within the known setting of the council."

"It would be a great opportunity for you."

"Definitely. I've not had any panic attacks at work since December, but I'm still afraid that one could kick off at any moment. I just wish I could get past this worry stage and feel more hope or joy or something positive."

"Think back to the verse about joy from the Christmas story – *'Do not be afraid. I bring you good news that will cause great joy for all the people'.*"

"That's the verse you got us to read each day in December. It seemed to crop up a few times in the run up to Christmas," she replied.

"Fear and joy don't coexist. It's one or the other. Everything you went through with Gary caused you to fear. And that fear has robbed you of your joy. Unfortunately, there's no magic wand to erase Gary and what he did. That's part of your story now. But it's up to you how the rest of your story plays out."

Her gaze drifted to the mountains. I didn't want to give her a hard time, especially as we were on holiday. I wanted good for my friend. To see her live life to the full and not just enduring things. A better future would only happen if she pursued it.

"Your future is ahead of you, Kirsty. And there can be joy in the future. And hope. But you need to step towards it."

"I know," she sighed. "But how?"

"It doesn't happen with a major step or with just willing it to happen. It starts with little steps. And as each little step takes you to a more expansive place you'll take another step then another. But the cool thing is you don't need to make the journey alone. Why do you think the Bible verse about joy stood out to you so much at Christmas time? It's Jesus nudging you forward. He wants you to live life in all its fullness. And he's given you friends to help you along."

"You've reminded me about something else that happened this week," Kirsty said, suddenly brightening up. "On Monday, as I was going to work, the song Joy to the World popped into my head. I selected it from my Christmas playlist and played it on repeat for the entire journey. The thought of listening to a Christmas song in January had me smiling the entire way to work."

"That's brilliant. Sometimes joy can surprise us, and that's all the encouragement we need to choose it the next time it comes along." She was holding my gaze now, hopefully, my words were encouraging her to believe in hope and joy. "You're on holiday in a beautiful setting with your best friends, Kirsty. Look for joy this week and don't shy away from it. And that includes joy in the small things."

She looked up to the mountains. Lost in her thoughts for a few seconds. "Do you think it comes down to my faith not being as strong as everyone else's? Even Paul, who's only been a Christian for a year, seems further on than me."

I hugged my friend. "Oh Kirsty, faith isn't something that should ever be compared. It's between you and God."

"You always make everything sound okay, Jennifer. You make me believe things will work out."

"Things will work out. Paul, career - it will all work out, we just don't know how yet. And in the journey you can find joy."

She smiled and hugged me. "Thanks, Jennifer."

I laughed and splashed water at her. "And this concludes today's hot tub therapy session."

Paul

The conditions were perfect. Clear skies, glorious sunshine, barely a breeze and just the right amount of iciness on the snow. It was invigorating to be back on the slopes. By the time we'd completed our afternoon runs, I was back up to speed. Boarding with Matt and Scott had been exactly what I needed. And not just because of the exercise, it was also good to have time to hang out. We sat watching other skiers and snowboarders as we took in the view and relaxed.

"Have you had a chance to look up the videos for the toboggan run yet?" Matt asked Scott.

"Nope. I'm leaving it as a complete surprise."

"Living life on the edge," joked Matt.

"That's a terrible joke for a ski holiday," replied Scott.

The banter between Matt and Scott added to the enjoyment of the afternoon. Was there a better place to be in life than with your mates on the slopes? I'd had my doubts about the timing of the holiday, however, sitting here with the guys I knew I had made the right choice.

Opening the salon was a dream come true, but that didn't mean it was stress-free. In fact, I hadn't been prepared for how stressful it could be. So right here, right now, I would enjoy the peace the mountains offered.

We got in another couple of runs before it was time to go back to the chalet. Our first day of snowboarding had been energising. But all that fresh air and exercise was creating quite the appetite. Mathieu's afternoon tea did not disappoint. This is the best ski holiday ever! Over hot drinks and a spread of bread, jam and freshly made biscuits, we exchanged stories of our first day on the slopes. I joined in the conversation less than usual, too busy eating my fill from the treats laid out in front of me. But sometimes, it's good to be a bystander and observe.

Kirsty was looking refreshed from her afternoon away from the slopes. As I watched her interact with the group a plan formed in my mind. I had already decided our holiday would be the perfect setting to ask her out, but my biggest challenge was getting time alone with her.

Tonight could work. A fun evening of fast sledging might be what she needed to get into her competitive psyche. I'd seen that Kirsty before. The one who took pure enjoyment out of her immediate setting and became who she was truly meant to be. I needed to speak to Matt.

Finishing my hot chocolate, I suggested to Matt that we go to our room to get our head torches and helmet cameras. As soon as we were alone, I enrolled him in my plan. "Mate, I need your help tonight?"

"What do you want me to do?"

"I want time alone with Kirsty. But it's proving trickier than I thought. So I was thinking we could wangle it so that me and Kirsty and you and Jo buddy up for tonight. Then you and Jo can split off and give me time with Kirsty."

"Sure. I'm willing to give it a go."

"Thanks. I'll owe you one."

We all got kitted up in our snowboots and puffy jackets and made our way to the cable car that would take us to the toboggan run. By some magic, my plan worked out without us even trying. There was only enough space in the first cable car to take Jennifer, Scott, Carol and Lynn. Leaving me, Matt, Jo and Kirsty waiting for the next one.

"Feel free to start when you get up there," I shouted over to Scott. "I bet we catch up."

"Ha! In your dreams," replied Scott. "We'll see you back down here."

I laughed as I waved them off. We didn't have to wait long for the next cable car and then it was our turn to ascend the mountain.

"Are you looking forward to this?" I asked Kirsty.

"I guess," she replied. "I mean they call it tobogganing but it's just sledging, right?"

"Of course. Kids do this. It's perfectly safe."

"Now, see. You say that, but I do have a poor track record with safety on activities."

"You'll be fine," I replied. "I'll look after you."

She glanced at me, questions in her eyes. Maybe my mum and Lauren had been right. When I told her how I felt about her last October, I thought I was being open and honest. But maybe I'd been selfish, leaving her hanging and not explaining things further. Tonight I would let her know how I felt.

The four of us sat side by side at the start of the run. Head torches on, ready to race each other down the six kilometre toboggan run.

"Go, go, go," shouted Matt, and the four of us scrambled, pushing our fists off the ground trying to get an initial burst of speed. It didn't take long to speed up, especially when we got to the first section with a decent slope. Matt and Jo were in the front and I was timing myself to stay next to Kirsty. The sledges had brakes at the sides, I'm not sure how effective they are, but they were enough to help me keep my speed at Kirsty's pace.

I glanced over to see how she was doing. "This is amazing," she said.

"Let's go faster," I yelled back.

At the next steeper section she used her brakes less and we gathered speed. We were even catching up on Matt and Jo. This was working out perfectly. Competitive Kirsty was back. I'm not sure if skiing is her thing, but at a resort like this, there are lots of other fun activities.

Matt and Jo were slowing down, and we came alongside them. "Why did you slow down?" I asked.

"The first light tunnel is just ahead," replied Matt. "We need to go through these. All part of the experience of doing the run at night time."

He led the way and we followed him to the right side of the slope for the light tunnel. It was weird. As we sledded through the tunnel, red, green, yellow and purple lights flashed through with us. It took a few seconds for our eyes to adjust to the dark after the tunnel lights, then we were on our way. Once again Matt and Jo led the way, leaving me to enjoy the experience with Kirsty.

"That was amazing," enthused Kirsty, when we reached the finish line. "I had no idea what to expect. I mean sledging for forty-five minutes? That's just strange. But I had so much fun and the time flew by."

Kirsty's eyes sparkled with the fun and excitement of the experience. I wanted to scoop her up and kiss her. But instead, I just agreed. Before I could say anything else, I heard Scott shouting. I looked around and located the rest of the group. Jennifer was clutching her arm, her face etched in pain.

"Jennifer?" exclaimed Kirsty, "What happened?"

"My arm caught on my sled at the last turn. I think I've done something to my wrist."

"We just got in before you," explained Scott. "Why don't you go back to the chalet and I'll take Jennifer to the medical centre."

"Do you need any help?" asked Kirsty.

"No, it's okay. You all head back to the chalet. Hopefully, we won't take too long."

We waited until they were out of sight then walked back to the chalet.

"Jennifer looked so pale," said Kirsty.

"She must be sore," replied Jo. "I don't think she's the kind of person to show pain easily."

We trudged back to the chalet, the euphoria of the toboggan run depleted. In silence, we sat around the dining table feeling useless as we waited for Scott and Jennifer to return. Mathieu opened a couple of bottles of wine for us and laid out a bowl with crisps as we waited.

Eventually, Scott and Jennifer returned, met with a chorus of questions from the girls.

"Thanks everyone, and sorry to mar our fun night. Apparently, I've sprained my wrist. I've got some strong pain relief to get me through the next couple of days.

Unfortunately, there will be no skiing for me for a few days."

Kirsty jumped up and hugged her friend. "I'm so sorry Jennifer."

"I can't believe I came on a ski holiday and got an injury from doing a toboggan run."

"At least you'll be able to gaze out at amazing scenery while you rest up. Maybe I should stay here with you, just to make sure you're okay," suggested Kirsty.

Jennifer laughed. "You're not getting out of your ski lessons that easily, Kirsty. I'll be fine. I'm sad to miss skiing time, but it will also be lovely to have some relaxing time to myself. I have a hot tub. I have books and I have coffee. What more could I need?"

Over dinner, we exchanged our stories of the toboggan run. When Kirsty talked about her experience, she was full of energy and enthusiasm. I loved to see her like this, but I was frustrated that the evening hadn't finished the way I had planned. Tomorrow was a new day with new opportunities.

JENNIFER

My wrist was throbbing. The medication was taking the edge off the pain but I was sore.

"I think we should all go out and relax our weary limbs in the hot tub," suggested Paul. "Do you think that will help your wrist, Jennifer?"

"Hopefully. It would be really sad if I had to avoid the hot tub and skiing! But let's wait another ten minutes. I still feel so full."

"I don't think it's like swimming where you need to wait an hour before going in," said Scott.

"I'm sure you don't," I countered. "But I still feel too full to go into water."

"Compromise," suggested Paul. "Why don't we play Switch for half an hour then it's hot tub time?" With agreement from everyone the game began. Instead of joining in, I lay on the couch and rested my arm. I was annoyed at myself for coming down with a sledging injury.

After the game we eased into the hot tub, all of us feeling the relief of the hot water on our aching muscles. I decided this was a good time to get the group's input about my worries over career/home balance. "Okay, everyone," I began. "I need your help with some research. I'm trying to work out how our family dynamic will be affected if I set up my own business and need to split my time between work and family. Who of you had mums that were out working and who had mums that were at home?"

"As you know," began Kirsty. "My mum stayed at home. But I don't have the best relationship with her. I honestly think she would have been a better mum if she'd had more of an interest out of the house."

"My mum worked full-time," said Paul. "She didn't have a choice. I guess I assumed it was normal and most of my friends' mums seemed to be out working at least part-time too. I'm really close with my mum."

"My mum worked part-time until my younger sister started school then went back to full-time hours," added Jo. "But it was always fine. Although my gran stayed with us too, so we didn't need to go to an after-school club as gran was there for us coming home from school. I feel quite close to both my parents. I never had any issues with them both working full-time."

"My mum worked part-time," said Lynn. "But because of her shift patterns, I would get confused about when she would be home and when she wouldn't. I didn't like that. And because she worked long shifts, she would be exhausted even when she had a day off. That was the worst."

"It's not something I've ever thought of," said Matt. "So I guess that means no issues from my side. My mum worked a couple of days a week, but sometimes she worked from home, so I probably didn't even notice when she was working. I was out playing with my brothers most of the time anyway."

"Thanks, everyone, that's been helpful. And it sounds like there is no one correct answer."

Paul spoke again. "Your girls are brilliant. I've no idea about parenting, but looking at my mum it was all about the atmosphere in the home. And you will always invest in your girls whether or not you're out working. I hear it from so many of my clients, always worrying about their kids and if they are doing the right thing for them. All you can do is the best as you see it."

"Just think," said Jo. "By going back to education and then setting up your own business you're providing a wonderful example of what is possible. That's a great lesson for your girls."

"Thanks everyone. It's good to have a really open chat about it. I'm just trying to work out what works for me but I worry that if I ask some of my mum-friends, it could turn into an emotive thing. There's always a level of guilt for us mums as we try to balance parenting and going out to work and I don't want to put any further pressure on anyone. It's about processing it for myself."

I rested my head back against the hot tub. Relaxing in the steaming water, stunning views all around and chatting with friends a wonderful peace surrounded me. It's easy to feel peace here, and this place was giving me space to process. I realised I had been using my role as mum as an excuse to slow down my dreams, but the reality was fear was the main stumbling block. And hadn't I just been telling Kirsty to push through her fear? In any new journey, there will always be potential negatives but there will also be gems of hope and new possibilities. It was up to me to choose between the safe path or risk a new adventure.

I smiled. Tonight it had been my turn for the hot tub therapy.

Jo

6 February

What a day! As soon as we walked out of the chalet, all kitted up ready for our morning of snowboarding, that wonderful mountain air caught my breath. There is something about air that has played with snow. It carries life and adventure with it. The very feel of it on my face had my heart beating in anticipation of ski runs and outdoor life at its best.

It's amazing to be snowboarding again. This morning was lots of fun with Matt and Paul. It was nice hanging out together and sharing our love of boarding. The guys are better than me, but not so much that I feel like I'm holding them back.

Tonight we did the toboggan run. It was hilarious. And, I got to go down with Matt. Paul was clearly orchestrating things to get time with Kirsty. The two of them are so into each other, hopefully they'll both realise it soon.

When Matt first started hanging out with us it was as Paul's friend. Paul was trying to make a good impression on Kirsty and he would bring Matt with him whenever he spent time with her, trying to convince her that their time together was purely platonic. Which worked out well for me as they included me in their get-togethers. The more time I spend with Matt the more I like him. I'm not sure if he likes me in the same way, but he seems happy to hang out. So I'll take that as a positive sign.

Tonight's the longest we've been on our own. And it went perfectly. We didn't even mention work and chatted on and off the entire way down the toboggan run. As well as snowboarding we're both fans of mountain biking. Nice to know that we share summer and winter pursuits.

It's looking like I'll get to spend more time with Matt over the next two days and we'll be travelling home together on Tuesday. Paul will be travelling back then too, but hopefully, I'll get time alone with Matt in amongst it all.

The only downside of today is that Jennifer had a bit of a tumble and can't ski for the next few days. Hopefully, she'll be back on her skis in no time.

Father, thank you for this holiday and for these friends.

Thank you, Father.

Amen

Kirsty

I am mortified!

Jennifer brought a selection of snow-themed movies with her. After our evening hot tub time, we settled down on the couches to enjoy the first movie. I was exhausted after a morning on the slopes and the toboggan run. I had no idea how everyone else could still be awake, except for Jennifer, they'd been on the slopes all day. Paul was sitting on one side of me and Jo was on the other. Between my tiredness and the distraction of sitting next to Paul, it was a struggle to keep my attention on the film. But as the hero and heroine of the movie trudged their way through knee-high snow, I could no longer keep my eyes open. As I slept my head must have nestled down on Paul's shoulder. The music from the closing credits woke me up. And why was I mortified? As I'd slept my mouth must have been slightly open and I had drooled on his shoulder!

Could my life be any more embarrassing? I was dreading seeing Paul at breakfast, but I needed a good level of nutrition in my body before I faced my morning ski lesson. Hopefully, I would leave for my lesson before I saw him. But no such luck. When I went through to the communal area, Paul was already there. And even worse, it was just him and Mathieu.

"Morning," I whispered. Trying not to draw attention to myself.

Paul and Mathieu paused their conversation and greeted me with friendly smiles. I picked up a plate and helped myself to a selection of breakfast goodies before retreating to the table, my back to the kitchen, setting my gaze to the snow-covered mountains.

I should have known there was no way I'd get away with it. Loaded with a full plate of breakfast treats, Paul sat next to me. We were the only two at the table, but he sat so close I could feel the warmth of his leg beside mine. In the closeness of his presence my appetite departed. My yummy breakfast selection was now bland and held no appeal.

"So what are your plans for today?" I asked, before he had time to make any jokes about last night.

"I'm not entirely sure yet. I need to wait and see who is up for what slopes before we make our plans. With Jennifer out of action, it might change how we spend the morning. As long as I'm out there I'll be happy."

You didn't need to be an expert on Paul to see how much pleasure he took from snowboarding. If only it was as easy to see how he felt about me. My insecurities were working overtime and having him sit next to me in shorts and t-shirt wasn't helping. Thankfully, the others started making their way through.

"How's Jennifer?" Paul asked Scott, as Scott entered the room.

"She's sore and in need of her pain meds. But she managed to sleep okay. I'm just going to take her some water for her tablets and a coffee and I'll be back."

Over breakfast, the group continued discussing their plans for the morning. Everyone in the group was comfortable with red slopes so they decided they would all stay together for the morning.

I sighed as I checked the time. Yesterday had gone better than expected but it didn't mean I was enthusiastic for round two.

Paul leaned into me, "You'll be great."

I blushed and smiled at his reassurance. How could one man confuse me so much? I had been hoping this holiday would clear things up. But I am still baffled. His actions confuse me. Sometimes he singles me out as if he's about to tell me how he feels and other times we're just friends in a group. However, I'm starting to realise I'm maybe not helping the situation much either. I seem to constantly flick between wanting him to ask me out and running for safety in the opposite direction. What am I scared of?

***

"Morning," greeted Chris, as we joined in the gathering ski lesson group. I smiled my response. "We'll be spending our morning on the nursery slope working on our turns."

Chris' words brought a mixture of thoughts. The positive was sticking to this nice small slope, the negative was working on turns. Why was this all so draining? Usually, I would rise to physical challenges. Although, if anyone can get me to enjoy skiing I'm convinced it's Chris.

"Did anyone do anything fun after yesterday's lesson?" asked Chris.

"We did the toboggan run last night," I replied. "Unfortunately, one of our group hurt her wrist during it."

"It does claim its fair share of injuries. Did you enjoy it?"

"I did. It was lots of fun."

"It is, isn't it? Now remember that feeling of fun and imagine you can experience it with skiing too."

I shot him a glance. I hadn't expected him to turn the chat about the toboggan run to my skiing ability, or lack of it.

"Stop looking so scared, Kirsty. I'm positive you can become an excellent skier, but I'm not convinced that you believe it."

I blushed at his words. How could he have me pegged so quickly? My stupid expressive face. I can't hide anything. But if Chris was convinced in my potential, maybe I should believe him. I will remember these words with every turn I attempt this morning.

As we had done yesterday, we made our way up the magic carpet and gathered together at the top. Chris skied down showing us how to use the width of the slope to take our turns, he left a marker at each turn to give us a guide to aim for. The first couple of people made it down without falling, they weren't graceful, but they kept upright. It was my turn. I managed the first couple of turns. Maybe I could do this. But by the third turn, something distracted me. I took my eye off the marker and panicked. Instead of turning I kept going and was getting close to the end of one of the blue runs coming back into the resort.

"Snowplough, Kirsty," shouted Chris.

I was mortified. Thankfully I remembered how to snowplough and brought myself to a stop before reaching the blue run. But now what? I looked down to Chris.

"Turn round, face downhill and snowplough back down to me," he instructed.

So much for the pep talk of earlier. I bet Chris has little expectation of me now.

"What happened?" he asked, as I came to a wobbling stop.

"I don't know. I took my eye off the marker."

"Every experience is a learning experience. Now you know to keep your eye on the marker and not get distracted by anything beyond your ski run."

"Maybe I'm not cut out to ski," I suggested.

"Nope, don't buy it," he replied. "By the end of this week, I will have you skiing down blue slopes. I guarantee it."

I sighed and stood with the others who had successfully completed their first runs. By the time everyone else joined us, I was still the only one who had been unsuccessful in my turns.

Carol gave me a reassuring hand squeeze, "You're doing great. Don't worry about the falls. That's just part of learning. No one learns to ski without falling over. And, even once you learn to ski you still fall over."

Sometimes words that are meant to encourage me have the opposite effect!

"Okay, let's all go back up and do it again. I'm going to go first. When I reach the first marker, Kirsty will follow me, then when she reaches the first marker Carol will follow and so on."

It was humiliating to be singled out as the one needing additional help. But, as I'd experienced on the indoor slope, when I could ski behind an instructor my skiing improved. I followed Chris' line perfectly and managed every turn without falling over and losing my concentration. When I reached the end of the run, he gave me a high-five. "See!" he said, "You are more than capable of skiing well. Believe in yourself, Kirsty, you can do this."

"Joshua, are you okay?" shouted Chris, as he looked back up the slope and noticed one of the teenagers had fallen over. My feeling of relief that someone else had made a mistake was ridiculous. Maybe I needed to give myself a talking to. However, this was a complex activity that defied the laws of normal life, so perhaps I should give myself permission to suck at it. At least for now.

For the next hour, Chris had us doing balancing exercises as we tentatively made our way down the slope. I couldn't work out if there was a reason to ski balancing on one leg or if he just took some warped pleasure in making his students look ridiculous. But whether or not it's a valid technique, he had me laughing and enjoying myself on skis. It wasn't as if I didn't make any mistakes, I made plenty, but I realised that none of us were perfect and we all had bad runs throughout the morning.

By the time the lesson came to an end, I was exhausted and looking forward to grabbing some lunch. All I wanted to do was relax in the hot tub. We hadn't discussed our plans for this afternoon yet, but even if everyone else was heading to the slopes, I would stay at the chalet and relax. Plus I didn't want to leave Jennifer on her own all day.

It was sad to think that today was the last day of us all being together. Jo, Matt and Paul would be leaving just after lunchtime tomorrow to travel home. Would I get any time alone with Paul before he left?

Jennifer

Who comes on a ski holiday and injures their wrist sledging? I'm not going to deny I felt sorry for myself. Although, I was looking forward to a lovely quiet morning.

After the others left for their morning adventures, I sauntered through to the living area. Mathieu was tidying up the table and kitchen. "Shall I make you some coffee?" he asked. "Would you like me to cook you anything?"

"Fresh coffee would be lovely thanks, Mathieu. But please don't cook me anything. I'll pick my way through a selection of these pastries and some fruit. Thank you." As I munched my way through more pastries than I should have and enjoyed a couple of mugs of freshly brewed coffee, I had a lovely chat with Mathieu. He told me lots of funny stories about his job and about his travel plans for when the season ended. And I told him about my hopes for interior design.

"What would you change about this design?" he asked, pointing to the living area.

"That's a good question. It looks beautiful as it is. Modern, clean, functional. Perfect for a ski lodge in the Alps. There are some extra touches you could do to increase its appeal. But I suppose the key selling points of this place are its location, the hot tub and the views. The décor can remain basic but attractive because the whole package is outstanding."

Mathieu's question had me thinking. My injured wrist gave me time to think about interior design. I put on my snowboots and sunglasses and walked round to the hotel. The atrium of the hotel was stunning. As with our chalet, it was all about location and the view. The check-in desks ran along one wall and at the end was a wall of windows making the most of the mountain view. The double-height ceiling and windows created a beautiful airy space full of natural light. It didn't seem there was much need for interior design when your natural surroundings provided so much beauty. There was an understated style in the hotel, and in our chalet. A style that complimented the natural area.

I walked away from the hotel and further into the resort. The resort comprised pretty chalet style buildings as well as standard hotels and apartment blocks. I looked up at the buildings, as well as taking in the sights at eye level. My morning was teaching me the importance of looking up and around, considering the exterior in relation to interior design. And taking cues and ideas from the surrounding area.

Back at the chalet, I made myself a coffee then sat on the terrace enjoying the winter sun. I'd bought a beautiful new notepad on my morning meander and now I would give it a special use. With my headphones on I got to work writing up notes from my morning musings. Lost in my music and the excitement of processing interior design ideas, I didn't notice the others had arrived back for lunch until Scott came out and told me it was lunch time.

When everyone left this morning, I'd felt the surge of panic that comes with the fear of missing out. But my time alone had been a chance to relax and dream about interior design. My morning hadn't been wasted instead it had been a precious gift of time.

Paul

We sat on the benches around the dining table catching up on everyone's news from the morning and making our plans for the afternoon. I needed this afternoon to be time with Kirsty, without making it too obvious. As we ate our sandwiches, we discussed various options.

"How has your wrist been this morning, Jennifer?" asked Carol. "Has it been boring being stuck here on your own?"

"It's been lovely. I had a pleasant walk around the resort. Plus Mathieu was keeping me entertained with stories of catering for ski groups. My arm is still sore and by the time I'm due my next pain meds, I can really feel it. But I'm trying to rest it as much as possible in the hope it speeds up the recovery. The chalet and resort are beautiful but I'm desperate to get back out skiing."

"Why don't I stay with you this afternoon?" suggested Kirsty. "I'd be more than happy to."

"It's fine Kirsty," replied Scott. "I'm going to spend the afternoon with Jennifer. We'll go for a walk then enjoy the hot tub."

"Why don't I take you out for a bit this afternoon," I suggested to Kirsty. "We can spend some time going over what you learned this morning."

"That would be great, Paul. But I can't take you away from your adrenalin slopes. You should be making the most of your time, not having to slow down for me."

"This holiday is about being together as much as the snowboarding. I've still got tomorrow morning."

"What about you, Jo?" asked Matt. "You up for some red slope fun this afternoon?"

"Absolutely. It was amazing this morning. And maybe we could take on a black slope for good measure."

"We'll head out with you guys," Lynn said to Jo, "But we'll leave you two daredevils to your adrenalin rush while Carol and I enjoy the regular sport of skiing."

And just like that we were all organised for the afternoon. The pairings had worked out perfectly. I had an afternoon with Kirsty.

"Thanks for taking the time to help me," said Kirsty, as we made our way to the gentle nursery slopes.

"No problem. Why don't we go over what you've been learning so far and then we can go to one of the terraces and enjoy coffee and cake?" I glanced up at the sky. Tufts of grey clouds were starting to form. Until now, we'd only had clear skies but it was inevitable that clouds would appear at some point.

"Sounds perfect."

On the travelator, Kirsty started fidgeting, working the Velcro fastening of her ski gloves. As we stood at the top of the slope, she checked her ski fastenings. "Kirsty, it's fine. You've been on this slope for the last few days. You know what to do." I wasn't sure why she was so nervous. This was barely a slope compared to my exhilarating runs of this morning, but I guess it's all new to her.

"Why don't you go first," I suggested, "and that way I can see how you're doing and what we can work on this afternoon."

"Okay, but don't laugh at how awful I am. I do better when I can follow someone, so this isn't going to be pretty."

"I'll be the judge of that," I said, laughing at her reaction. "Seriously, it's fine. Just go for it and let's have fun."

I followed behind as she tentatively set off and skied down the slope. Kirsty is the kind of woman who looks good no matter what she's wearing. I had to keep reminding myself that I was supposed to be concentrating on her skiing. "Kirsty, that was good. I think the key thing to work on is your confidence. If you put a bit more speed into it you'll do better,"

"Easy for you to say."

She was looking a bit more nervous again. I bent down and picked up a handful of snow. "Don't you dare!" she screamed, just as I threw the snowball at her. Immediately she tried to grab some snow, but the movement caused her to fall over and she ended up in a heap in the snow. I laughed as I manoeuvred over to help her. But as I held out my hand, she threw a handful of snow in my face. The surprise made me lose my balance and I was down on the snow beside her. We lay next to each other on the snow laughing.

After all the misunderstandings of the last few months, lying here in the snow felt perfect. The sound of skiers and snowboarders drifted away. It was only the two of us. Our laughter faded as we continued to gaze at each other. It would be so natural to lean over and kiss her. In hindsight, I should have taken that moment to kiss her and tell her exactly how I felt. But I didn't.

"Right, come on lazy," I said, as I stood up. "Back to it. And this time with fun and speed."

Jennifer

Spending the morning lost in my dreams reminded me of the harsh reality that Scott and I needed to have an honest conversation about how we would adapt to this new season in our marriage. He hadn't engaged in the conversation last night as I asked the other if their mums had worked. And I needed to know what he was thinking.

After lunch we wondered around the gift shops of Val Thorens, choosing gifts for the girls and our parents. The aromas of coffee and cake drifting from the terraces tempted us to stop and enjoy some afternoon treats but there were still plenty of food at the chalet and we were looking forward to getting time alone in the hot tub.

Relaxing in the warmth of the bubbles with cold drinks beside us I questioned if now was the time for the much-needed conversation. Scott looked so relaxed, leaning against the head support with his eyes closed and a smile tugging at the corners of his lips. Was it fair to spoil this moment for him? But there would always be an excuse to put it off.

"How's your arm?" asked Scott.

"It's okay."

"You seem a bit quiet, so I thought it was maybe getting sore again. Do you need some pain meds?"

"No, it's not my arm."

He glanced over at me.

"I've been thinking about how we operate as a family. Because I've been at home with the girls, you've been free to work as many hours as you want. But that needs to change now I'm starting to pursue a new career."

"Is that what you were getting at last night with the others?"

I nodded.

"But you're not there yet. At the moment it's just night classes."

"Scott!" I almost shouted. I couldn't believe he had been so insensitive about my course. I took a breath and looked to the mountains. Clouds now covered the peaks and the sky was getting gradually darker.

I looked over to Scott. He was sitting upright, no longer relaxed. "What did I say?"

"You've just made it sound as if you don't take my dream of interior design seriously. It's not just taking a course to fill in time and get my brain engaged. This is something I want to do."

"I know that. All I meant was that you're at the studying stage just now so what needs to change?"

A few flakes of snow drifted down. I watched them as they floated through the sky. As soon as the flakes came near the water they melted, becoming part of the bubbling mass.

"My very first evening class you were late home."

"And I said I was sorry. And last week I was on time."

"I know. But don't you see. My very first evening of classes your work took priority. I'm not asking you to leave early. I'm asking you to leave on time. Do you realise how many hours you put in at the office?"

"It's a busy time of year for me."

"But that's just it. It always seems to be a busy time of year for you. Will you ever be able to make space for me to have a career?" Scott didn't reply. I wasn't even sure he understood my worries.

Before he could formulate any reply our phones rang.

PAUL

Kirsty was happy going up and down the nursery slope, but the gathering clouds were bringing a chill and I was desperate to get to the café. "You've done very well and have earned your hot chocolate," I informed her, guiding her away from the slope.

The cafes were unusually quiet and we were able to get a table at the edge of a terrace, affording uninterrupted views towards the slopes. As we waited for our order to arrive, Kirsty looked toward the ski runs and smiled. "I think I'm finally starting to understand the appeal of skiing."

"Just wait till you can make it up to the longer runs. You'll love it. The views, the speed, the feeling. There's nothing like it."

"Slow down there, I'm almost enjoying these safe runs. Don't be scaring me with tales of long, steep slopes."

I laughed. "Just think of it as a great way to see more of God's amazing creation."

"Good point."

For a few moments, we sat in silence, enjoying our hot chocolates and looking out over the vista before us. In the midst of our silence snowflakes gently started falling. Kirsty looked up and smiled. I watched as she followed the course of a snowflake as it fluttered past her face and landed on one of the marshmallows in her mug. We both watched, transfixed, as it melted in the steam of her hot drink.

As the snow started coming more quickly, she held out her ungloved hand, letting the snow land on her fingers as if a flutter of butterflies were landing on her.

"It's so beautiful," she whispered. "How many snowflakes need to land on your hand before you feel their weight?"

I laughed at her question. The setting, the snow, it was all lending itself perfectly to asking her out. At that moment a snowflake landed on her nose. I reached over to wipe it away. My hand rested on her cheek.

"Kirsty?"

"Yes," she barely whispered.

"I'm really glad it worked out for us to get time together this afternoon."

"Me too."

But before I could say anything else. Before I could tell her how I felt, our phones rang simultaneously. We looked at each other then grabbed our phones.

PAUL

The phone call was a group call from Jo.

We both answered.

"It's Matt!" she said. "He's being stretchered off the slope. Can you meet us at the medical centre? I've no idea how bad it is. I'm not sure if he's broken his leg."

"On our way," we both replied.

We left our half-drunk hot chocolates and made our way over to the medical centre. It sounded as if Matt's injury could be serious. Scott was already waiting outside the clinic. A few minutes later the stretcher sled arrived with Matt. Jo snowboarding down just behind.

There was no time for questions as the responders rushed him into the clinic. We followed them to the waiting area. As soon as they took Matt through to the examination area, we turned our attention to Jo.

"What happened?" asked Kirsty, as she hugged her friend.

"I don't know. One minute we were racing each other and the next he was a crumpled heap. By the time I realised he'd fallen over I was further down the slope. I stopped and waited for him. But he didn't get up. I could see him clutching his leg so I took my board off and walked back to him. Some people had stopped beside him by the time I got to him. One of the men who had stopped offered to ski down to the centre and send the first aiders up. Thankfully we were quite near the end of the run when it happened. But it's crazy. We had just aced a difficult section and were easing down to the end."

"That can happen," I replied. I put my hand on Jo's shoulder. She looked quite shaken up by the whole thing. "Why don't you and Kirsty head back to the chalet and we'll wait for Matt?"

"No way," she replied. "I'm waiting here. I was the one with him when it happened. I need to know how he's doing."

We sat in silence. No one quite sure what to do or say. "Why don't I go get us all coffees," I suggested. Everyone grunted their agreement.

"I'll come and help," volunteered Carol.

By the time we got back with the coffee, that no one wanted, there was still no word on Matt. "Why is it taking so long?" questioned Jo.

"It will take time," replied Scott. "I don't know if they have x-ray equipment here, but if they do that takes time. Why don't we pray for Matt, and for you? You do look pale. You've had a bit of a fright too."

We gathered together and prayed for Matt and for the medical staff working out what was wrong. A peace came over our group as we prayed. The peace in the unknown.

The most difficult thing about a medical waiting area is not knowing how long it will be until someone is able to give you information. And also, not knowing what the news will be. Eventually, Matt hobbled through to us on crutches. A medical person came out in front of him and handed Scott a bag and instructions. "He's torn ligaments in his right leg. There are pain meds in this bag. He should walk as little as possible and keep the leg elevated. When he returns to Scotland, he should go to his doctor."

"Thanks," replied Scott. "Will he be okay to fly back to the UK tomorrow?"

"Yes. He should take aspirin from now till the day after flying. Keep rotating his ankle every fifteen minutes to keep the blood flowing and wear compression socks and drink plenty of water. Also, book in for extra assistance at the airport and inform your airline of the crutches."

Scott shook hands with the man and thanked him. As the sky darkened and the snowfall increased, Scott and I helped Matt into a waiting taxi for the short ride back to the chalet.

Mathieu helped Scott make all the necessary arrangements and changes for getting back to Scotland. While they were making the arrangements, I glanced over to Matt. He looked exhausted and sore. "Come on, mate, let me help you through to bed. I'll bring you dinner once it's ready." I helped him hobble through and into bed. He would probably be asleep before I could return with his dinner.

I walked back to the living area, frustrated that once again my plan to kiss Kirsty had been sabotaged. But as I walked into the room, she looked up and smiled at me. In that smile there was hope.

Kirsty

For two nights in a row our group had been at the medical centre. But tonight was different, we all knew it was more serious. The chalet was strangely quiet. There was no banter or joking around. No music played through the speakers. Paul had gone to sit with Matt but Jo was also missing, I went in search of her. She was sitting on her bed writing in her journal.

"Hey, how are you?" I asked her.

"I'm doing okay."

"What's wrong?"

"I'm worried about Matt. I can't help thinking his accident was my fault."

"We're on a ski holiday. I'm no expert, but it does seem the kind of holiday where accidents can easily happen. Why would you think it was your fault?"

"I was the one who suggested we race."

"Are you kidding? Those guys always find an excuse to see who can go fastest. This is not on you Jo."

"I know you're right. I just need to convince myself."

It was strange to hear Jo doubt herself so much. She's usually the confident one who just gets on with things. I know from my own experience that having a friend try to talk you round doesn't always achieve much. You need to believe it for yourself.

"Will you be okay travelling home tomorrow?"

"It'll be fine. Just as well Paul is travelling with us." Jo swiped away a tear. "I still can't believe he had such a nasty fall. I hope he'll be okay with no lasting damage."

I suddenly realised what was going on. "Jo, do you have a thing for Matt?"

She looked over to me with watery eyes and nodded.

I leapt over beside her and put my arm around her. "I can't believe you didn't tell me."

"I know. I should have. But before this week I was still trying to figure out how I felt about him. Now I know."

I hugged my friend. "I'm so excited for you. You'll make a fab couple."

"Only if he doesn't blame me for his injury."

"It's Matt. He wouldn't blame anyone for an accident. Now why don't we go out and make use of that hot tub?"

"Okay," she shrugged.

We sat silently for a few minutes. Enjoying the warmth and comfort of the hot, soothing bubbles. I looked towards the mountains, but the clouds hid them from view. Now and then a flutter of snow would descend.

In the comfort of the hot tub Jo returned to her usual, cheery self. "How are you feeling about the rest of the holiday?"

"I'm going to miss you so much," I replied.

"Me too. And is there anyone else you're sad about leaving tomorrow?"

"You know there is."

"Have you and Paul had any time to discuss relationships since we got here?"

"I think he might have been building up to it this afternoon when we got your call."

"Oh no! You mean I interrupted 'the chat'?"

"Who knows? There have been a few times I thought he wanted to talk about us, but something always gets in the way. Maybe we're not actually meant to be together."

"That's silly talk," laughed Jo. "You two are meant to be together. Trust me, Kirsty, it will happen. The time just isn't right yet. Give the boy time, he'll catch up."

I looked down to the resort as I considered what to say next. It was time to be honest. Jo is my best friend, the person I trust most with my secrets. "I'm scared," I admitted. I wasn't sure how Jo would react to my statement, but it was a relief to express my doubts to someone.

"Scared of what?"

"Scared about me and Paul. Scared we work out. Scared we don't work out. I know it doesn't make sense but I'm scared to hope that things could work for us. When I look to the future, I want to be with him but how do we get there."

"Aww, Kirsty," said Jo, as she pushed through the water to come and hug me. "Don't fear hope. Hope is what you need. Hope and joy. I have hope that you will get together but for now, be his friend. It's not fair on Paul to leave it all on him. Be a friend. He needs his friends around him, he's in a stressful and vulnerable place with his business. Don't spend your time waiting and wishing for the future, enjoy your last few weeks, or months, of being a singleton!"

Before we could discuss things any further we were interrupted by the rest of the group, minus Matt, coming out to join us in the hot tub. I avoided eye contact with Paul. Jo's comments had made me feel shy around him again. There was no denying I was attracted to him, but it was time to rediscover the confidence that faith and joy offered and give Paul the space he needed.

In the freezing night air, we enjoyed the heat of the hot tub and friendship. I was sad that Jo, Matt and Paul would be leaving tomorrow. But it was also time for some soul searching and sorting out my attitude to Paul. Jo was right. It was time to be Paul's friend.

Jo

7 February

I am exhausted. Father, today went so wrong.

I was buzzing as we returned to the chalet for lunch after an invigorating morning of boarding. And then, things got even better when the lunchtime chat led to me and Matt pairing off for the afternoon. As we stood next to each other in the cable car we talked about how much we were enjoying our holiday and how excited we were for another afternoon of perfect conditions. He even suggested we relax in the hot tub once we had completed our afternoon boarding.

The first run went so well. We raced each other down. He won, but only just. After another run, we had a break at one of the mountain cafes. We grabbed a couple of loungers and ordered hot chocolate. As we enjoyed our drinks and the views we chatted about our work. I told him about my love for geography and how it opened up my understanding of the world and he told me about being a computing teacher. We compared notes on our schools, the way they were run and their catchment areas.

As we prepared to push off from the café, I informed him I would beat him to the bottom of the run. The speed, the conditions, it was all so invigorating. I was ahead. We were both laughing. And then it all went wrong. I'm not sure what, but something made me look back, and when I saw him in a crumpled heap, I felt an incredible sense of dread. I'm so grateful for the skiers who stopped to check on him then went for the help he needed.

I'm wracked with guilt. Was the crash my fault? Did I goad him into going too fast? I felt awful as I just stood there, watching as the first responders strapped him into the sled. I could tell from his face he was in pain. If only I hadn't made our afternoon competitive. We should have enjoyed the thrill of boarding without making it a race.

Thank goodness Paul is travelling back to Glasgow tomorrow too. I must confess, at first I was frustrated that he would be with us. I'd had been dreaming of time alone with Matt. But now I'm very grateful Paul will be with us. I'm not sure that my five foot two inches could handle Matt's six foot one inch all by myself. At least we can share the responsibility of looking after Matt. I'm also very grateful for Scott and Mathieu sorting things out for the Geneva end for us. It was always going to be a long day, but with Matt's injury, it's going to feel like the longest journey ever.

And, as if that wasn't enough drama, Kirsty has guessed I like Matt. I think she might have been a bit miffed that I didn't tell her. I should have spoken to her about it before but I've been so busy trying to work out how I feel it didn't occur to me to talk to her about it. But it was lovely to confide in her about Matt. Somehow it makes my feelings for him more real. I just hope I haven't blown things with him.

Father, I pray that Matt's injury isn't serious. That he heals quickly and fully.

Father, even though Matt's been hurt, I still thank you for this holiday and for these friends. Amen

2am

I can't get to sleep. My mind keeps going over the events of the afternoon. I keep seeing Matt in that crumpled heap, pain etched across his face. How are we going to manage the journey home tomorrow? I hope Matt is asleep and getting some much-needed rest. My head knows it was an accident but my heart feels guilty. Matt barely acknowledged me after the fall, will he even speak to me on the journey home?

Help me, Father. Thank you that you are my refuge.

Thank you, Father.

Amen

PAUL

I woke up full of frustration. Frustration that things hadn't gone according to plan with Kirsty yesterday. Frustration that I needed to travel back home today. And frustration that Matt was hurt. The smell of breakfast distracted me from my irritations. I looked over to Matt's bed "How you doing this morning? Do you want me to bring you through some breakfast?"

"Breakfast would be much appreciated. Thanks." Matt sat up and took his pain meds.

Mathieu was alone in the kitchen. "Bonjour," he greeted me, as I walked in. I felt ravenous at the sight of all the food he was preparing.

"Once again you're giving us an amazing feast to start our day," I said. "I'll make up a plate to take to Matt."

"How is he feeling this morning?"

"He looks quite sore. It'll be an interesting journey home today."

"It will not be easy, but I think you will be fine."

As I selected food and coffee for Matt, Mathieu finished laying out breakfast. On our first morning Matt and myself had hung out with him in the kitchen, intrigued to find out more about our chef. He had completed his studies the previous year and wanted a year out before joining the corporate world. Being employed in the resort gave him afternoons off to enjoy the slopes and after our evening meals were cleared away, he was out enjoying the Après-ski. With the money he made over the winter, he planned to go travelling at the end of the season. It sounded like an ideal lifestyle. When I was Mathieu's age, I was driven to succeed at hairdressing and nothing slowed me down as I clambered to make myself known as an up-and-coming stylist. Had I missed out on something by pushing my career? Where had it got me? Here I am almost thirty and only now opening my own salon. It almost feels like I'm starting from scratch. The thought unsettled my already discontented mood.

After I dropped off Matt's breakfast, I knocked on Scott's door. "Hey Scott, you up for some boarding action?" I decided the best way to finish my holiday was on an adrenalin high.

A muffled grunt replied that he would be ready in ten minutes. Last night I couldn't be bothered with the idea of snowboarding this morning. But now I was desperate to be on the slopes. My head was full of confusion and I needed activity to sort me out.

We left the chalet just as the others were appearing for breakfast. An awkward smile passing between Kirsty and myself.

It was a relief to be outside in the chilly mountain air. A bit of speed and physical exertion on a clear, sunny morning would ease my mood. After a couple of runs down our favourite red slope we took a break, sitting to the side of the slope, our boards beside us. We sat in silence enjoying the setting as boards and skis swooshed past and people shouted and laughed.

"Thanks again for taking this holiday to the next level for us. These last few days have been brilliant and the energy-laden fun I needed."

"You're welcome. It's a shame you need to leave early but you've made the right decision to get back to your new business. How much have you thought about the salon while you've been here?"

"A few times. And I confess I texted Brian to ask him how everything was."

"I'm sure it's all good."

"Yep. He said it was all fine. I'm missing it and looking forward to getting back. But I'll be sad to leave all this today," I sighed.

"Despite all the accidents, it has been a good few days," replied Scott.

"It has, but I think I'm still leaving with regrets." I hadn't meant to be so honest in my comment.

"And do those regrets pertain to a certain new skier?"

"I had planned to speak to her yesterday afternoon. I had it all thought out. Then just as I was about to tell her how I felt we got the phone call from Jo about Matt. It was the same at Hogmanay, I decided to make my move at midnight and then the power cut got in the way. It's never been this hard for me to ask someone out before!"

"So what are you going to do about it?"

"What do you mean? What can I do?"

"Tell her how you feel."

"I'm trying."

"Are you?"

"Of course. If it wasn't for power cuts and snowboarding accidents, I would have asked her out by now."

"Were those the only two times you had the opportunity to ask her out in the last few months?"

My attention retreated to the view. This conversation was getting uncomfortable. Was Scott in league with my mum and sister? Why was this all on me?

I don't know if it was the snowy scene, but my thoughts drifted back to the Christmas Eve service and the carol O Little Town of Bethlehem. It seemed strange to be thinking of Christmas in February. But on Christmas Eve something clicked about what God's love meant. Not some nostalgic Christmas card picture but something so much deeper. Love that wasn't self-serving and false but lasting and deep. I was beginning to realise that depth of love wasn't just between me and God but flowed out to other people too. It was the basis for a relationship with Kirsty.

"I'm trying to figure it out, Scott. It's like a whole new world and outlook for me. I want to get it right with Kirsty. In the past, I lusted selfishly but now it's time to love selflessly. That's the love I see in the Bible. I need to prove to Kirsty she's *the* one and not just another one."

"And that's good. But don't blow it out of proportion either. Kirsty doesn't need perfect. She just needs you."

As we began the final descent of my holiday, I thought over Scott's words. They offered a different perspective. Could it be as simple as just asking her out? But I didn't want to merely ask her out. I wanted the big romantic gesture. I wanted Kirsty to know how special she is. I set my sights on Valentine's Day.

Jennifer

"I hope they get home okay," I said, as we waved off Jo, Matt and Paul.

"They'll be fine," reassured Scott.

"And how are you doing?" I asked Kirsty, as I put my arm around her shoulders. This afternoon was probably a double blow for her with both Jo and Paul leaving.

"I'm okay." She didn't sound or look okay.

"Why don't we plan a fun afternoon? Do you want to do something active or something more relaxed?"

Kirsty shrugged her shoulders. "I don't know. What are you thinking?"

"Well if you want an active thing there are sled dogs or the zip line. Or to relax we could make the most of the hotel facilities and enjoy the swimming pool and steam room. Then get a coffee on a terrace."

"Let's do the hotel and coffee option. I like the sound of that."

"Carol and Lynn? Are you up for it too?"

"Sounds great," the girls replied.

"I'm going to leave you girls to it," said Scott. "The slopes are calling to me. Maybe I'll meet you for coffee. Let me know when you're at the café."

After a light lunch, we put on our snowboots and sunglasses and walked round to the hotel. "I can't believe how lucky we've been with the weather this week," I said.

"If we get a whiteout tomorrow it's your fault," joked Lynn. "It is so beautiful here. I'm glad we can stay on till the end of the week. I feel sorry for the others having to travel home today. Hopefully, they have an easy journey."

"I don't envy them their day of travel, especially when Matt is still so uncomfortable," I replied.

We booked ourselves in and collected our towels. With a beautiful sunny afternoon, most people were outside enjoying the conditions, which meant we had the pool and facilities to ourselves. "How amazing is this?" I said as we entered the pool. "Usually when I'm at a swimming pool, it's for the girls' swimming lessons. The pool is full of kids and the surrounding area full of overheated parents waiting for the lessons to finish. This is sheer luxury."

"It is fabulous getting a swimming pool to yourself," replied Kirsty. "Especially when it looks as nice as this one."

It felt wonderfully decadent spending time in such fabulous surroundings. I swam a few lengths then let myself float in the middle of the pool. While the girls chatted at the side of the pool, I enjoyed the quiet of the moment. *"Peace to those on whom his favour rests."* I wanted to stay in that peace, but my mind kept replaying the conversation with Scott from yesterday. I was annoyed that it had been cut short, although I'm not convinced he really got what I was trying to say. Maybe he needed some time for it to sink it. I needed him to understand how important it all was to me. He needed to understand interior design was my future career and that meant changes for his working habits. I'm not sure if he's able to change, of if he even wants to.

The others swam a few laps and then we congregated at the shallow end. "How's your arm when you're swimming?" Kirsty asked.

I put my unease to the side. This afternoon was time with friends. The disagreement was between me and Scott. I smiled at Kirsty. "It feels good, I think it'll be fine for getting back to skiing tomorrow."

"I am so glad to hear you say that," replied Kirsty.

"And how are your lessons going?"

"I am enjoying them more now. I thought it would be scarier in amongst the mountains, but maybe being in the natural setting, rather than inside, makes it all feel more fun."

"Yes!" exclaimed Lynn. "We'll get her fully converted to skiing by the end of this holiday."

For the next hour we swam laps and took in the heat of the steam room. We were fully relaxed, and perhaps a bit too wrinkly, by the time we made our way outside to the terrace. Our timing was perfect. A group vacated a table just as we arrived.

I looked out over the resort. After my comment of earlier about the weather, I noticed clouds were starting to form around the mountain peaks. But even with the gathering clouds, the scenery was stunning. With my friends chattering beside me, my thoughts drifted. I realised I'd finally reached the point where I'd stopped worrying about the girls. I was grateful for internet connections that meant we could check in on them daily, but I'd now settled to the idea of being separated from them. On last night's call, they only stayed on long enough to tell us they were having a great time with my parents.

Mum and dad looked quite tired, which made me feel guilty, but they reassured me that even though they were tired, they were having a great time.

As our steaming drinks arrived we let out a collective sigh. "Well girls," I said, raising my mug, "here's to us and the rest of our holiday." We clinked our mugs together. "I for one am loving our snowboots and sunglasses holiday."

Paul

It wasn't easy waving goodbye to the rest of the group. I had unfinished business with Kirsty. And before us lay a long day of travel, complicated by Matt's injury. The first part of our journey was easy, yet we were all quiet. Each of us lost in our own thoughts. I kept replaying my time with Kirsty yesterday afternoon. It had been so perfect then disaster. I had to make this work but all I could think of were our missed opportunities.

We checked ourselves on to our flight, then requested support to get Matt to the gate. I let Jo ride on the buggy with him and I plodded along to the gate. After the laid-back vibes of the resort, the airport seemed frantic, travellers on a mission to get to their gates as quickly as possible. I didn't want to be here. I wanted to be on a ski slope with Kirsty.

I meandered up to where Matt and Jo sat. The holiday was over, there was no point in being grumpy the entire trip home.

"Do you want me to get you any food or drink?" I asked Matt.

"Can you get me a coffee and a bottle of water?"

"You get yours then I'll go," said Jo.

"Guys, I'm fine. I'm okay to be left on my own. You can both go. I'll be fine." Matt stared at us, defying either of us to contradict him. It wasn't a look I often saw from Matt, but I knew enough to give him space.

I exchanged glances with Jo and we walked over to the nearest café together. "I think he's quite sore," I started. "He's not usually so blunt."

"I get it," replied Jo. "He must be in pain and feeling anxious about flying with his limited mobility."

Her acceptance of the situation impressed me. Kirsty is my primary focus when it comes to this group of friends. But over the holiday I'd gotten a deeper insight into their group dynamic. Jo was the stable influence in their midst.

"I think I'm going to have a wander around the Duty-Free shop. I'll see you back at the gate," said Jo. I bought coffees and water and returned to Matt.

"You okay, mate?" I asked.

"Just feeling a bit tired and useless," he sighed.

"It's fine. We've got this far with no hassle. We can do this." I checked my watch, "Why don't you take your aspirin now? It shouldn't be too much longer till we board."

One advantage of travelling with someone on crunches is that you get to board first and claim your overhead baggage space. I couldn't believe how busy a Tuesday afternoon flight from Geneva to Edinburgh was. As soon as the flight attendant had run through the safety brief, Matt put his headphones on and closed his eyes. He needed to sleep when he could. In just over two hours we would be in Edinburgh and then we would need to make our way to Glasgow. I looked round to see what Jo was doing. She was also sitting with her headphones on and her eyes closed. My brain felt too alert to sleep. I flicked through the inflight magazine not noticing anything. Why had I put my book in my hold luggage? Probably because I expected at least one of my travelling companions to talk to me on the flight.

I flicked through the inflight magazine again, already bored. There was a middle-page spread about Valentine's weekend destinations. I stopped flicking and gazed at the images in front of me. Frustration pumped through me as I thought of the wasted opportunity of this holiday. I had been so close to asking Kirsty out in the perfect setting. None of these images came close to the location we'd had.

I closed my eyes and tried to come up with the ultimate Valentine's for a relationship that had still to begin. Nothing came to me.

I put the magazine back in the seat pocket and took my phone out. It would be a long flight if my thoughts kept replaying missed opportunities. I tried a couple of games but none of them could hold my attention. I opened my Bible app and began reading the gospel of Luke. I've read through the gospels a couple of times in the past year and I would say Luke is my favourite. Reading the first couple of chapters of Luke my thoughts returned to the love that surrounds the Christmas Story. I almost laughed out loud. It was like the song said, 'love is all around'.

The next thing I knew the flight attendant came over the intercom to instruct us to return our seats to the upright position and ensure our seat belts were fastened.

I must have dozed off. I glanced out the window but there was nothing to see in the darkness.

Matt stirred. I was glad he had slept. While our fellow passengers disembarked we remained in our seats, waiting for the all clear from the air stewards to leave the plane. I was grateful the plane was attached to the terminal with the enclosed walkway. This was not a journey to have to get a bus from the plane to the building. When we got into the building, a mobility cart was waiting for Matt. As in Geneva, I said to Jo to take the extra passenger space and I'd meet them at baggage reclaim.

Once we had collected our bags, we made our way, very slowly, to the bus stops. We timed it perfectly. A bus for Glasgow waited in its allotted place. We threw our bags into the hold and then helped Matt onto the bus. Our good fortune continued with the front seat being available for him. Jo and myself made our way further up the bus to the next free seats.

"I don't want to jinx anything," started Jo. "But the journey is going much better than I feared it would."

"I know what you mean." As we sat down, I realised how tired she looked. "How are you doing? Will you survive your first day back in the classroom tomorrow?"

"Thankfully it's an in-service day, which will involve trying to take in a bunch of information, but at least I'm not teaching the whole day. I'm so tired, I don't think I would be able to string a sentence together. What about you? Have you got any clients tomorrow?"

"I think my first booking for tomorrow is eleven, but I'll probably go in earlier to get settled and find out what's been happening. Our next few days should be good and busy. Valentine's is a busy time for hairdressers."

"And do you have any plans for Valentine's yourself?" asked Jo, with a mischievous grin on her face.

"That would be telling," I replied.

This Valentine's Day was more important than any other. What did the perfect date with Kirsty look like? I had no idea. By Monday I needed to produce the biggest romantic gesture of my life. The holiday had convinced me I had a future with Kirsty. But how would that future begin?

Jo

8 February

Geneva airport.

The first part of the journey home went smoothly. The customer service at the airport has been excellent. Paul let me go in the buggy with Matt to the departure gate. To be honest, I would have preferred Paul went with him. I feel guilty every time I look at Matt and see him hobbling about. He still looks in pain but I can tell he's trying to be brave. Paul is so helpful. He seems to know what to do to help Matt, and he's able to keep the chat going. Whereas, I've no idea what to say.

Edinburgh airport.

Thank goodness the flight is over. It went okay. I pretended to sleep as I didn't want to talk to either Paul or Matt. We're waiting for the bus to get us back to Glasgow. Suffice to say, we're all looking forward to getting home.

Home.

Phew, we made it home! Thank you Father that things went relatively smoothly for the journey. It's been a long day, but we finally made it home. The taxi dropped Matt and Paul off before bringing me home. I didn't want to end the day without apologising to Matt, but Paul was with us the whole time and I never got the chance.

It's been a strange holiday. We've had a wonderful time away together. The chalet, the hot tub, the snowboarding, the food, the views, the company. But it has been a holiday wracked with accidents. I can't believe I'm back at work tomorrow. I'm going to need so much strength for tomorrow to survive the in-service day. I'm tired.

Before we went on this holiday, I knew I liked Matt, but I wasn't sure how much it meant. Despite my current levels of guilt, I know I like him a lot. We've had days of laughter and discovering our shared interests. But have I ruined it all by causing his accident? Will he want to talk to me again? Maybe tomorrow I'll pop in and see him on my way home from work and check he's okay.

Father, thank you for the ski holiday. Thank you for my friends. Please guide me with Matt.

Thank you, Father.

Amen

Kirsty

The chalet seemed strangely quiet when I woke up. I looked over to Jo's empty bed. How much fun would the rest of the holiday be without them? Although to be fair, after they left yesterday we had a lovely day. As far as resorts go, I was enjoying Val Thorens. There was always something going on. After dinner last night we went to the nearest bar. I couldn't believe people had the energy to go dancing after a day on the slopes. Between the fresh mountain air and my limited skiing, I was exhausted. How did these people do it?

After another delicious breakfast, it was time to get to my lesson. As I embarked on the now familiar routine of clambering into all my ski clothing, I hummed the verse of a worship song Jennifer had been listening to. "You sound upbeat," said Carol.

"I think I'm actually looking forward to this morning's lesson."

"Don't sound so shocked." Carol laughed as she put on her jacket. "Skiing is a fun activity. We all told you you'd love it once you got here."

I smiled at Carol as I wiggled my feet into my boots. Jennifer was right. This holiday was the perfect place to experience joy. It was time to embrace joy and take hold of the confidence it offered.

"Wow, you're doing really well this morning," enthused Carol, after we had completed a few exercises.

Carol's words buoyed me up. And on top of my decision to fully enjoy myself, I felt ready to take on the world. "Thanks. I think I'm starting to enjoy it now."

"Okay, everyone," shouted Chris. "We're going to do another couple of exercises then we're taking it to a blue run."

My resolve wavered. Maybe I wasn't ready to take on the world. A blue slope felt a bit beyond my happy place. Was I competent enough to be on an actual slope with actual skiers? My next run down the nursery slope was a disaster. When I tried a turn, I fell over. When I tried to snowplough to a stop, I kept going. How could I graduate to the next level?

"Kirsty," said Chris, skiing up beside me. "You can do this. Stop letting your head dictate to your body. You've been skiing beautifully the last two days and as soon as I mention a change you've forgotten everything. Believe in yourself. You can do this."

Why was skiing beating me? Whenever I tried a new activity, I would be reasonably good at it because I would push through and believe I could do it. Maybe the problem was skiing was counter-intuitive. You had to do the opposite of what felt safe – lean away from the mountain, go faster – it all seemed wrong. I looked around the group. If they could all rise to the challenge so could I.

My nerves were on high alert as we made our way to the ski lift. A spike of fear went through me as I watched people being scooped up by the metal benches. "It's fine," reassured Carol. "I'll tell you where to stand and what to do."

When our turn came, Carol directed my positioning and before I knew what was happening, I was sitting on a ski lift with the safety bar over me. "See, it's not so bad," said Carol. As the chair took us higher into the mountains, I worried about how we would get back off. But at the same time I was excited to experience more of the mountains. I was going to where skiing really happened, no longer confined to the nursery slope in the resort.

The top of the lift came into view. What if I wasn't able to get off? Would I go round and round for the rest of the day? As we approached the top we passed the sign instructing us to lift the safety bar. "Edge forward just a little bit," instructed Carol. I eased myself forward and then jumped when she told me to. I did it! The first hurdle over, I felt a bit more confident about getting down my first blue run.

Carol and I stood to the side with Chris. As we waited for the rest of the group to join us I watched skiers hop off the lift and immediately take off down the slope, making it all look so effortless.

"Okay," shouted Chris. "We're going to take this nice and slow. You can all do this. I'll lead off and then stop us partway down to make sure everyone is okay. Everyone ready?"

Most of the group were enthusiastic while a few of us were apprehensive. Chris set off followed by the other members of the group. Carol and myself were the last to go. "Let's do this," enthused Carol. She pushed off and I tentatively followed. But in my fear, I didn't go fast enough and fell over at my first turn. Thankfully Carol had been checking on me and stopped. "Just push yourself up and keep coming," she shouted. I did as she instructed and started skiing again. "Go faster," she continued, "or you'll not make your next turn."

Against all my instincts, I pushed myself to go faster. It worked! I took the next turn without falling. "That's it," cheered on Carol. "You can do this." We made it down to Chris' stop point without any further falls.

"How was that for everyone?" asked Chris.

He was met with enthusiasm from some and non-committal replies from the rest of us. He laughed at the mix of responses. "For those enjoying it, keep enjoying it. And for those of you who aren't sure yet, fun is waiting for you. Again, I'll stop partway down and check how you're all doing."

We set off again. Following the same order as before. Once again I fell over at the first turn. Carol turned around just as I tumbled. "You can do this, Kirsty," she shouted back. "Remember to push off more quickly and get your speed up by the first turn."

I got up and pushed myself off. I was starting to feel tired and less than enthusiastic about completing this run. My negative vibe conspired against me and I took another tumble at the next turn. Ugh! I was back to not enjoying skiing. Carol hadn't noticed my fall so quickly this time and was further down the hill. Now, what would I do? There wasn't anyone from our group behind me.

Some snowboarders came swooshing down beside me. The noise of the boards implying they were going faster than they were. I let them get past before I even contemplated trying to get up again. Just as I was about to attempt to push myself up another couple of snowboarders approached. But this pair stopped. "Can we help you?" asked the first guy.

"Yes, please," I responded, lifting my arms up so they could help me back up to a standing position. As I looked over to thank my good Samaritans, two things struck me. One, I was lucky that they were Welsh and had spoken to me in English. And, two, they were a couple of hot guys.

"We saw you fall," said the second guy. "You've got great form, you just need to go faster and you'll be fine."

"That's so funny. That's what my friend said to me too." As I spoke, I pointed towards Carol. She was waving me down to her. "Sorry, I don't want to be rude, but I need to keep going. I'm the last one from my ski lesson and everyone will be waiting for me."

"After you," replied the first guy. "We'll stay behind you and make sure you make it down okay."

"Thanks," I said, trying desperately hard not to giggle.

The interaction with the snowboarders had given me a new lease of confidence and the encouragement to go faster. It wasn't long before we reached our waiting group. As the snowboarders continued down they shouted over, "Good luck with the lessons." Chris looked at me with a raised eyebrow. I blushed.

"How was that for everyone?" asked Chris.

This time his question was met with more enthusiasm. "I knew you could all do it," he continued. "We're going to finish today's lessons with you all skiing into the resort. One word of caution. It gets busier as you approach the resort as a few of the runs converge but just be aware of your surroundings and you'll be fine. Don't try to slalom out of people's way or you'll end up colliding. I'll go last to make sure you all make it down. As soon as you finish the run, go to our meeting point and we'll have a brief chat to end this morning's session."

As the others pushed off, Chris edged over to me. "You okay, Kirsty?"

"Yes, thanks," I replied. "I think I was being too cautious on the turns and then I fell over a few times. But I think I'm getting the hang of it."

"Do you want me to go in front of you or behind you?" he asked.

"Maybe behind and then you can let me know what I'm doing wrong."

"Okay. Carol, you go then Kirsty and I'll follow."

Somehow I completed the final section without any more falls. "Great job, everyone," said Chris. "We'll meet here in the morning and have another day of blue slope fun."

My first ever blue slope had been a bit of a mix of emotions – fear, exhaustion, joy. I had been so nervous about the new challenge I'd lost my confidence but between Carol, the snowboarders and Chris cheering me on I'd done it. It wasn't pretty, but neither was I dreading doing it again.

"You are oblivious to everything, aren't you?" asked Carol.

"What do you mean?"

"Like the way those snowboarders looked at you. Or how Chris was put out that someone else was helping you."

"What do you mean?"

Carol laughed. "You really are clueless sometimes, Kirsty. All those guys are attracted to you."

Carol's comments annoyed me. Normally I could rely on her to be the nice one in the group. I pushed back. "No. They're all just nice guys."

"Trust me. They like you."

She was wrong. People are friendlier when you're out in the mountains. And anyway, there was only one guy I wanted to like me. But when it comes to Paul, I am clueless.

Kirsty

"Would you two mind if I bailed on this afternoon? I don't think I've got the energy to move from this table."

"But you were doing so well this morning," said Carol.

"It's not about the skiing. It's more about wanting to sleep."

The plan for the afternoon had been for the three of us to go skiing together. But my first encounter with a blue slope had left me quite exhausted. "We'll stay with you," volunteered Lynn.

"No. I'll be fine on my own. You go off and enjoy your afternoon of skiing. And don't come back early on my account."

After everyone left, I crawled through to my room and into bed. The duvet moulded around me and I snuggled into its comfort. There's something wonderfully decadent about an afternoon nap on holiday, and this treat was even more enjoyable because my tired body had earned it. I only slept for about forty minutes, but the brief nap had done wonders to revive me. I was tempted to relax in the hot tub, but exploring our surroundings was probably a more constructive use of my time.

I clambered into my snow gear, complete with snowboots and sunglasses and set out for some quality me time. It was another stunningly beautiful afternoon in the French Alps. With some uplifting music playing through my iPhone, I felt invigorated. After walking for a while I sat down in the snow and enjoyed the scenery. I paused my music, closed my eyes and rested in the silence. One downside of living in Glasgow is the constant noise, it had taken me a while to get used to. But here in the Alps, there was a beautiful peace and stillness.

The fear associated with Gary, the questions about Paul all faded away in the grandeur of the mountains. My faith had felt weak for months, but here in the Alps, it felt bolstered. I took out my phone and put on some worship music. Sitting in the snow, surrounded by awe-inspiring mountains, I was at peace. Even as my thoughts returned to Paul, I felt a peace. I smiled at the memory of our snowball fight. I was done with worrying about tomorrow. It was time to enjoy today. Throwing myself back in the snow I made a snow angel.

When I returned to the chalet, the hot tub beckoned. Sitting in the bubbles, my music playing beside me, sunglasses on and my drink chilling in the cold Alps air I felt very spoiled. I smiled. A deep-down happy smile. Nothing had changed. I was still unsure about work. I had no idea what was going to happen with Paul. But I had hope, and the hope brought joy.

The boisterous arrival of Lynn and Carol disturbed my peaceful setting.

"Great idea," shouted out Lynn, when she saw me in the hot tub. "Stay there, we're coming to join you."

"You look so content and relaxed lounging about," commented Lynn, when they were in the tub with me.

"I am. And Lynn I owe you an apology."

"You do? What for?"

"When I started going to ski lessons, I had *very* negative thoughts about you and your suggestion for this holiday. But turns out you were right. A snowboots and sunglasses holiday is exactly what I needed."

Jennifer

I should have been excited about an afternoon skiing with Scott but I was still mad at him from our unfinished conversation of Monday. Had he thought any more about it? Or did he think we had said all that needed to be said on the subject?

It was sunny as we made our way to the ski lift, but a few clouds were gathering around the mountain peaks. We spent some time meandering around the various routes, taking in some red and blue slopes, before stopping for a break at one of the mountain top cafes. I grabbed us a couple of sun loungers while Scott made his way inside to get us coffee and cake. The terrace was busy with skiers and snowboarders enjoying their afternoon rest.

"How's your wrist?" asked Scott, as he settled in his sun lounger.

"I'm happy to report it is coping well with its first day back in use."

We sat in silence enjoying our coffees and the buzz of the mountain terrace, watching people come and go.

I couldn't wait any longer, I needed to know what Scott was thinking. "Have you had a chance to think about our conversation of Monday? About what it would look like for us a family, as a couple, for me to pursue interior design?"

The silence that followed offered little hope. I was beginning to wonder if I needed to push for an answer when he finally replied. "You took me by surprise when you brought it up the other day. To be honest I hadn't thought about it. I guess I selfishly assumed it was something you would work on while the girls were at school."

Where was this conversation going? At least he was being honest.

"When I took on the new partner last year, I'd planned on reducing my client list but somehow nothing changed."

"Are you willing for it to change?"

Scott glanced over to me. He shifted about in his chair, focussing on his coffee. I wasn't sure I wanted to hear his answer. "I thought I was but maybe I'm not. I enjoy being busy. I like being the one clients come to with their questions and concerns for their businesses."

"And I love that you care so much. But you also have a family. We need your time too."

"I know you're right. We've been in this routine for so long and it's one I'm comfortable with. I don't think I know how to change."

I smiled over to Scott. This was going to be tricky to navigate but as long as we were both willing to make changes we could do it. "We take it one step at a time. We look at what needs to adjust now and work on that. And when we get to the next stage, we adjust again."

"And what is this stage?"

"For now it's you being home early on Tuesday nights so I can get to my evening classes without running out the door."

"Sounds simple, but I let you down on your first night."

"But not last week. Maybe this gradual change gives us both time to adjust."

"And what would the next step be?"

"I honestly don't know. I think I need more than just an evening class certificate but I don't know what. However, I won't have time for anything else over the next few months. The evening classes run until Easter and then it's the Easter holidays. After the Easter holidays, there's the combination of holiday weekends and all the leavers' things for Amy. So I'm looking at August/September before I can make my next move in interior design."

Scott stood up and held out his hand, I took it and he pulled me into his arms, kissing me. "I am so proud of you. We will work this out."

I hugged him. Practicalities could be sorted out later, today was about attitude of heart. With renewed hope for the future, I could enjoy the present. We put our skies on and pushed off from the terrace, excited for fun on the slopes together.

After another delicious dinner from Mathieu, the others took advantage of the hot tub. Left to ourselves, Scott and I sat by the fire with glasses of wine and opened our laptop. "Why don't we look into Interior Design courses," said Scott, as he tapped on his keyboard. His search brought up a page of results. Clicking on various links highlighted how many choices I had. I could choose online diploma courses that would take six to twelve months, depending on how long I took to complete each module, all the way to BA and Honours degrees.

"I didn't realise I would have so many options. How will I choose?"

"Once we're back home, take some time to investigate the various courses then speak to your tutor and ask her to recommend the best option. I would expect she has a good idea of what you need and what the courses offer."

"That's a good idea." I walked over to the kitchen and brought the bottle of wine back to our seats. I smiled to myself, Scott had gone into 'fix it mode'. I didn't need him to work it out for me, but it was his way of saying he was on board and that he was part of this journey.

I leaned over and kissed Scott. "Why don't we put the laptop away now?" He grinned and sat it on the table and pulled me into his arms. A day on the slopes, delicious food and dreams for the future wove their tapestry of peace around me.

Paul

The dreams of snowboarding and Kirsty were brought to an untimely end by my alarm clock. There was no leaping out of bed this morning, instead frustration had me hitting snooze too often. Not that I achieved much once I finally left the warmth of my bed, the heat of the shower now held me captive. With the flat lacking in food, I skipped making myself breakfast and headed off to the salon. I left a note for Matt, I didn't want to disturb him if he was getting some much-needed sleep.

It was a cold, grey February morning, quite the contrast to the bright white setting of my holiday, I couldn't wait to get to the salon. I opened the door and inhaled the familiar smell of hair products. The salon was decorated for Valentine's Day. Red and pink love hearts were everywhere – on the windows, on strings dangling from the ceiling and stuck to all the mirrors. Brian and Trish laughed as I took in the decorations.

"Happy Valentine's season," they chorused.

"Great job on the decorations. How've things been?"

"Yeah, it's going great," replied Trish. "Saturday we were full. And even yesterday wasn't too bad. The run-up to Valentine's is good for the business, even if personally it's a complete non-event."

"Well, at least you can enjoy the day with us," I replied. We had decided not to work on Mondays as a general rule, but with Valentine's Day falling on a Monday this year it seemed too good an opportunity to miss. Our businesses needed all the money they could get right now.

"You two are probably the best guys for me to spend the day with anyway," she replied.

"How are the bookings for Monday?" I asked.

"We're fully booked," replied Brian.

"The three of us?" I checked.

"Yep."

"That's brilliant. It's definitely the right decision for us to be open then."

"We're also both working on Sunday. Are you wanting to work Sunday too?" asked Trish.

"Yes, let's go for it."

"Also," continued Brian. "Elsie's moving ahead with the student night she suggested. She's got a potential date she's working towards and putting together a list of ideas for it. She seems really keen on the idea."

"That's brilliant," I replied. "Are you happy to work on it with her?"

"Absolutely."

The busy day in the salon revived my spirits. With barely a break for food, the day was a blur of chats with clients as I cut, styled and coloured. I was getting to live my dream, and it was more than I hoped for. How many people were able to say that? I'd felt a pang of jealously at Mathieu's year-out adventure. But right here was where I belonged. And with business worries decreasing it was time to move things forward with Kirsty. Valentine's Day was only a few days away. We had missed our perfect moment in the French Alps but I would make it up to her in Glasgow.

At some point during the day, it occurred to me to ask my clients what they were doing for Valentine's Day. Hopefully within these conversations would be the beginnings of the perfect plan. I got a variety of answers to my question: trips to the cinema, romantic meals, weekends away. The weekend away seemed to be quite a popular option today, which also explained why I had so many clients mid-week.

Dinner and cinema trips sounded so commonplace and lacking in imagination. I needed something special. But nothing was springing to mind. Thankfully I still had a few days to plan the perfect Valentine's Day.

By the time I waved off my last client I was exhausted and couldn't wait to get home and collapse on the couch. I sent Matt a text to ask what he wanted to do for dinner. But he replied to say it was covered. That got me curious.

I heard muffled voices in the living room as I entered the flat. I wondered if someone from church had heard about Matt's accident and had brought dinner for us. It was the kind of thing our church would do.

"Paul, great timing," said Jo, as I entered the living room. "I'm just about to make dinner."

I glanced over at Matt. He gave nothing away, sprawled out on the couch, his leg raised on cushions. "Good day at work?" he asked.

So that's how he was going to play it. As soon as Jo left, I would have plenty of questions for Matt!

"Do you want a drink?" I asked him.

"I'm okay, I've got water here."

I followed Jo through to the kitchen. "Do you want a drink?" I asked her, as I grabbed a beer from the fridge.

"I'm good thanks," she replied.

I leaned against the kitchen counter. "You know you don't need to cook for us. We would manage, but I do appreciate it."

"It's no bother at all. Plus with the others still spoiling themselves in Val Thorens what else am I going to do?"

"Still, I'm sure you've got other things you could be doing, so thank you. How was work today?"

"It was okay. I was relieved it was an in-service day but I think I might have got more energy from a classroom full of kids."

"I don't know how you and Matt do it. Teaching must be one of the hardest jobs out there."

"Says the man starting his own business. Each to their own!"

"I guess so." I took a sip of my beer and looked around the kitchen. "Did you clean and tidy in here?"

Jo nodded her answer. I wondered how long she'd been here and what else she had achieved. By the time Matt went back to work our flat would be cleaner than it had ever been. Plus, if she kept cooking for us, we'd be eating better than usual too. Matt was a lucky guy.

I smiled at the thought of Matt and Jo. They make a perfect couple.

Jo

9 February

Boo to the first day back after a holiday. It was even worse this morning because I knew Kirsty and the others were still enjoying Val Thorens. But the thing that did motivate me throughout the day was the thought of seeing Matt after work.

As soon as school was over, I did some food shopping and took it round to his flat. He looked so pale and in pain when he answered the door. Thankfully he got an appointment with his doctor this morning and then got an x-ray this afternoon. I think it all confirmed the diagnosis of the doctor in the ski resort. He needs to keep his leg rested as much as possible and has been signed off work for the rest of this week.

Over drinks (non-alcoholic while medication is involved), we chatted about the joys of in-service days. As we reached a natural pause in conversation, I apologised for causing the accident. Gentleman that he is, he told me it was not my fault. He assured me he was the one who was trying to beat me and he was the only one responsible for his accident. It was kind of him to say so, but I still feel guilty.

At that point, Paul arrived home. I excused myself and retreated to the kitchen to make dinner. It was nice to cook for more than just myself. Plus, cooking and cleaning their kitchen eased my conscience.

Over dinner, the conversation stayed on safe ground. General conversation about everyone's day. With Paul back home there was a safety in the conversation but also frustration. It sounds such a cliché, but it is so easy to spend time with Matt and as soon as I leave him I look forward to the next time I'll see him. We get on well and seem comfortable in each other's company; I certainly am with him.

How do we move beyond friendship? And should we? If we started going out and then split up, it would be awkward for our friends. But I won't lose out on something for fear of what if.

Father, thank you for today. Please guide me with Matt.

Thank you, Father.

Amen

KIRSTY

"Congratulations everyone," cheered Chris, as we clinked our glasses. "You've all done really well." Chris had insisted on treating us to a celebratory drink as soon as our last lesson was over. It was strange being out socially with the group.

Judging by the other groupings on the terrace, we weren't the only ski class enjoying post-lesson drinks. The other groupings were as noisy as ours, cheering and celebrating the end of their lessons. There was a definite appeal to the Après-ski lifestyle.

"Will you all come on ski holidays again?" asked Chris.

Everyone expressed their enjoyment of the week and most people were keen to return to the slopes in the future. A week had converted me from being terrified of skiing to being optimistic about what could be possible. I'm sure a big part of my enjoyment has been staying in a beautiful chalet complete with cooked meals and a hot tub, but I admit skiing is growing on me.

Over another round of drinks, Chris entertained us with stories of his unusual lifestyle of chasing the snow from the southern hemisphere to the north. For the months void of skiing he picked up work on building sites. His lifestyle fascinated me, it was so different from anything I knew. As he followed his dreams he experienced so much more than just skiing. My life felt very sheltered and small in comparison.

"So have I won you over to the joys of skiing, Kirsty?" he asked. I blushed at the attention, even though he had also asked some of the others.

"You have. Thank you for making this week fun." Everyone else joined in with their agreement.

"As long as I see people smiling I feel like I'm doing my job well. And, on that note, I'm going to say farewell. Friday afternoons are a time for the ski instructors to escape to the high slopes before we party. If any of you are out and about tonight, feel free to come and hang out with us on our pub crawl. Or alternatively, run off in the opposite direction."

I might have thought it was my imagination that he looked at me as he talked about tonight if it hadn't been for Carol sitting beside me, nudging me and throwing me a knowing look.

After lunch, I went out with Lynn and Carol for my last blue run of the holiday. As we queued for the chair lift, I realised how quickly I'd gone from being fearful of these contraptions to enjoying them. It was an opportunity to sit back and enjoy the views. As the three of us jumped off the chair lift, we shuffled to the side and asked a fellow skier to take our photo. When the man handed my phone back to me, I checked the photo and smiled. With a backdrop of dazzling snow and blue skies, the three of us stood side by side, looking quite the part in our ski outfits and matching sunglasses. But the best thing about the photo was how happy I looked.

My last run of the holiday involved a few falls, of course, but instead of being down on myself I was determined to enjoy every second. I knew the falls were a result of holding back on speed, but at least the falls weren't sore. There was a safety to the nursery slope but these longer blue runs offered a view and excitement you didn't get staying close to home.

At the end of the run I hugged my friends and waved them off as they made their way back over to the chair lift. The others wanted to ski until the last possible moment, but my weary limbs were quite happy to call it a day. Back at the chalet I swapped my ski boots for my snowboots and returned all my ski equipment. I walked around Val Thorens enjoying the sights and sounds. Most afternoons the resort had been relatively quiet, but with the approach of the weekend, it was getting busier. I meandered along the various streets, looking in shop windows, taking photos and enjoying the energy of the place.

I felt a tinge of sadness that our holiday was coming to an end. Turns out snowboots and sunglasses do equate to a wonderful holiday! My first ever ski holiday has been quite successful and I'm pleasantly surprised at how much I've enjoyed it. My skiing ability is nowhere near as good as anyone else in our group, but it has come on leaps and bounds. And, despite the number of incidents on our holiday, I have remained intact and injury-free. I'm sure everyone was expecting me to be the one to go tumbling downhill.

The chalet was empty and quiet when I arrived back. The hot tub beckoned. It seemed like the perfect way to finish off my last afternoon. I lay back in the soothing bubbles, savouring the scene before me. I was going to miss this spectacular setting of snowy mountains with the background noise of people enjoying life. My aching muscles had appreciated their daily hot tub therapy. And my soul had appreciated the stunning views.

My thoughts returned once again to the Bible verse about fear and joy. '*Do not be afraid. I bring you good news that will cause great joy for all the people*'. The angel's words of joy were for everyone, not a chosen few. And, if joy is for everyone, then it's for me too. As Jennifer said, fear and joy don't coexist. It was time to choose joy over fear. It was time to engage with work again. Hopefully, I'd get the PR job, but even if I didn't the new manager seemed okay. I shouldn't assume working for him would be an issue because of my experience with Gary.

And when it comes to Paul, it was time to be patient with the guy. Look at all he's achieved in the last few months while I'd been wallowing around. Okay, that was probably a bit harsh on myself, but he was pushing ahead and making considered choices. I should have been at his salon opening. That's what friends do. They don't take the easy way out.

Being here, in the Alps, with my best friends had nourished my faith too. A reminder of the beauty of creation and that I have people in my life who love and support me. But most of all it's about me and Jesus.

Almost as soon as we had booked the holiday it represented decision time for so many areas of my life. Things would be different from now on. Or more accurately, my attitude to them would be different. I'd wasted enough time feeling sorry for myself. It was time to get on with life and choose joy.

***

After dinner we decided to go out and celebrate the last night of our holiday. On a terrace with friends, drinking beer in the snow, soaking in the atmosphere of the outdoor lifestyle was the perfect way to end our ski holiday. The resort was bustling with snow enthusiasts but despite the crowds we got a table at the front of the terrace. All wrapped up in our puffy jackets and snowboots, we clinked our beer bottles together and saluted our fabulous holiday.

"Have you enjoyed your holiday?" asked Jennifer.

"It has been surprisingly good. Thank you so much. I have to say I wasn't convinced when Lynn suggested it, but it's been amazing. I even think I've made quite a bit of progress over the week."

"You really have. It was fun skiing with you yesterday afternoon and seeing how much you've come on."

I looked around the terrace, it was full of groups of people laughing and chatting, everyone ready to party in big puffy jackets, padded gloves and woolly hats. Strings of fairy lights sparkled above us and further along the street. At the sound of a band starting their set people made their way inside, but we were happy to stay outside and enjoy the atmosphere of the terrace. If someone suggested a ski holiday again in the future, I think I would be enthusiastic about it.

Finishing our beers, I heard some familiar Welsh voices behind me. I turned around. Standing immediately behind me were the snowboarders who had stopped to help me the other day.

"Hello again," they greeted.

"Hi," I replied. Not sure what else to say. Had they seen me before I turned around, I wasn't sure. They didn't seem overly surprised to see me.

"Can we get you a drink?" they asked.

"Thanks, but we've just finished and are heading back to our chalet," I responded.

"The night's still young," said the one with the beard. "Why not stay out a bit longer?"

"We only came out for one," I replied. "We're travelling home tomorrow, so we need to go back and pack."

"Too bad," he replied.

Walking away I felt quite self-conscious, especially when I heard Carol say to Lynn, "See I told you." I spun round, trying to glare at them but they grinned back at me. "And our ski instructor was strongly hinting that she join the ski instructors on their pub crawl tonight too."

I was mortified. My friends were always there for me, but sometimes I was the butt of their jokes. I missed Jo.

When we returned to the chalet Mathieu had already cleared up and left. His parting gift was a box of chocolate treats. We wouldn't see him tomorrow morning as breakfast would be pastries delivered from the hotel. The end of holiday sadness was descending. But I wouldn't let myself get sad, there were still a few hours to enjoy.

"Why don't we make up some tea and coffee and enjoy these chocolates around the fire," suggested Jennifer, as she went into the kitchen area and started organising coffee and cups.

"Great idea," I replied and walked over to help her.

We turned off the lights and opened the curtains. Once again we were rewarded with a beautiful clear night. The stars glittered in the sky and the outline of the mountains cast their grandeur over the resort. It felt magical sitting by firelight, hugging our mugs and savouring the chocolate with a snow-covered mountain range before us.

I let out a satisfied sigh. "I'm going to be sad to leave tomorrow. I am so content right now."

"Me too," replied Jennifer.

PAUL

By the time I finished work on Friday, I was shattered. All I wanted was to crash on my couch with beer and a pizza. But once again as I entered my flat I heard Jo and Matt talking.

It was interesting observing the interactions between the two of them. They were so comfortable in each other's company. Which was good for them, but I was beginning to feel like a third wheel in my own flat. Last night was late opening at the salon and I didn't get home until after nine. As I walked into the living room, they were sitting right next to each other on the sofa. Matt was teaching Jo how to play one of his computer games. I don't even think they noticed my presence until I sat down on the armchair across from them.

Tonight was back to regular finish time. As with the previous nights, I wandered into the kitchen and grabbed a beer. "How's the leg today?" I asked Matt, as I motioned to his leg. "It's good to see you up and about."

"Getting there. I was feeling sore from too much sitting so I've tried to hobble about a few times."

"When do you next see the doc?"

"I've got an appointment for Monday. So we'll see what she says then about me getting back to work. Although I'm not sure how safe it would be hobbling through the school corridors with a swarm of teenagers darting about."

He and Jo both laughed at his school joke. I laughed too, but not at Matt's joke. Before me, I was witnessing the start of a new relationship.

"And how was school today?" I asked Jo.

"All good. I had more senior classes today. They are always better. There are still behavioural issues, but it's different to the first and second years."

"I don't know how you both do it. Much respect to you both."

"Well thank you. And how was the salon today?"

"Brilliant. Another good and busy day. Tomorrow is even more jam-packed. I'm also working on Sunday and Monday, which are usually my days off. But we're all fully booked with people getting themselves glammed up for Valentine's Day."

"I'm not a fan of the day myself," replied Jo. "But it's always fun watching the kids at school on Valentine's Day. A lot of them ignore it but there are always some who go way over the top. In general, I have a rule that I don't laugh at the kids, but it's so hard not to sometimes." She started laughing, no doubt thinking about incidents from previous years. "One of the best ones was when a first-year boy gave the head girl a single red rose. He met her at the main doors as all the kids were gathering for the start of school. She was mortified and had to endure an entire day of being laughed at. I'm not sure whether the boy was considered a hero or delusional."

We laughed at the story. "So do you have any plans for Monday?" I asked.

"Nope. I'll probably go round to Kirsty's and we'll hang out together." She paused and glanced up at me. "Unless, of course, she has something else to do on Monday night."

There was no awkwardness or tension between Jo and Matt at the mention of Valentine's Day. It made me wonder if something had already happened between them.

With regard to my own plans, Jo was getting ahead of me. I was still struggling to come up with something. Where could I take Kirsty? How would I navigate around the plans she had with her friends?

A few minutes later we were sitting around the TV, enjoying our pasta. "The best thing to come from your accident is Jo cooking us all these amazing dinners," I said to Matt. "Thanks for everything you've done this week, Jo. All the cooking and cleaning. It's all very much appreciated.

"It's the least I could do after causing Matt's injury."

"Don't start that again," replied Matt.

"What?" I asked. "Why would you think you caused the accident, Jo? Matt told me what happened. You weren't even next to him at the time. You had him beat."

"Exactly. I pushed him into racing. And it caused the accident."

"Are you kidding? Surely you've realised by now that this guy is the one who starts all the competitions? The accident is all on him and his need to win. Or maybe, in this case, show off."

You could almost see a wave of relief wash over Jo. Meanwhile, Matt was glaring at me. Time for a speedy exit. "I think I'm going to head to bed. It's been a tiring few days and I've got a full schedule tomorrow."

I tried not to laugh as I left the two of them to pick up the conversation. I wasn't tired yet. But while there was much to appreciate with Jo coming over, I needed my own space. If I hadn't just devoured a large helping of pasta, I would have gone for a run. But I had, so my room was the only place to go. My thoughts returned to Kirsty and the best way to ask her out. It had to be perfect.

My mind drifted back to the time I'd spent with Kirsty on holiday. My favourite memory was our time on the terrace just before we learned of Matt's accident. It had almost been our first kiss. There was joy in that moment. There had also been a lot of laughter and fun during the toboggan run. She could be so competitive with the right challenge. Maybe I could do something to recreate our holiday. I could take her to the indoor snow area and we could do some sledging then have dinner in the bar. It wasn't as romantic as Val Thorens but it was as close as I could get to recreating the magic of the holiday. And hopefully, because it wasn't the most romantic plan, it wouldn't be too busy. Would I finally get the chance to move us to the dating phase?

The next thing I had to work out was whether to surprise her with it all or arrange to meet her. But if I arranged to meet her was that already asking her out? Surprising her would be best. I could either meet her coming out of work or at her flat. I know she makes use of the flexi system which means she doesn't always finish up at the same time, especially on her first day back from a holiday. No, that would be too risky. I would turn up at her flat.

However, what if she had plans with her friends for Monday night? The sound of laughter from the living room interrupted my thoughts and reminded me that I probably had two willing accomplices close by. I would get Matt involved in my planning. Despite the lack of answers to my questions, I know those two like each other. Taking Kirsty out on Monday could end up doing the two of them a favour too. Because if Matt hooked up with Jo the odds of Kirsty being on her own on Monday night increased dramatically. Yes, this would work.

Freak storms and torn ligaments had completely sabotaged my plans for Hogmanay and the ski holiday, but nothing could go wrong with my new plans.

Jo

11 February

I can't believe it's just a week since I was getting ready to go on holiday. How much has happened in one week? The travel. The snowboarding.

Matt. We've spent so much time together this week. First on holiday and then each evening since we've been home. I think his leg is improving slightly, but it still seems sore and uncomfortable for him. Every night he's insisted that the accident was nothing to do with me. I'm starting to believe him. And Paul told me tonight that it wasn't my fault. He said Matt is the one who is always pushing the competition. Paul's comments probably helped me most as he didn't need to say anything.

I started teaching Matt to cook tonight. It was funny seeing him so useless around the kitchen. I've no idea what those two live on. I suspect more takeaways than is healthy for anyone. They can do some of the basics and they can always fall back on the 'throw in the oven' offerings, but it's time they stepped up and started cooking healthy options and looked after themselves.

This week has confirmed that I like Matt as more than just a friend. It's been fun to see how much we have in common and he's even got me playing computer games! Most nights this week I've fallen asleep thinking about him. But what should I do about it? I think he likes me too. I give Kirsty a hard time for being this indecisive about guys and now I'm doing it. I get it now. It's hard when it's about yourself. How do you trust yourself to read the signs accurately? Is it wishful thinking or more?

The rest of the group are back from holiday tomorrow. Just as well as I think Paul might be getting fed up with me constantly being at their flat. As soon as he finished dinner, he went to his room. I don't want him to feel uncomfortable in his own flat. Time for some double-dating???

Father, help me get this right. And please help Matt recover from his injury. Don't let there be any lasting damage.

Thank you, Father.

Amen

Jennifer

The winter scene flashed by as we were driven to the airport. I was sad to leave the mountains. At least on this journey, there was snow in the lower-lying region, bringing a wintery beauty that had been missing on our arrival. We had been lucky with the snowfall this week. There had been fresh snow during our stay but it mostly happened as we'd been snuggled up in our beds. The result was an abundance of snow without losing time to whiteout conditions.

The self-check-in machines at the airport transported us from the joy of our holiday to the reality of normal life. As we waited for our gate number we chatted about our favourite parts of the holiday. By the time we boarded the plane, everyone was quiet. I kicked off my snowboots and prepared to sleep on our journey home. I had loved every minute of our holiday, apart from my injury. But I was also leaving this holiday with renewed dreams for my future as well as fun skiing memories.

On the taxi ride home, I snuggled into Scott. "That was a lovely holiday, but I am looking forward to being back in our own home."

"Me too," he replied.

"Maybe we should go away again next year. But take the girls. I'm sure they would love it."

"I like that idea. It was fun being with everyone this week, but it would be good to have a family ski holiday."

"It's funny. Before we went I was excited to go on holiday with a younger grouping and have an escape from the boring grown-up conversations, but it's just reminded me that every age group has its conversation staples. And we're not in the same stage as them."

"What do you mean?"

"It might be down to the fact they are all single, but all the conversation around dating got old pretty quickly. And then all the tension between Kirsty and Paul, and Jo and Matt."

"Wait! What? What's the reference to Jo and Matt?"

I laughed at Scott's expression. It had all seemed so obvious, I couldn't believe he'd missed it.

"Do you need me to explain it to you?"

"I'm scared to say yes, but I don't know what you're talking about."

"And you were the one who was on the slopes with Jo and Matt." I laughed. "I had my suspicions before we went on holiday that they liked each other. Seeing them together confirmed it. Although I think they'll progress through this stage more smoothly than Kirsty and Paul. They don't have so much baggage."

"Okay. I was unaware of all that. Did you see or hear anything or is this a feminine intuition thing?"

"A feminine intuition thing?" I laughed. "Scott! Really!"

"We're definitely just going with the girls next year," he continued. "This is all too confusing for me."

Walking through our front door three energetic girls almost bowled us over. It was hugs all round and non-stop chatter as the girls tried to speak to us at the same time. My parents looked tired and after some catch-up chat, they retreated to the sanctuary of their own quiet house.

Back to our little family unit, we cuddled up together in the family room. Over hot chocolate, we gave them their presents and listened to their stories of the week, even though we'd already heard most of them at least once.

With the hot chocolates consumed and the girls all busy with their gifts, I went upstairs to unpack the bags. Which for the most part meant emptying the contents into the laundry basket. I sat on my bed and enjoyed a moment of calm in my room. In the quietness, I realised how peaceful I felt. Since Chloe has started school in August, life had been either off-kilter or full-on. The ski holiday had given me the perfect opportunity to stop and catch my breath. A time to take in the beauty around me and collect my thoughts. Interior design was the career I wanted to pursue. When I initially made my decision, I felt so much joy, and there was still joy but now it was accompanied by peace. I don't know how I'll balance work and motherhood, but I know it's possible. And I'm hopeful that Scott will try to reduce his workload. We would take these new steps together. This was a season of learning and that was definitely something the family could accommodate.

My mum, the hero, had loaded up our slow cooker with a chilli for our dinner. I was getting quite used to not having to cook. After dinner, the five of us curled up together to watch a family movie. It was good to be home. Tomorrow I would switch on my computer and look at what I needed to do for Tuesday's evening class. But tonight was about family and being thankful for what I have.

KIRSTY

I woke myself up sneezing. I'd started sneezing on the flight home, hopefully, it wasn't the start of a cold. Checking the time, I curled up under my duvet, I didn't need to get up for church for another half hour. As I lay in the early morning darkness of my room, my thoughts returned to Val Thorens, specifically the moments with Paul. Our first time in the hot tub, the toboggan run, the snowball fight and the terrace. Each one a wonderful memory to hold on to and hopefully build on.

When I walked into church, I looked around the hall, hoping to see Paul. I had resolved not to fixate on him, but I missed him and wanted to see him. As usual, I sat with Jo, Lynn and Carol. I kept glancing about hoping to see Paul. He doesn't come every Sunday as sometimes he and Matt still go to Matt's church. But more and more often the two of them are here. "He's not coming this morning," whispered Jo.

"Who?" I whispered back?

Jo replied with a raised eyebrow. "Clients had asked for appointments today so he's at the salon. Apparently, Valentine's is good for the hairdressing business."

I sighed, louder than I meant to, attracting the attention of a few people sitting close by. If he was already busy with Valentine's Day then I probably wouldn't get to see him anytime soon.

By the time the service ended, my sneezing returned with a vengeance and my head was starting to hurt. "I need to get home, you guys. My head is hurting."

Jo gave me a sympathetic smile. "Take care. I'll call you later."

I'd had great plans of going grocery shopping, doing a load of laundry and even cooking a few meals for the week ahead, but all I wanted to do was sleep. When I got home, I changed into my pjs and cocooned myself in my duvet on the settee. Hugging a hot, steaming mug of cup-a-soup I switched on my TV, ready to spend a few mindless hours catching up on some of my favourite comedy box sets.

Thankfully I finished my soup before I fell asleep because the next thing I knew it was dark outside and I was several episodes ahead in the box set. I felt awful. A search of my bathroom cabinet rewarded me with two paracetamol and one lemon drink, I'd take the drink now and save the paracetamol for bedtime. Returning to the settee I hid under my duvet, this time I wrapped my hands around the foul lemon drink, instead of tasty soup.

The next time I woke up it was three o'clock! I was still on the settee and I'd missed the rest of the box set. With my duvet wrapped around me, I shuffled through to my bed, taking the paracetamol before going back to sleep. There was no way I'd make it to work. I quickly sent

Irene a text to let her know I had a cold and wouldn't make it to work in the morning. Even sending a quick text felt exhausting. I collapsed into bed, not even caring that it looked bad to phone in sick after a holiday.

PAUL

Work had been non-stop today. I appreciated the business, it would help clear some of our start-up debt, but I was tired. Tomorrow would be another busy day but tomorrow night would be all about Kirsty. I still wasn't sure that sledging was the most romantic way to spend Valentine's Evening, but I liked the idea of trying to recreate our holiday vibe.

Once again I entered my flat to the sound of Matt and Jo talking. All I wanted was to unwind and switch off. I said my hello's and trudged through to the bathroom. A long hot shower would give me alone space and hopefully a better attitude. However, when I got out of the shower the sound of their laughter invaded my space. My attitude had not improved. Looked like it would be another evening hiding in my room.

"We've already had our dinner," said Matt, as I walked back to the living room. "But we left you some if you want it."

Jo got up and followed me through to the kitchen. "Have you made any plans for tomorrow night with Kirsty?"

"I've got a couple of things booked but I haven't spoken to her yet," I said, as I opened the fridge in search of a beer.

"I hate to tell you, but she's coming down with a cold."

"You're kidding!" I slammed the fridge door shut. It was wrong to take my frustration out on Jo, but I was in no mood to apologise. Every time I decided to ask Kirsty out something went wrong. Why should tomorrow night be any different?

But Jo wasn't prepared to back away from my mood. "You can feel sorry for yourself or do something about it."

"What can I do? If she's sick, she's sick. It'll be another missed opportunity."

"Only if you think your plan was the only way to show Kirsty how you feel."

"What do you mean?"

"Of course Kirsty would love a big romantic fuss but maybe the small gesture is the one with the bigger meaning."

"I don't understand what you're getting at."

"You keep trying to think up all these perfect ways to ask Kirsty out. Grand gestures, romantic settings. But what if you forgot about all that and focussed on just being together?"

"But how does that resolve anything?"

"As we all know, Kirsty has lots of insecurities she's constantly battling through. She knows you've been with lots of glamorous women in the past and she's never going to feel she can measure up to them. So you've got to make it clear to her that she is *the one*."

"She knows she's the one I want to be with. I told her that before."

"Do you really think she believes it?"

Jo had called my bluff. I know Kirsty has doubts, but that's a conversation for me and Kirsty. Right now I was willing to say anything to get away from this uncomfortable conversation. I took a step towards the door but Jo blocked my way, or at least as much as her small frame could block a doorway. "As you seem to have all the answers, what do you suggest?"

"Ditch your plans for tomorrow night. Go to her flat and just be with her. Let her know you're happy to sit with her even when she's not well. It might not be the most romantic Valentine's Night ever, but it will show her you care more about her than anything you have planned."

I couldn't decide if Jo's idea was brilliant or stupid. Plus in my exhausted state of mind I wasn't in the best place to process this conversation. "That's not a date that's just hanging out with a friend. Valentine's is cancelled this year!" I'd had enough of this conversation and Jo telling me what to do. I picked up my beer and the pizza box and escaped to my room, slamming my door behind me.

Jo

13 February

I had been hoping to chat with Kirsty about Matt but she's down with a cold. So no girl chat with her about boys. But do I really need that? I know exactly how I feel!

Paul was working all day yesterday and today. So I've spent most of the weekend with Matt. And all this time together isn't just instigated by me. Every night as I've said goodbye he's asked if I'll be round the next day. Yesterday I arrived with snacks to keep us going through our pre-arranged gaming afternoon. I've surprised myself at how much I'm enjoying the games. Although I suspect my enjoyment is more about spending time with Matt.

Today I persuaded him to try a little walk outside. The stairs were a bit of a challenge for him. Despite his efforts to hide it, I noticed how much he braced himself for each step and the grimace on his face as another stab of pain must have coursed through him. To cheer him up, I agreed to more gaming time. And then he suggested takeaway for dinner so we could spend more time gaming instead of cooking. His comment made me laugh, but it was nice to treat ourselves to pizza.

We decided to take a break from the gaming and watched a movie as we scoffed our dinner. It wasn't even a romantic film, nor was the setting of Matt's flat particularly romantic, but there was a sparkle in the atmosphere as we sat side by side eating pizza and watching the movie.

I think I might have blown things for Kirsty though. I talked to Paul about her and told him she didn't need grand gestures just him, but I don't think he appreciated my input. I probably overstepped a boundary or two. Because I think he's now given up on the idea of even seeing her tomorrow which means I'll not be able to see Matt as I'll need to go and console my poor friend!

I'm sure Matt will understand. This week has been amazing, despite, or maybe because of, his accident. I'm not the kind of girl to have a list of boyfriend requirements but Matt seems perfect for me. We've covered so much ground over the last few days. Our family stories, reasons for choosing teaching as our profession, faith. But it's also about the laughter we've been able to share, even with his leg injury. The only downside I can see to a potential relationship is our height difference. But then again it's another reason to stick with my beloved high heels. Snowboots were an essential item for a ski holiday but they did nothing to mask the height difference between us.

I really think Matt is the one for me.

Thank you, Father.

Amen

Valentine's Day

Paul

I can safely say I have never listened to Christmas songs in February before. But I needed something inspirational for my journey to work and O Little Town of Bethlehem caught my attention. I put the song on repeat and closed my eyes. It was the perfect reminder of what genuine love was. Not fake holiday love but deep, true love. I thought about Jo's suggestion of yesterday. Was I overcomplicating things with Kirsty? I'd never put so much thought into asking someone out before. Maybe it was time to just ask her out regardless of the setting. But for today I had a full schedule of clients to concentrate on.

Despite my exhaustion of yesterday, Valentine's Day in the salon was fun. With Trish's decorations the salon had a party vibe. We played cheesy love songs and joked with clients all morning. Each client excitedly filled me in on their expectations and plans for the day. Of course there was excitement at the prospect of romantic dinners, tickets to the theatre and the possibility of diamond rings, but for most, it was about the person they would spend the evening with.

By the time I got to my short early afternoon break, I had come up with a new plan for tonight. For this plan to succeed I needed Jo's help. I sent Jo a text asking her to let me know when she had time to talk. As it turned out, she was on her lunch break. I apologised for my grumpy attitude of last night. Then we hatched a plan that would work in both our favours…

Kirsty

It was lunchtime before I shuffled through from my bedroom to the settee. I felt awful. My head was bunged up, and I was feeling well and truly sorry for myself. My rumbling stomach sent me to the kitchen cupboards in search of food. But my post-holiday cupboards held nothing of worth. Thank goodness for the array of home delivery options. Healthy or junk? Chicken nuggets won over some healthier option and half an hour later I was wolfing through my chicken nuggets and chips and savouring the lovely warm coffee. And just to make the delivery cost worthwhile I added a muffin to the order. By the end of my feast, I felt slightly better.

The good thing about being laid low with the cold was it gave me the perfect excuse to avoid Valentine's Day. I could even pretend my low mood was purely down to not feeling well rather than another reminder of my lack of love.

By the time I'd finished lunch my eyes were able to focus enough to check my phone. I had a text from Irene asking how I was feeling. I sent a quick text back thanking her for asking and telling her I'd slept all morning. I had also missed a call from Jennifer, she had left a voice mail to ask how I was feeling. I called her back to fill her in. That one call then resulted in text messages from Jo, Lynn and Carol. I love my friends.

An hour later there was a knock on my door and the sound of it being unlocked. "Come in, Jennifer," I shouted, or at least attempted to shout, I didn't quite have the energy to cast my voice very far.

"How are you feeling?" she asked, as she walked into my living room. She was laden with carrier bags. This woman is amazing. "I've brought you some shopping. Just some bits and pieces to get you through the next few days."

I pushed myself up, planning to take the bags from her.

"You stay there," she instructed. "I'll deal with this. I've brought you some soup, tissues, pain relief and some microwave meals, as well as bread and milk."

"Thank you so much. My cupboards and fridge are all empty. I can't tell you how much I appreciate it."

"Sorry I can't stay," she said, "I need to pick the girls up from school."

"Don't worry about it. You've done more than enough."

After Jennifer left, I stayed in the living room and enjoyed some mindless box set viewing. But it wasn't long before I started feeling sleepy again. Just as I made my way through to my bed, Jo called me.

"Hey, how you feeling?"

"I'm okay. Jennifer came by with a bunch of shopping, so at least my kitchen is replenished. I'm feeling tired again, though, so I'm going to have another nap."

"I'm glad I caught you then. Listen, why don't I come round and hang out with you tonight. Make sure you're sorted for dinner?"

"Don't you want to spend time with Matt?"

She gave an awkward laugh. "I've seen him every day this week, it's time to be with my buddy. Plus you're not well, you need company."

Our conversation batted back and forth with a few more rounds of us holding our own. By the time we brought our conversation to a close, I wasn't sure what we had agreed to. My head was feeling fuzzy, I needed to sleep.

I woke up with a start at the sound of a buzzer. It took me a few seconds to realise someone was buzzing the downstairs door. I stumbled out of bed, flipping on lights to combat the darkness now filling my flat. I felt a bit dizzy as I made my way to the intercom and pressed the release button for the outside door. I opened my flat door before retreating to my settee. It didn't even occur to me to check who it was. I assumed it was Jo.

I was just wrapping myself up in a blanket when my front door closed and footsteps approached my living room. Those weren't Jo's footsteps.

Jennifer

I had little expectation for Valentine's Day. Not because we've been married for fifteen years, but because we're just back from our wonderful ski holiday. The skiing was energising but even more life giving was the time with Scott. Time to talk through some of the issues we'll face as I pursue my new career. I'm not naïve, I know there will be more disagreements and comprises. But I know I have his support.

Today had been a deflating back-to-reality day – the school run, grocery shopping, checking in on Kirsty, laundry, making dinner, helping with homework. Normally I enjoy the ordinary, but it made me a little bit sad today, it was all part of the emotional adjustment from a great holiday. Sometimes it's okay to let the slow days be slow and mundane.

By the time it got to ten o'clock, I could barely keep my eyes open. "Looks like bedtime for you," said Scott, as I stifled another yawn. "It's evening class night tomorrow, so you need a good sleep to set you up for all that learning."

I laughed at his reasoning. He held out his hand and led me upstairs to our bedroom. There on my pillow was a single red rose. Scott took me in his arms. "My December Rose. No matter what you do – whether being the glue that keeps this family together or creating amazing interior designers – you'll always be my December Rose. I pray God's peace over you this coming year."

"Thank you," I replied, as I hugged him.

He lifted up my chin and kissed me. Fifteen years of marriage and Valentine's Day is still romantic.

Jo

14 February – Valentine's Day!

Best Valentine's Day EVER!

Usually, I don't give Valentine's Day too much thought. But this year is different.

Paul's scheming to be with Kirsty worked out perfectly for Matt and me. Paul and I talked at lunchtime and hatched a plan. I would phone Kirsty and tell her I would spend the evening with her but then Paul would take my place and that would leave their flat free for Matt and me. I liked his way of thinking. But it made me a terrible teacher all afternoon as my mind wandered around a flurry of ideas. How could I pull off a Valentine's date with such little planning time?

At six o'clock on the dot, I was standing at Matt's door. When he heard the doorbell, he thought Paul had forgotten his keys again and was shouting insults at him as he hobbled along the corridor to the door. I had bought a bunch of balloons and positioned them so that when he opened the door all he could see were the red balloons.

As I peeked through the balloons and he registered it was me, his face went through several emotions. Because yes, guys do have emotions too! The lasting emotion was joy.

I set up a picnic on the floor of his living room. A blanket, candles and a starry sky cast onto his TV set the mood. Sitting on the floor wasn't the easiest for him, but it was time he was moving about more. The fish and chips were the comedy value, I didn't want to scare him.

As we finished our fish suppers, I handed him his gift. I knew a box of chocolates wasn't the way to this guy's heart, so instead, I'd rushed to the shops to get him a new game for his games console – one that we could play together. After he opened it he pushed himself up and hobbled through to his room. When he returned, he handed me a small gift box. Inside was a beautiful snowboard pendant.

He held out his hand and drew me up to him. Taking the pendant from the box he put in round my neck. I had to remind myself to breathe as I gazed into his eyes. He ran his finger along the chain and then he kissed me. The most romantic kiss in the history of romantic kisses!

I hadn't been looking for love but it found me. I'm so grateful for our snowboots and sunglasses holiday and discovering love.

Thank you, Father.

Amen

Paul

I entered Kirsty's flat not knowing what to expect of the night. Was tonight just friendship or something more?

As I walked into her living room a snuffling Kirsty greeted me. I tried not to feel too disappointed. Despite the hint of a ski-holiday tan she was pale. Her hair was sticking out at strange angles, which gave me the horrible feeling that I had woken her up. She was wearing baggy, flannel pyjamas. But despite all of that, my heart still beat faster at seeing her. Proof, if it were still needed, that this was love.

I tried to lay aside my disappointment, this was not the way I had planned to spend tonight. I didn't mind losing the money on the sledging, but I missed the fun of being out together. Tonight was about just being here with Kirsty instead of recreating our Val Thorens moment.

Once she was feeling better, we would get this relationship moving forward.

"Is it okay for me to stay or do you need to rest?"

Before she could reply she started coughing. I handed her the glass of water sitting beside her. She took a sip then looked up at me through watery eyes. "Please stay. I'm glad you came. My day has consisted of sleeping and feeling sorry for myself."

I shrugged off my jacket and sat beside her. "Can I get you anything? Do you want something to eat? Will I order takeaway or do you have anything in?"

"Jennifer dropped off some soup earlier. Would you be okay with just having that?"

"Sounds great." Okay, so the soup part isn't great but hanging out with Kirsty is.

"Do you want to watch a movie together?"

Sitting next to each other, eating soup and watching an old movie was a nice way to spend a Sunday afternoon, but not Valentine's Evening. I glanced over at Kirsty. She really was bunged up with her cold and she didn't sound great. "Maybe I should go now?" I suggested. I didn't want to make her any worse.

She put her hand onto my arm. "Please stay, at least until the end of the movie? Honestly, I've slept so much today I'm not sure how early I'll get to sleep tonight."

"Only if you're sure." I smiled as I settled back down to watch the rest of the film.

As soon as the final credits began to roll, Kirsty turned round to me. "How about a coffee before you go?"

My initial frustration had now evaporated. I was enjoying the closeness of our friendship. "I'm in no rush as long as you're okay for me to stay. Plus, I think Jo is at my flat and I don't want to walk in on anything between her and Matt."

"Tell me everything! What's been happening between the two of them?"

I laughed as Kirsty sat upright, ready for some news. "No point in asking me. All I can tell you is Jo's been at our flat every night since we got back from France."

"I can't believe I'm missing all this! We had a brief chat about it when we were in Val Thorens but it sounds like things are happening now they're back home."

"You can laugh, but I'm starting to feel like a stranger in my own flat."

"Well you're welcome here anytime," said Kirsty. A blush spread over her face in record time. She started pushing herself up from the settee. "I'll go make us those coffees."

"You stay where you are," I said, placing my hand on her shoulder. "I'll get the coffees."

Over coffee, we chatted about the ski holiday, with Kirsty filling me in on what they'd done after we left. "It was a great holiday," I replied. "I just wish we'd had more time together."

That blush brightened her cheeks again. "I was pleasantly surprised by how much I ended up enjoying skiing. I could probably be persuaded to do it again. Although we were spoiled by the serviced chalet and the perfect skiing conditions."

I smiled at Kirsty's attempt to keep the conversation on neutral ground. "I'm glad you enjoyed it. My favourite part was our snowball fight." I glanced over to her, but she kept her eyes focussed on her coffee, giving nothing away.

We drank our coffees with the natural pause in the conversation, both of us taking small sips, keeping our drinks going as long as possible. She may not have responded to my comment, but she was in no rush for me to leave.

I was trying to figure out what to say next when she started coughing again. It didn't make sense to stay when she was ill, but I didn't want to leave. I reached my hand over and smoothed a bit of hair away from her face, my fingers lingering on her cheek. We gazed into each other's eyes. And in that moment I knew…

No more excuses. No more putting off being with Kirsty. This was our moment.

"Kirsty, I'm sorry."

She looked at me, her brow furrowed. "What for?"

"Back in October I told you I wanted to be with you in the future. But that was vague and unfair. I expected you to fit in with my timings. I'm sorry."

She silently gazed into her coffee cup.

"When I asked you out, I wanted it to be perfect. I wanted to whisk you off your feet and let you know how much you meant to me. But every time I tried something got in the way. And then I realised the perfect moment doesn't exist. Christmas taught me that. The truth of Christmas is that love doesn't need a perfect setting."

I sat round to face her and took her hands in mine. She looked into my eyes. Those beautiful eyes sparkled with hope. "I know I have a poor track record with dating but I want to start over with you, Kirsty. I've never found it so hard to ask someone out. But it's never mattered this much."

Kirsty's hand started shaking in mine.

"I love you Kirsty Price. I noticed you the second you walked into ByDesign all those months ago. And every time I'm with you I want to spend more time with you."

"Kirsty, will you be my Valentine?"

As she nodded her head, I leaned in and kissed her.

Kirsty

I have a boyfriend!

I can't believe it! It's Valentine's Day and I have a boyfriend. I look awful. I'm in old, flannel pjs. My hair is a mess and I am makeup free. But the hottest guy I know has asked me out. I'm not sure if I'm happy or disappointed this is how I looked for our first kiss.

But is there anything more affirming than having a totally hot guy ask you out and kiss you when you look this bad? Especially when I had to cut our first kiss short so I could cough! The imperfect setting somehow made it all the more perfect.

My holiday in snowboots and sunglasses restored my faith and gave me a new perspective. Now I know joy and hope surround me.

There were magical moments with Paul on holiday. But tonight has proven beyond doubt that Paul is the perfect guy for me. He is my Valentine, and so much more.

As soon as my coughing fit ended, I initiated our second kiss…

The End

Acknowledgements

Thank you so much to everyone who has helped in bringing this book to print. Your input and encouragement is truly valued.

Innes, Calum, Cameron and Cara. Thank you so much my fab wee family for being part of this journey. And thank you for always cheering me on.

Thanks to the Snowboots & Sunglasses 'first responders' team. To Lorna, Joy, Fiona, Joan, Mark, Mandy, Stacy, Innes and Mary. Your insight and feedback challenged me, inspired me and encouraged me.

Thanks also to competition winner Jane. Thank you for naming The Smith Salon. I hope you enjoy reading about Jane and Elsie. x

Thanks to the fabulous Tanya Rochat. Once again you have produced a stunning cover. Thank you for your friendship and amazing creativity.

And thank you to you the reader for buying this book and encouraging an aspiring author. Enjoy

xxx

A couple of notes about Snowboots & Sunglasses:

Originally, Raincoats & Sunglasses was going to be a stand-alone book, but several of you asked 'what happens next?'. And then my friend, Manja, posted pictures of her ski holiday and sent me a message saying 'sunglasses in snow' and within minutes I knew there would be a second book and it would take the characters on a ski holiday.

When Jennifer and Scott go to UnderGround for her birthday celebration, they meet Scott Nicol. Scott is a good friend of mine and a fab singer – check out his website www.scottnicol.us

And, just in case any of you try to find Lochcala on a map, I'm afraid to tell you it's made up! But it is inspired by some of the beautiful harbour villages of Argyll.

Keep In Touch

Check out my website for further information and my online shop. Why not sign up to receive regular newsletters?

www.carolinejohnston.co.uk

Follow me on social media for updates and news:

www.facebook.com/carolinejohnstonauthor

www.twitter.com/author_caroline

www.instagram.com/carolinej_author